OCT 0 7 2008

HAYNER PLD ALTON SQUARE

Lydia Bennet's
STORY

The continuing adventures of Mrs. Darcy's youngest sister
A sequel to Jane Austen's *Pride and Prejudice*

jane odiwe

SOURCEBOOKS LANDMARK™
AN IMPRINT OF SOURCEBOOKS, INC.®
NAPERVILLE, ILLINOIS

Published by Sourcebooks Landmark, an imprint of Sourcebooks, Inc.
P.O. Box 4410, Naperville, Illinois 60567-4410
(630) 961-3900
FAX: (630) 961-2168
www.sourcebooks.com

Library of Congress Cataloging-in-Publication Data

Odiwe, Jane.
  Lydia Bennet's story : the adventures of Pride and prejudice's naughty youngest sister /
Jane Odiwe.
    p. cm.
  ISBN-13: 978-1-4022-1475-2
  ISBN-10: 1-4022-1475-8
  1.   Austen, Jane, 1775-1817. Pride and prejudice—Fiction. 2.   Young women—
England—Fiction. 3.   England—Social life and customs—Fiction. I. Title.
  PR6115.D55L93 2008
  823'.92—dc22
                          2008022772

          Printed and bound in the United States of America
            VP 10 9 8 7 6 5 4 3 2 1

To the memory of my mother Val,
To my father David,
and to Annette, Gaynor, and Richard, with love

Part One

Tuesday, April 13th

I have quite worn out my silk dancing slippers at the Assembly Ball tonight by standing up with several very handsome officers for every country jig and figure. Indeed, on entering the Rooms, I had barely cast my eye about before I was applied to by a string of gentlemen, though sadly, they were not all officers. I must say there is something about a soldier which makes an excellent partner—I am quite giddy in their company!

I wore my tamboured muslin, which becomes me extraordinarily well, and received so many compliments I was quite the belle of the ball. So smitten by my saucy looks were the officers of the Derbyshire militia, I swear I sat down not once! I danced the first two with Mr Maybury, then Mr Denny, Mr Wooton, Mr Blount, and Mr Wooton again; then, a simpering coxcomb, Mr Cavendish, followed by Mr Wickham. That gentleman danced and teased me by turns—he has a way of looking into my eyes which I find most disconcerting. Mr Wooton begged to dance again, but I was heartily sick of him, so as the supper bell rang, I affected a fainting seizure with an attack of the vapours, which had the opposite of the desired outcome, making him attend me all the more. It also meant that I missed dancing the Allemande, which I love—hateful man!!

Mr Blount took me quite unawares at the supper table by presenting me with a small package. On closer examination, I guessed it had been sent from Mr Howett who was indisposed this evening. Enfolded in a piece of violet scented paper was what I can only imagine to be a lock of his hair (nasty, wispy sort of stuff), with a page of sentimental poetry (clearly not of his own invention). As soon as I had the opportunity, I disposed of this unwanted gift as I happened to be passing the huge chimneypiece on one side of the room. Unfortunately, I had not taken into consideration the stench a large lock of hair like that would make or that the paper would smoulder and only half burn. It caught the attention of my mother who is generally not so observant but she has a suspicious nature. However, I managed to convince her that it was merely a lock of my own hair, which I had cut off because it was being unruly, wrapped in an old laundry bill. Fortunately, I am the apple of her eye and she is easily placated.

Mr Maybury asked me to take a turn with him in the grounds as he suddenly became overheated whilst conversing by the fire. No sooner had we stepped through the French doors than the naughty man was begging to steal a kiss and, as I was thus constrained between a jagged wall and a rugged man, I was forced to surrender. Note to myself—will hereafter forbear kissing gentlemen with whiskers—they tickle too much!

Mr Wooton is threatening to pay court and at the very least will call tomorrow. His eyes are too close together and he has damp palms, bad teeth, and breath reminiscent of a stable-yard privy. No doubt he will bring Mr Blount for my poor sister, Kitty. He is equally captivating, being two feet nothing, with more fat than a hind of pork, and with eyes that squint out from a florid visage like a slapped behind. Mr Edwards will be dragged along in tow to plead their case—we must visit Aunt Phillips and escape the deputation.

His whiskers might tickle but he is so gallant. I long to see Mr Maybury again! Mrs Lydia Maybury—there, that looks very well!

Thursday, April 22nd

As a result of certain incidents that have lately taken place, I have decided to reside quietly at home and forgo any trips to Meryton or flirtations with officers for a month at the very least. Likewise, when the time comes for me to step out into Meryton again, I will be more cautious in my choice of company and look for more than a handsome face amongst the gentlemen. I shall not let Mr Maybury know he has quite broke my heart— I daresay I shall never look at a fellow again! He is a very sly young man and, as Kitty pointed out, not only is his nose too long for sincerity of character, but I have also had a narrow escape from an alliance which surely would never have been happy. She quite rightly says that I am none the worse for the experience; only she and Mr Wickham know of his dallying with my heart, and I can trust both of THEM implicitly.

It is my greatest desire to fall in love and catch myself a husband, yet, whilst I am truly proficient in the art of becoming enamoured, so far finding my partner in life eludes me, however vigilant I have been in the endeavour. My fondness for an officer as befitting exactly what I require in a husband is so well established that it would take a good looking man indeed to capture my affections if he had not the added attraction of a scarlet coat. But to tell the truth, I am fast learning that not all soldiers are the marrying kind!

I have decided to devote the next few weeks to refining and polishing my accomplishments, which, due to my good fortune, I am already liberally blessed. I am to give more time and effort to preserving my Beauty, Health, and Loveliness, whilst exercising a Graceful Attitude in Deportment and cultivating my Superior and Beautiful mind. Kitty and I have drawn up some ideas and instructions (gleaned from some Ladies' books on the Art of Beauty and Accomplishments) for a new plan, and we have both agreed that we will not entertain any officers even if they should call!

Friday, April 23rd

Kitty and I have had a most wonderful day devoted to ourselves. Hill woke us at a little before five as requested, but we decided it might be more fortuitous to our walk and our constitutions if we could actually see where we were going. We had not considered the lack of daylight on a cold April morning, and so we determined to delay our ramble until eight, thereby shortening the time and distance to be covered and thus being duly returned by the breakfast hour. We set off in the direction of Holly Knoll but had only got half way when the sun disappeared behind a black cloud; we then had the misfortune to be caught in a sharp shower and were drenched through with rain. We have decided that in future, we may just as well lie in bed and postpone our brisk walking until June at least, as tramping through mud, rain, and cowpats is strictly injurious to a graceful carriage of the body.

We sat down to breakfast at the appointed hour, but it was a rather poor affair: toast and tea instead of the requested steak and ale. Mama was in ill humour.

It has to be said that Rebecca and Mrs Hill were not as delighted to see us in their kitchen as we might have expected but were very helpful, especially with the recipe for a face mask. Lord how we laughed; the breadcrumbs kept falling off, despite *the sticking effect of egg whites and vinegar. Finally, Rebecca suggested that we sit round with our heads lain upon the tabletop. Just as we were made comfortable, Mr Hill came in and asked if he should cut off our heads to match the chickens that were lying on the other side awaiting plucking. We could not help but laugh at him, although his manner of speaking was such that, if you didn't know better, you might think he meant it.*

Rebecca was sweetness itself in making up our faces and declaring she had never seen such beauties. For her kindness, we returned the favour, but I am not so sure that she was as pleased with our efforts as we were with hers. It has to be said that the canvas we were working on is no painting in oils, and Kitty's insistence on applying the "Liquid Bloom of Roses" was rather too artistic. Rebecca looked more likely to be at home in Drury Lane, but Ned the stable boy seemed rather to like it and chased her around the kitchen begging for a kiss from her ruby lips!

We pressed on with our dancing practice, and Kitty had the marvellous idea of asking Rebecca and Ned to join us. The poor boy was quite worn out before we had finished with him and played the part of the gentleman exceptionally well, though I had to scold him for his insolence. As Rebecca and Kitty were whirling one another round in a very dizzy fashion, he whispered in my ear that he had never seen such pretty ankles as mine in the dance. I did not like to admonish him too much; after all, I am sure what he says is perfectly true!

Still, our performances certainly cheered up mama, who laughed and clapped and hummed songs for us until Mary deigned to give us a few tunes on the pianoforte.

We have spent the evening in refined conversation with papa, who did not attend to a word we said, so just to vex him we took turns about the drawing room, walking with great Fluidity and Elegance. Mama was in such excellent spirits that the workbox did not make an appearance and we three were all in high spirits. Kitty and I are determined to keep up our admirable routine, though we have been persuaded to venture out tomorrow by a missive from dear Harriet Forster who has promised news and gossip not to be missed. I do not think I shall come to any harm just by strolling out to Meryton and have cause to think that a little exercise and company can only do me good!

Chapter 1

THE TRUE MISFORTUNE, WHICH besets any young lady who believes herself destined for fortune and favour, is to find that she has been born into an unsuitable family. Lydia Bennet of Longbourn, Hertfordshire, not only believed that her mama and papa had most likely stolen her from noble parents, but also considered it a small miracle that they could have produced between them her own fair self and four comely girls—Jane, Lizzy, Mary, and Kitty—though to tell the truth, she felt herself most blessed in looks. Lydia's greatest desire in life was to be married before any of her sisters, but a lack of marriageable beaux in the county and her papa's reluctance to accompany her to as many Assembly Balls as she wished had thwarted her efforts thus far.

The youngest Longbourn ladies, Lydia and Kitty, were employed in preparations for a trip out into the nearby town of Meryton. Their bedchamber was strewn with cambrics, muslins, and ribbons, all cast aside for want of something better. Slippers and shoes, sashes and shawls spilled over the bed and onto the floor. Feathers, fans, and frills flowed from open drawers like a fountain cascade. Amongst the spoils, Kitty reclined against propped, plump cushions to regard her sibling, one arm resting behind her head whilst the other held back the heavy bed drapes, so as not to obscure her view. Lydia sat before the glass on her dressing table, scrutinising her reflection as she put the last touches to her toilette. She dusted a little powder over her full, rosy cheeks and twisted the dark curls on her forehead with a finger, patting them into place until she was satisfied with her appearance.

"Is it not a face designed for love?" she asked Kitty with a chuckle, practising several expressions she thought might stand her in good stead with the officers, or at the very least amuse her sister for five minutes. She was perfecting what she could only describe as a "passion promoter" to great comic effect, pouting her generous mouth and flashing her wide, black eyes with slow sweeps of her lashes, which had Kitty reeling on the bed with laughter. "No doubt, I shall capture Mr Denny's heart once and for all!"

"I do not think making faces at Denny will make one jot of difference to his regard for you," Kitty declared, spying a bauble amongst the strewn bedclothes and sitting up to clasp the necklace about her throat. "But, in any case, is it wise to spend so much time on a young man who has such a glad eye? I should have thought you would have learned your lesson by now!" Kitty was the sister with whom Lydia shared all her fears and secrets, cares and woes, secure in the knowledge that she was acquainted with as many of Kitty's confidences, as her sister was of her own. Lydia would never divulge what followed when Charles Palmer detained Kitty in the conservatory and proposed to show her the illuminations, nor disclose intelligence of the letters that passed between them afterwards. Their confidence was absolute.

"I do hope Denny will like my new hairstyle," Lydia went on, tying a length of coral silk around her tresses and ignoring her sister's comments. "I daresay he will; he is always very attentive to every little thing. Why, I only changed the ribbons on my straw bonnet from white to coquelicot last Sunday and he had noticed before the first hymn was sung in church. Oh, Denny, he is so very sweet, though perhaps he is not quite so gallant as Mr Wickham, whose compliments are without doubt the most accomplished. I wonder what he will have to say. Do you think Mr Wickham will notice my hair?"

Kitty did not think Lydia really expected an answer to her question but ventured to comment on the fact that Mr Wickham, one of the best looking officers of their acquaintance, might have his attentions engaged elsewhere. "I do not think Mr Wickham's notice extends much beyond that of his present interest in Miss Mary King. I hate to disappoint you, Lydia, but quite frankly, you could have Jane's best bonnet on your head and he would not notice you! Pen Harrington believes he is quite in love."

"Well, I am not convinced he is in love with Mary King," said Lydia, liberally sprinkling Steele's lavender water on her wrists, "but with her ten thousand pounds! Money will certainly give a girl all the charm she needs to attract any suitor. If you and I had half so much, do you think we should still be single?"

"Well, be that as it may, whatever Mr Wickham's true feelings are on the matter, I declare that I shall never forgive him for his conduct to our sister. I think he used our Lizzy very ill," Kitty cried, as she drew a white chip bonnet from its pink and white striped box and pulled it on over her ebony locks. "No wonder Lizzy went off to Hunsford to visit Charlotte Collins. I think Mr Wickham quite broke her heart."

"Mr Wickham is a very amiable, but wicked, man and if he were not so charming or so handsome, I swear I would snub him forever," Lydia replied. She stood up to smooth her muslin gown over her hips, pulling it down as hard as she could and sighing at its length in despair. Jane, the eldest of the Bennet daughters was a little shorter than herself, Lydia reflected, tugging at her cast-off gown. Indeed, none of her sisters were as tall. And whilst she enjoyed her superior height, she knew that nobody else had to suffer the indignity of wearing clothes that were too small. If only she could persuade her papa that she really needed a new dress for herself alone, she knew she would be the happiest girl alive. But that was impossible. There was never enough money and, if there was any left over for the occasional luxury, as the youngest of five daughters, Lydia knew she would be the last to feel its effects. Tacking on another length of fabric from the workbox was the only answer, but there just wasn't time for that now. If they were not careful, they would be late and miss all the fun.

"If I know Lizzy, she will not be downhearted for long and her letters from Hunsford parsonage are cheerful enough," Lydia added, pinching her cheeks between thumbs and forefingers for added bloom. "She expresses no feelings of regret and certainly there is no mention of moping for Mr Wickham, though how she can possibly be having fun with our dreary cousin Collins is quite beyond me. Poor Charlotte! I know you and I used to joke about the 'Lovebirds of Longbourn' but, now that she is married, I cannot help but feel sorry for her. Can you imagine having to live with William Collins for the rest of your life? Well, at least

Lizzy managed to avoid that, although I am not sure our mother will ever completely forgive her for refusing to marry him."

"Even sister Mary was not keen on the idea of becoming a parson's wife, despite her penchant for bible study and religious tracts," added Kitty, tying blue ribbons under her chin. "Although as I recall, if pressed, she might have consented to the match."

"But Mr Collins never asked her!" Lydia giggled. She adjusted her bonnet, setting it at a jaunty angle before winking at her sister. "To be married with a house of my own is my ambition, I admit, but I declare I could never love a clergyman, not in a million years. Come, Kitty," Lydia urged, picking up her reticule with one hand and taking her sister's arm with the other. "Let us make haste. If we delay much longer, the morning will be gone and we will miss all the gossip!

Such a pretty scene met Lydia's eyes on their arrival in town that she didn't know which way to look: at the ravishing bonnets in straw and silk in the milliner's bow-fronted windows or at the figured muslins, crêpes, and linens ruched and draped across the width and length of the tall windows of the mercer's warehouse. Vying for her attention was a highway teeming with those captivating visions in scarlet; officers were everywhere, strutting the pavements and swaggering in step. A whole regiment of soldiers had arrived in Meryton several months ago, along with the changeable autumn winds, blowing every maiden's saucy kisses like copper leaves down upon their handsome heads. Lydia and Kitty had been far from disappointed when line upon line of handsome soldiers and debonair officers had come parading along the High Street, a blaze of scarlet and gleaming gold buttons, laden with muskets and swords, clanking in rhythm as they marched. It had not been very long before both girls had made firm friends with all the officers, helped along by the introductions from their Aunt and Uncle Phillips, who lived in the town.

Harriet Forster, the Colonel's wife, was fast becoming Lydia's most particular friend, and it was to her elegant lodgings that the Bennet sisters now hastened on this spring morning. As was expected, they found her in good company. Penelope Harrington and Harriet's sister, Isabella Fitzalan, were regaling Harriet with the latest news. The three ladies were most elegantly dressed to Lydia's mind: Harriet in a white muslin, Penelope in blue with lace let into the sleeves, and Isabella in lilac, to match the blossoms on the trees outside. Lydia thought Miss Fitzalan was elegance personified, with her golden curls dressed just like the portrait of Madame Recamier she had seen in her mother's monthly periodical.

"I am so glad you have arrived at last, Lydia and Kitty," Harriet exclaimed, as she rang the bell for tea, "for I have some news which cannot wait to be told. You will never guess what has happened!"

Chapter 2

HARRIET PAUSED, HER CHESTNUT curls trembling with animation and her eyes sparkling with amusement. "Just as we thought a certain couple on the point of announcing their betrothal, Mary King has left to stay with her uncle in Liverpool! It is reported that she had so many bandboxes, it looked as if she was going for good!

"George Wickham is said to be suffering her absence greatly," added Isabella, "as he has been seen going around the town with an air of despondency the like of which has never been seen in him before. I daresay you may have seen it for yourself if you chanced to pass him in the High Street this morning."

"We have not had that misfortune thankfully, though I have a mind to say that I would not expect him to be mourning the loss of Miss King's affection," Lydia immediately answered, unbuttoning her pelisse. "It is far more likely that he is feeling the deprivation to his pocketbook. No wonder you say he looks as though he's lost a shilling and found a groat!"

"So, Lizzy may get him after all," said Kitty, voicing her thoughts out loud.

"They will be able to marry in Longbourn church before the summer is out; how delightful!" Harriet exclaimed, pouring tea into china bowls. "I do love a happy ending."

Lydia could not think why the idea of her sister marrying Mr Wickham did not fill her mind with the same enrapt effusions, but she admitted to herself that it did not. Perhaps it was the idea that her sister might be the first to marry and, therefore, enjoy all the attention that would bring. Try as she might, Lydia felt most jealous of the notice and affection that was bestowed upon Elizabeth, particularly by her father. Except to tell her how silly she was, Lydia could not recall a single comment that her papa had ever made in her favour. Despite the appearance Lydia gave of caring little for his remarks, she longed for him to say a kind word. By every unlucky turn of fate, her attempts to please him always ended in disaster, which had the effect of vexing him all the more. And apart from Mr Bennet's unconcealed adoration of Lydia's eldest sisters, it appeared that every young man in Hertfordshire was smitten with Jane and Lizzy. Not only were her sisters considered to be great beauties, but they also enjoyed countless opportunities to exhibit their loveliness to its greatest potential. If a new gown or a new bonnet were to be had, it seemed to Lydia that Jane and Elizabeth were treated first. It was very hard sometimes, Lydia thought, not to be envious when the best compliment she ever received was that she was tall and "handsome" and her best dress was a hand-me-down that even Mary, who had no interest in fashion, had turned down.

Well, apart from her own feelings, she felt she knew her sister Lizzy well enough, and Lydia was not convinced that the latter still held a torch for Mr Wickham. "I would not be surprised if Elizabeth has fallen in love with someone in Hunsford," she said out loud.

"Has Mr Collins a brother?" asked Harriet, who had them all falling about with laughter at the very idea.

"Lord, no!" Lydia cried. "Thank goodness that there is only one such odious gentleman as Mr Collins in this world, though I daresay if he had a brother, he would have proposed to my sister Lizzy also. No, there is another gentleman, I believe, who is courting my sister. She has been in the company of Mr Darcy and his cousin, Colonel Fitzwilliam, very much of late, and I am inclined to think that the Colonel may be the man. After all, it could not very well be Mr Darcy!"

They all laughed again at the idea of Mr Darcy being Elizabeth's suitor. This particular gentleman had lately been staying in Hertfordshire with his friend, Mr Bingley, and though the neighbourhood (and Lydia's sister Jane in particular) had warmed to the latter, Mr Darcy had been found to be very proud and disagreeable, fancying himself above all the company.

"Well, now I have a tale to cheer us all up," Penelope started. "I will tell you all about my friend Caroline and her brother Edward, twins and alike as two peas in a pod. They were invited to a fancy costume ball and, having no particular apparel, decided to dress as one another. Edward was squeezed into his sister's gown!"

"And what did Caroline wear?" begged Lydia. "Did she don her brother's breeches?"

"Yes she did! Can you think of anything more shocking?" cried Penelope. "And not only did she completely look the part of a man, but Edward fooled the entire party."

"Did they really think he was his sister?" asked Kitty.

"Well, I'm told none doubted him for a moment," Penelope replied. "He was applied to for ever so many dances!"

Penelope's description of Edward's dress and toilette diverted them so excessively, that when one of the officers, Mr Chamberlayne, called half an hour later, he was not only kidnapped for the rest of the day but forced into allowing them to dress him likewise. Kitty ran to her Aunt Phillips's house just around the corner to procure a gown and a wig, whilst the rest of them prepared to get him ready.

Lydia and Harriet trapped young Chamberlayne in Harriet's dressing room as soon as he could be persuaded to accompany them upstairs.

"We promise we won't come in until you are ready to have your corset laced," Lydia called through the door, to the amusement of the other girls who hovered outside, "but do not take too long. We would not wish to take you by surprise. In any case, there is no need to be so shy, Mr Chamberlayne. Harriet has seen it all before. Just say the word if you need any help; we're awfully good at undoing buttons, you know!"

Harriet, Penelope, and Isabella did all they could to smother their giggles. Lydia was in her element. "I'll lace his corset so long as you all help to pull," she commanded as the door opened to admit them. Penelope and Isabella stood on the threshold with their mouths gaping wide open, unsure whether they should join in. "Don't just stand there, Pen, give me a hand,"

Lydia cried, as the young officer was set upon before he knew what was happening. "Isabella, help me pull harder. Quick, before he changes his mind! It will all be over in a minute, Mr Chamberlayne; stand still, I beg you."

By the time they had done with him, they were all feeling rather jealous of his pretty looks and even he admitted he was a beauty. He was laced and frocked in a muslin gown with a scarlet cloak and a bonnet topped with feathers and flowers. He had eyelashes that any young miss would be proud to possess and they all agreed (even he) that a little rouge and powder went a very long way to improve the complexion! Colonel Forster came in just ten minutes later, after being disturbed by all the noise, and was almost fooled until Lydia could not resist telling him the truth.

A while later some of the other officers arrived, all looking quite as splendid in their regimentals as ever. Lydia thought Mr Wickham looked particularly dashing this morning, his brown curls waving over his head to fall on his stiff, braided collar. His eyes met hers as he entered the room. So brazen was his expression that she caught her breath and felt obliged to turn immediately to Kitty as if she had remembered something of great importance.

"Have you heard any interesting or diverting snippets of gossip lately, Mr Wickham?" quipped Mr Denny as he walked through the door.

"Why, now you come to mention it, dear fellow," Wickham replied, taking up his stance for all to see him, "I did hear two handsome young ladies in earnest conversation on my way here."

"How splendid! Pray, Wickham, were these delightful creatures known to you?"

"Why yes, two of the fairest girls in Meryton struck up a most enchanting discourse." Mr Wickham laughed at his own comic efforts and pitching his voice several octaves higher, with his lips pursed, he played his joke, impersonating Kitty and Lydia by turns.

"Kitty, that fellow over there is vexing me greatly," he smirked and simpered, looking straight into Lydia's eyes, with a pat of his curls, before he leapt around on the other side to take up Kitty's corner. "How can that be, Lydia, when he is not even looking at you?" he trilled next, with one hand on his hip. He paused, as they all started to shout, before delivering his final assault. "That, my dear Kitty, is precisely what's vexing me!"

The entire company could not, or would not, scold him because they were laughing so much. Lydia thought him shameless and had soon told him so, as she did her best to disguise her embarrassment. She felt him watching her, but when she dared to look again, she was disappointed to see that she no longer held his attention. Suddenly, every eye was turned upon the young lady whom the officers had not seen before. Lydia was highly amused to see every soldier smooth his hair and adjust his cuffs, before vying for a position where they could admire her more closely.

Colonel Forster performed the introductions so seriously that it was near impossible for Lydia and the others to keep their countenances. "I am particularly pleased to be able to present our own dear Chamberlayne's sister, Miss Lucy, who has come to enjoy Meryton's society for a few days."

"Lucy" bobbed a curtsey and fluttered her eyelashes, paying particular attention to Denny, and said, "I have heard so much about you all and much of you, Mr Denny, sir, but indeed no one prepared me for such handsome soldiers nor for such gallantry. I declare I love a redcoat more than I ever knew."

"She is rather shy," whispered the Colonel in Denny's ear, "but I am sure you will put Chamberlayne's little sister at her ease. Unfortunately, the man himself has had to pop out to see the saddler on business in the town, leaving her to our tender charge. I do not think he will be long, but she has been fretting for him ever since he left."

Of course "Lucy" was not upset or in the least bit reserved and immediately took to flirting and teasing and making such a play for Mr Denny that his complexion took on the same hue as his scarlet coat. They were all excessively amused to observe how he became increasingly attentive as the morning wore on. How they did not immediately laugh out loud Lydia was unable to account.

"Do tell me all about yourself, Mr Denny," begged "Lucy," seating herself next to him in very close proximity on the sofa. "I have heard there is not another soldier so brave as you."

"I am sure we are all as courageous as one another here, Miss Lucy," Denny answered, twisting his hat nervously. "May I say what a pleasure it is to be introduced? It is always felicitous to meet with such handsome relations of one's fellow officers, and indeed, the word handsome does you no credit. I had no idea Chamberlayne had such a beautiful sister. Where has he been hiding you?"

"It is too true, kind sir," answered "Miss Lucy," "I have, until recently, been much hidden away at home, but now I have come to Meryton I hope I shall be able to enjoy every society . . . and your company would be truly beneficial to me I believe, Mr Denny."

"Do you care to dance?" Denny simpered. "It would be my pleasure to partner you at our party this evening if you would be so kind as to consider a humble soldier's wishes."

"Mr Denny!" "Lucy" cried, jumping up excitedly. "I could not wish for anything better; you may engage me for all of my dances," she declared, forcing all observers to snigger behind hands and into handkerchiefs. They were in stitches holding onto their sides from mirth. Mr Chamberlayne was so convincing, such a talented mimic whose voice was pitched just like a young girl's.

Mr Wickham, who had not been enjoying the fact that his efforts to attract "Miss Lucy" had been impeded, took over Denny's part, and it was only when he remarked on the likeness between "Lucy" and her brother that Harriet and Lydia could bear it no longer. They laughed till they thought they should each suffer a seizure, which of course, made the men very suspicious.

"Lucy" broke down and declared that he could not endure such a falsetto modulation any longer but begged he might be allowed to keep the dress on for dancing later, to which there was a vast deal of laughter and jeers of derision. Mr Chamberlayne was made to part with his gown and wash his face before the evening party began. Lydia danced with all the officers, three times with Mr Denny and four with Mr Wickham. Considering the absence of his sweetheart, Mary, Mr Wickham appeared to be in reasonable good humour. Lydia wondered if he had heard that her sister Lizzy was leaving for London at the end of the week and would be back in Longbourn by the middle of next month. Perhaps it was this very fact that had raised his spirits.

Admitting to herself how much she had enjoyed having all of Mr Wickham's attention to herself for a while, Lydia was forced to confess that the prospect of sharing his company once more with her elder sister was not entirely welcome. Elizabeth had been his favourite once before and could become so again, she was sure.

Although she did not look forward to this unwelcome likelihood, Lydia felt there could not be a happier or more contented creature. Life was good and with friends such as hers, she was certain of constant amusement!

Saturday, May 8th

My world as I know it has ended! I have received such dreadful news today that I do not think I shall ever recover! I met with Mr Wickham (who looked as handsome as ever in his scarlet coat) in the High Street in Meryton this morning, and he informed me that the regiment is leaving to be encamped at Brighton for the summer! I could not believe it, nor disguise my disappointment, and asked him what on earth we shall all do without the society of all the officers we have come to know so well. His replies were gentlemanly and thoughtful, yet he seems keen to be gone and spoke of little regret. I daresay he is anxious to take his disappointed hopes away with him, though it has to be said, his excitement for the Brighton venture was plainly evident, especially when he spoke of an appointment he must keep at his tailor. New clothes for the seaside would be absolutely vital, he explained. It could not be said that the militia did not know how to dress, and the entertainments would be such that he would be letting the Colonel down if he was not turned out just right. Oh, if only I could go to Brighton and sample its delights! Lord! Life is so unfair!!!

I do wonder what Mr Wickham will feel when he sees my sister Lizzy again—what will she have to say on the matter? Her hopes of marriage may yet be doomed with the man she so clearly admires. I could not help but watch his progress down the street as he left me—oh, how many times will I have that pleasure left?

I hastened on to Harriet's, hoping that by some small chance, the report might have been a false one, only to have it confirmed and find my dear friend in a state betwixt excitement at the prospect of spending several weeks in Brighton and distress at leaving all her friends behind. She had the most wonderful idea to persuade papa to take a house for the summer and, although my mother and I have petitioned him with the details, he is adamant in his renouncement of any such plan. If only Jane and Lizzy were here, I am sure they could persuade him of the benefits to the entire household.

I cannot live with the idea of Meryton devoid of all its dear redcoats. How I shall miss darling Denny, Pratt, and Chamberlayne. I will never dance with Mr Wickham again. I think I shall die!

Sunday, May 9th

The weather and my spirits are well matched today. There has been nothing but rain, and a sense of misery and desolation is felt by every single lady in the parish. The mood was very subdued in church today and the little groups that formed outside were apt to speak in whispers; it is as though the very soul of the place has died. The only people who do not seem to be affected in any way by our dreadful news are Mary and papa, though quite why I am so upset by their lack of interest in the whole proceedings I do not know. I declare, if I myself were to say I was leaving, it would not trouble them in the least, and they would go on as always.

Mr Wickham was not in church—I feel his absence most pertinently.

Tuesday, May 11th

I am torn between wanting to spend every moment with my friends and feeling that to have them leave might lessen this pain I suffer. Every time I look upon their sweet countenances, I try to memorise every feature, every hair on their head. It is too cruel, and papa has no idea what we suffer!!!

Kitty has sat on my best bonnet and crushed it beyond repair. She clearly has no feeling in her nether parts, for the abundantly large cherries adorning it would have alerted a more sensible person with immediate effect. I have appealed to mama for recompense!

Wednesday, May 12th

Tomorrow, Jane and Lizzy are to return at last. Papa, in his eagerness to have Kitty and I out of the house (he has likened the house to a mausoleum and has hinted that the company of Mr Collins would provide more cheerful diversion), has suggested that we may have the carriage to meet our sisters at the George in Hoddesdon. He has even provided us with the means to do a little shopping and procure a meal for us all to enjoy before returning home. I would think him a very kind papa if it were not for the fact that he is so very keen to be rid of us!

I own I am quite excited at the prospect of a little jaunt out. What fun!!!

Thursday, May 13th

We reached Hoddesdon within three quarters of an hour and were unceremoniously handed out of the coach with little decorum by that insolent stable boy Ned, who left to see his cousin at the Black Lion as soon as he could shift himself, it being market day, his cousin being a maltman, and the Lion being a favourite haunt.

We entered the George and were shown a commodious dining room just fit to receive our sisters by a "glad-eyed" serving boy with a hideously long chin and then ordered some platters of cold meat and salad to be brought up at midday. We ventured into the High Street, where, despite Kitty's scolding, I could not resist a chip and satin bonnet with a plume of green feathers on the top, although it has to be said that as soon as I had made purchase of the hat, it became a very ugly object. Kitty, not to be outdone, spent the rest of our money on a tortoiseshell hair comb and a piece of lace trimming, and so the problem of how to pay for the awaiting repast at the inn soon arose. However, it immediately occurred to me that Jane and Lizzy would no doubt be flush from receiving a generous pocket allowance from our affable uncle and be pleased to lend the money for the food, so thoughtfully and kindly ordered on their behalf by their dutiful sisters.

By midday, having run out of money and with no familiar beaux to abuse, we returned to the George to sit by the window and spent an amusing half hour trying to catch the eye of and waving at the sentinel opposite, who ignored all our gesticulations and marched up and down when he became troubled at losing his resolve.

The serving boy appeared once more and thought he would frighten us with local tales of madman Tommy Simmons, a knife-wielding murderer responsible for slitting the throats of three Hoddesdon ladies a few years back. Having entertained us with an amusing interpretation of the poor unfortunates, doomed forever to wail in the upper rooms of the Black Lion, he called our attention to the window.

Dear Jane, Lizzy, and Maria had arrived and joined us in five minutes, only to abuse my new bonnet and express little surprise when I announced that the nuncheon treat must be paid by themselves. I informed them about the regiment being encamped near Brighton and of our hopes of spending the summer there, but Lizzy did not seem to be as excited at the prospect as I had hoped. I kept my news about Mary King and Mr Wickham till last, divulging that Lizzy's favourite is safe at last, now that Mary has gone to her uncle in Liverpool. Of course, I added that he had not cared for her in any case, but Lizzy very typically made little comment.

We had such a giggle trying to accommodate us all into the carriage, with so many bandboxes and purchases, but at length we were off, stopping to pick up Ned from the Black Lion (where I scanned the upper storey for signs of bloody apparitions) and joining the other coaches that were now *leaving together for fear of meeting highwaymen on Hertford Heath. We were soon home safely, unravaged by masked men of any description on the journey home, despite having to stop near that wasteland so that Ned, who had consumed too much porter, could be sick into a wayside ditch!*

What happy scenes there were on our return. My father became the jovial, playful pater we have not seen these last two months, so glad was he to see his girls, and especially his Lizzy. We had a noisy dinner with the Lucases who came to meet their Maria, and the atmosphere was only spoiled when my suggestion to go to Meryton to see the officers was flatly refuted by Lizzy. Her sojourn with the serious Collinses has not improved her humour. She declared that it would be noted by all of Meryton's residents that the Miss Bennets could not be at home for half a day before they were off chasing officers. What else is there for a girl to do, I ask?

Friday, May 14th

Since returning home, Elizabeth has been no assistance in our scheme for an expedition to Brighton, although mama and I have frequently brought up this topic in conversation, indeed at almost every opportunity! We were counting on her help with papa, but though he looks to be attending and nodding in all the right places, his affirmation of the scheme is not firm and he has become so vague in his answers that it is impossible to know what will be the outcome. Mama thinks he may yet give way but I know him better; unless Jane and Elizabeth insist upon us going, we are done for. Whatever shall I do?

Saturday, May 15th

Jane and Elizabeth have soon slipped into their old ways and are forever closeted within the chamber of one or the other of them and speak in such inaudible whispers that it is impossible to know what they are about.

Lizzy has only walked into Meryton on one occasion to visit our aunt to relate her gossip. Jane is almost as unsociable, but I suspect she is still suffering from her disappointment. As far as we can tell, she saw nothing of Mr Bingley and not very much of his sister when she was staying with my aunt and uncle in London. She has a melancholy air, which, added to our own, makes our home seem quite miserable. Oh! For the happy times of our carefree youth—that they could be revisited, when all was gaiety and laughter resounding!!!

Tuesday, May 25th

I am the happiest creature alive! Long live the Colonel and his adorable wife! I am to go to Brighton!!!

My dearest, most wonderful friend Harriet has arranged it all with an invitation to accompany her, the Colonel, and the entire regiment to that haven of pleasure, that paradise by the sea, beautiful, brilliant Brighton!! I know how it all will be, lines of gaily coloured tents, thousands of handsome redcoats, everyone of them in splendid admiration of me at my most scintillating best, as surely I shall be in such company. I am so excited I cannot speak and I just want to laugh out loud at everything today. Nothing and no one can upset me, not even Kitty who is vexed not to have received an invitation also. I cannot feel too sorry for my sister; after all, I am Mrs Forster's particular friend whom she cannot do without!

I am to go to Brighton—even as I write the words, I cannot believe it. Oh! Should something happen to prevent my going I should just die!!!!!

Monday, May 31st

Harriet and I have at last said goodnight and come to bed, so that we may be up early tomorrow for the long journey to Brighton. How I shall sleep when my feelings are so aroused with anticipation I can only wonder; with such flutterings all over me that I know I shall not be able to close my eyes.

Mama gave a farewell dinner for our favourites at Longbourn this evening before I left for the Forsters, and everyone was in high spirits, except of course for Kitty who has become exceedingly tiresome on the subject of her misfortunes. It is not my fault that she cannot come with me!

Lizzy and Mr Wickham spoke together for not more than five minutes during the whole evening, and their manner of speaking was such that I was left in no doubt that my sister does not want him to resume paying his addresses to her; more than that, although perfectly civil, I would go so far as to say that their behaviour towards one another was quite cold. I am convinced it will come out sooner or later: Lizzy must have a secret passion; she must be in love with Colonel Fitzwilliam. Why else would she give up on her only chance to become a bride and ignore the only good looking man in the room?

Mr Wickham said he would like to show me Brighton, especially as I am a stranger to that part of the world and have never even seen the sea, but I do not know if I shall accept his invitation, kindly meant or not. That gentleman has a habit of teasing me, and though he can be the most diverting company, I am determined to find myself new favourites.

I cannot wait for tomorrow. I am the luckiest girl in the world!

Chapter 3

LYDIA WAS AWAKE JUST after dawn for the start of the journey to Brighton, checking her luggage twice through in case she had forgotten anything. Harriet was up early too, having said goodbye to Colonel Forster, who was obliged to travel with his regiment, leaving in the small hours by horse, carriage, and wagon train to set up camp on Brighton's Downs. "Poor things," Lydia cried, "what an arduous journey they will have to endure and what's more, it will not be eased by the delight of our company!"

The girls set off in the Colonel's coach for London, along dry roads in good weather, and soon entered the yard of the Bell Inn at Holborn to change the horses and take some much needed refreshment, for having been so excited before leaving Meryton, they found that they could not face a morsel on rising. "Lord, I'm starving," Lydia shouted above the din. "I hope there will be some food left after these wretches have gone."

"Do not worry. I am sure we will be well catered for," Harriet insisted, "and we have plenty of time. How I long for a cup of chocolate and some hot buttered toast!"

All was bustle and confusion. A stagecoach was leaving for Brighton as they alighted; young maids dashed about with pitchers of porter, snatching them from the hands of those about to be bundled into and onto their conveyances, lovers were unwillingly prised apart, babies bawled and children mizzled, whilst a red-faced coachman twitched and snapped the ribbons to the call of the horn and the clatter of hooves on the cobbles. A very smart curricle, all gleam and polish, arrived just as Lydia and Harriet were handed out of the carriage by a surly boy who offered them breakfast, newspapers, and a chair in which to rest. The owner of this splendid vehicle was clearly not only a soldier of rank but a man of fashion, impeccably dressed from head to foot in beautifully cut and fitted apparel, with his curricle, horses, and even his boy servant all in shades of the same buff and blue to match his uniform. The small boy who held the ribbons leapt down before his master had stirred and, with a one-handed flourish, accomplished the task of quieting the horses and opening the door. All eyes were turned on this gentleman, for it was clear he was a rich man with a very decided air, and as he rose out of his seat, he caught Lydia's eye and stared at her in a way that she confessed was not unpleasant to her.

"Did you ever see such a fine-looking gentleman, Lydia?" Harriet indulged in another fit of giggles, punctuated with winks and nudges in the direction of the beau in blue as they made their way into the breakfast room. A few passengers were seated at a large table by the window, hurriedly consuming their rolls and coffee before they were called to the next coach.

"He is rather handsome, I grant you," Lydia agreed, "and next to a scarlet coat, I would say that blue is very becoming!"

They sat in a corner which afforded an excellent view of the company and noted that their fellow traveller, who had followed them in, sat opposite, where he continued to quiz them and unnerved Lydia to the point where she could scarcely meet his eyes. This encouraged Harriet to abuse her further.

"You've made a pretty conquest there," said Harriet, out of the corner of her mouth, as she spread her toast with thick yellow butter. "I've never seen such behaviour in all my life; such open admiration, he can hardly keep his eyes off you. I do hope that he is for Brighton and that we shall see him again, do not you?"

Lydia fiddled with her napkin. "I do not think he is looking particularly at me; he is looking at you just as much," she whispered, knowing that this was not entirely true. Indeed, she was quite taken aback, as she did not remember inciting such interest since Captain Carter had decided to look her way. She tried not to stare back but the man really was a most prepossessing gent, with blond locks, a firm chin, and eyes the colour of an Italian lake (at least the colour that she imagined that might be). He was obviously in a hurry, drinking two large cups of thick black coffee before he was on his way in a most urgent manner, with a nod and a bow in their direction.

"I will ask the boy if he knows who that gentleman is and where he is headed. It would be interesting to know a little more, don't you think, Lydia? Such a manner as one never sees in Hertfordshire, and he was so absorbed in his observation of you that I swear I could see Cupid's arrow sticking out of his heart! Clearly he is a single man, he is of a very suitable age, and he certainly has the appearance of wealth and good fortune too by the look of him!" Before Lydia had a chance to speak, she had summoned over their glum waiter and made her enquiries.

"That was Captain Trayton-Camfield, ma'am," he answered. "Captain James Trayton-Camfield. A very wealthy gentleman by all accounts. He has a big estate somewhere near Brighton at Wilderwick, I believe, and is an officer in Prince George's own regiment. He keeps horses for racing, which I know to be one of his passions."

"And is Mrs Trayton-Camfield at home at present?" asked Lydia's devious friend.

"I can't say as I have ever heard about the gentleman having a wife, ma'am. He is always busy hunting, shooting, and racing his horses with the Prince of Wales and his set. He is up and down from Brighton to London a vast deal and is a regular here. I cannot tell you any more, except to say he owns a fine set of horses." The boy, who had become almost animated when started on the subject of horses and of his being once invited to watch them race on White Hawk Down near Brighton, was soon dismissed by Harriet who could not keep her countenance much longer.

"The perfect match," she declared. "Lydia, with her wit and beauty, captivates the race-horse-owning Captain who has royal connections. I can see it now: Lady Lydia Trayton-Camfield—at home to her friends, who include Prince George and his lady, Lord Alvanley, Lord Barrymore, and Letty Lade, who exhibits her highwayman's manners by riding at break-neck speed around Wilderwick estate in her phaeton!" Lydia could not help but laugh at her companion's enthusiasm for this ridiculous picture of matrimonial bliss but admonished her when she persisted.

"Harriet, our paths will likely never cross again. I daresay he only looked at me because I am in your coach and he naturally assumes that I am a lady of means. He is probably a huge flirt and philanderer, which all young men seem to be! I will not even join you in your musings. Lord, now I have eaten too many muffins, and I shall have to sleep them off in the coach. Shall we go? You never know, perhaps we may catch up with him and he can make his offer as we pass by!"

With Harriet's scolding retort assailing her ears, Lydia settled back into the coach for the next leg of the journey, and, as they crossed Blackfriars Bridge and took the road south, they felt they were really on their way. The tantalising rows of London's shops were soon far behind, and now they were bowling along the quieter country roads of the old route, Harriet eager to avoid the worst of the stagecoaches and military wagons that would be descending on Brighton from all over the country. Even so, the presence of several officers, driving in their own curricles, was to be seen as they stopped in Croydon at the Crown. They too were of Prince George's own regiment, all very handsome, very merry with liquor, and not in the least too abashed to give Lydia and Harriet the "glad eye."

Back on the road, they cantered through the hills onto Godstone Green where they sat in the beautiful flower garden of the inn for luncheon just before noon. After a refreshing glass of lemonade and some bread and cheese, they travelled up the long hill and headed for East Grinstead. Through picturesque woodland and forest, over heathland and past huge black, rugged rocks, they journeyed through Uckfield and down the valley into Lewes, with its castle and pretty shops. From here, winding their way up and between the hills of the South Downs, Lydia started to feel most excited; everywhere was bathed in sunshine, the beautiful landscape was verdantly green, and the hills dotted with sheep. Then, as they neared their destination, they saw their first views of the encampment, row upon row of military tents, flags waving, horses braying, and soldiers marching. Lydia hung out of the window, trying to take it all in.

"Cannot we stop to find the Colonel?" she asked. "I'm longing to see our friends."

"No, Lydia," Harriet replied laughing. "We should never find Henry's regiment on our own, and in any case, he is to come to us later, when he has made sure that the men are comfortable."

Just as Lydia thought the views could not be improved and their felicity complete, they took in their first real glimpse of the sea, and the town of Brighton unfurled like a Chinese carpet of shimmering silks before them. The Marine Pavilion nestled at its heart, a range of bow windows gracing either side of a domed building, faced with cream glazed tiles. Along the Steyne they trotted, past elegant houses, past people parading and coming and going from their doors with such an air of fashionable disdain as to make Lydia ache to be one of them. Salty breezes wafted away the girls' fatigue as they turned onto the seafront, and so dense were the crowds that one might have thought they were in London but for the purity of the air and the freshness of the scene. They were soon admiring the sweet bow-windowed houses on one side and the handsome visions of the redcoats against the watery backdrop on the other, as they stepped out to find their rooms at the Ship Inn at five o'clock on the seafront at Brighton!

Chapter 4

"HARRIET, WE HAVE ARRIVED in paradise," cried Lydia, watching the throng from her window promenading in an unceasing procession along the cliff edge. Carriages, coaches, curricles, and phaetons, setting down new arrivals or departing with sad-faced passengers, were displayed in a series of pictures through every pane of glass, providing a constant panorama. She could do nothing but look out at the mesmerising mass of water and the waves ruffled by the wind, turquoise and white-capped with the sun glittering on the water, inviting the gulls to wheel between the fishing boats and sailing ships. What a sight! How her mama would have loved it here; the air was so invigorating, she was sure her nerves would be improved with a single sniff.

Within the hour the Colonel arrived to greet them, bestowing kisses of affection upon them both and joining them for dinner. "The officers are dining in the mess, my dears, but will join us on the Steyne later for an evening walk," Henry Forster announced. "Now, what's for dinner? I hope we'll have some fish, though I can't abide bloaters; they don't agree with me!"

They sat down at a window table in the dining room to a splendid repast of baked fish, prawn pies, and syllabubs, all the more delicious for being eaten as they gazed at the ever-changing sea view and their more immediate surroundings.

"There are a great number of people staying here and several tables are occupied with an assortment of interesting characters," Harriet observed. She had been silent for some time, preoccupied with the pursuit of watching her fellow guests. "I would say the lady at that table to your left, Lydia, must be a duchess at the very least, judging by her dress, her manner, and her voice, which by all accounts is the loudest I ever heard!"

Lydia was sure she had assumed correctly. "She is certainly proud enough; it is clear, from what I have heard, that she is acquainted with at least a dozen lords and ladies. And she has a very aristocratic nose, which is vital for looking down at her neighbours," she laughed.

As the dishes were being cleared and they were partaking of some excellent tea, who should they spy, swaggering along, looking into every carriage that contained a lady, but their old favourites: Wickham, Denny, Pratt, and Chamberlayne. The men were in high spirits, following the gaze of every maid who looked their way. They bowed, nodded, and clicked their heels at a dozen or more before the dinner party saw them cross the road to enter the inn. All was as Lydia had hoped it would be; she inspired such attention, everyone fighting to accompany her on the walk, that she soon settled on them taking turns.

"Please allow me to offer my arm first, Miss Bennet," proclaimed Mr Denny as he stepped alongside. "Did you have a good journey?"

"Oh, yes. It was so exciting to see so many places," said Lydia, "but you poor officers, your travels cannot have been agreeable. And are your quarters comfortable? I long to hear about the camp."

"The camp is quite excellent, everything splendidly fitted up, and I think we shall be very happy. Though to tell the truth, we are not so sure about the company we shall have to keep. We ran into some of the Prince's own regiment this afternoon," he explained.

"I confess I am surprised," cried Lydia. "The fellows we saw on the road seemed affable enough."

"I assure you, Miss Bennet, they are not in the least sociable or pleasant but think themselves far above their company," complained Mr Denny. "You've never witnessed such swaggering in your life, and though I hate to shock you, every one of them has a mistress encamped up there too. Miss Bennet, they are not the gentlemen one would presume."

These revelations did not seem to have disturbed the high spirits of her favourite beaux too much, and with the exception of the Colonel and Mr Wickham, who talked of Ramsgate, it was everyone's first visit to the coast, and Lydia owned there could be no match anywhere for fashion and gaiety like that seen walking on the Steyne in Brighton!

Lydia and Harriet were dressed and downstairs by seven o'clock next morning to go bathing. They left the Colonel snoring away, as he was not due to inspect his troops till one o'clock, and hastened down to the beach to be dipped by Martha Gunn and her ladies. The girls decided to share a bathing machine for changing, but as there was hardly any room to manoeuvre, they kept falling over, partly because of the necessity of standing on one leg to undress and partly because they were laughing so much. Once they had on their flannel gowns and caps, it was time to face Martha Gunn, chief dipper and a woman not to be opposed. She stood in the water whilst her servant and helper led them hand in hand down the steps, but as soon as they hesitated with a first toe in the freezing water, she stepped up and very firmly took charge. She was a strong woman, and before they realised what was happening, they were submerged. Lydia would never forget that first occasion. She declared the horror of it would stay with her forever. Such was her surprise at being forcibly plunged into the icy brine, she forgot to hold her nose as instructed and as she emerged, coughing, feeling half drowned, she was convinced she had drunk several day's dosage of the recommended amount.

"I cannot imagine any circumstance where I would be induced to try this heinous activity again, unless I was desirous of drowning myself and anxious to have done with my life," she spluttered.

"I cannot agree, Lydia," Harriet declared, splashing her friend till she shrieked for mercy. "I find it most refreshing and invigorating, and I profess that the water is exactly the temperature I prefer."

"You are clearly most insensible, my friend. I always knew that, of the two of us, I was the most sound of mind and feeling," shouted Lydia, as she escaped another assault and ascended the steps, dripping and cold.

Getting dried, dressed, and changed into one's clothes, not to mention trying to dress one's hair so as not to appear a complete fright, was a skill which they had not yet mastered after sea bathing. They almost ran back to the inn, which fortunately was opposite the steps they had descended, but as they reached the summit and were stepping out to cross the thoroughfare, they were intercepted by a curricle which swerved, making the horse rear, forcing Harriet to fall backwards, sending Lydia reeling to the ground. As she recovered herself, she saw that the driver had at least had the courtesy to stop, but she could have died as she slowly recognised the buff and blue livery of his servant, the buff and blue paint of his carriage, and, finally, the blue cloth of his coat, his buff breeches, and cockaded hat, a picture of perfection and in great contrast to the one which the girls presented.

Lydia scrambled to her feet, aware not only of her unkempt hair poking under her bonnet but of her general appearance of dishevelment, now that her white muslin was covered in grime and dust. She bit her lower lip, tasting the salt encrusted there, and cast her eyes down to the floor in the vain hope that he would not recognise them.

"Dear ladies," Captain Trayton-Camfield declared, leaping to the floor and bowing before them, "forgive me, I did not see you. I hope you are well. Please tell me that you are not injured at all, for I shall never forgive myself if you are harmed in any way."

"Please, sir, do not be alarmed, and thank you for your concern," said Harriet, "but we are just returned from a little sea bathing, and I am afraid that in our haste to return to our inn, we did not see you."

"Would you allow me to insist that you rest awhile in my chariot or may I escort you to a safe haven? Are you staying near? Please let me take you to your home," the Captain entreated.

"Sir," replied Harriet, "we are entirely at fault. It is we who should be apologising to you, sir. Pray, do be easy; we are not harmed in any way, though a touch shaken, to be sure, but nothing that a little rest in our rooms over the way will not cure." Harriet brushed at Lydia's gown and thrust her forward.

Captain Trayton-Camfield looked across to the Ship Inn. "I should have known that two such genteel ladies would be accommodated in refined surroundings. Please, may I beg your permission to introduce myself. I insist that it is quite the thing in Brighton to dispense with the formality of waiting for Mr Wade to perform the introductions! Indeed, I feel I know you already as I never forget a pretty face; haven't we already met on the Brighton Road?"

Lydia was inclined to giggle at his forthrightness. I must admit, I like his open manner, she thought. But Harriet had suddenly become more than a little reticent in her replies. She clearly thought the Captain was overstepping the bounds of propriety and was keen to make her escape. She dismissed him as politely as she could; he took his leave, jumped onto his seat, and with a wave of his hat, cantered off in the direction of the Marine Parade.

"That wasn't very friendly, Harriet," Lydia protested. "He was nice, very pleasant in fact; he was only trying to make amends."

"Yes, I know," said Harriet, "and if you are to keep him interested, then it is not a good idea to go throwing yourself completely in his path, although," she added with a chuckle, "you could not have succeeded better in that! Do not worry,

Lydia. I am sure we shall meet with Captain Trayton-Camfield and be introduced with all due decorum as a matter of course, and I do not think you will have to wait very long before we will be assured of seeing him again! I would lay a bet that he will see to it himself. Mark my words, Lydia: if we do not formally meet before the week is out, I shall forfeit my subscription to the Castle assemblies!"

"He is very handsome, almost as good looking as Mr Wickham," Lydia said sighing, "whose eyes are the most beautiful of anyone I have ever known, deep brown like a cup of chocolate, all velvety on the bottom."

"Lydia, I believe you are quite right," Harriet replied. "Next to my darling Henry, George Wickham has the sort of eyes that could command one to do almost anything, but perhaps as a married woman, I should not say so," she giggled. They laughed so loudly that the "duchess," who was passing out of the inn as they were entering it, glared in their direction, pursed her lips as though she had detected a nasty stink, and announced in a loud voice that she was concerned that the Ship Inn was not continuing to attract the right sort of clientele, that in its heyday there had not been a single personage accommodated there under the rank of a duke, and that in future, she was considering a move to Worthing, which she deemed far more refined!

Tuesday, June 1st
How wonderful is the sight of the sea, its sound so delicious on the ear, and its vast waters swimming with gentleman bathers! We have rooms overlooking the water, which provide the most excellent looking post! It is heaven, indeed!

There is an odd assortment of people staying here: Mr and Mrs Rand are a very jolly pair, though she must spend a small fortune on rouge, which I fear is daubed on in vast quantities in an effort to match her husband's ruddy cheeks. Mrs Falkener, "the duchess," enjoys snubbing us whenever she can, which only has the effect of making me want to behave outrageously whenever we see her. Harriet has discovered that she is a close friend of a royal duke, but I think if I describe that relationship as "intimate" that will be nearer to it! She is not a titled lady of any description but likes to give the impression that she is of great rank. Dr Blair is a man with a permanent cold who hides whenever he sees "the duchess" approaching— she has a habit of engaging him in conversation on her ailments, of which there are many; the poor man can be seen glazing over as soon as she starts. Then there is Signor Ricardo, the Italian opera singer with a cockney accent who performs once a week at the Promenade Grove. Captain and Mrs Montague are gentility itself—I am tempted to change my allegiance to the navy he looks so well in his uniform. And finally, there is the beautiful Miss Westlake. She appears to be a pleasant enough young woman and is a fount of gossip about the notables in Donaldson's and Tuppen's. Mr Wickham has wasted no time in introducing himself to that lady!

Wednesday, June 2nd

We have been to Donaldson's library to sign the arrivals book and take out our subscriptions for all the entertainments. Everybody who is newly arrived is quizzed to an extent that is enough to unnerve all but the most confident creature. We have taken out subscriptions for the Castle and Ship assemblies, will attend card parties, the Promenade Grove, and public teas for our delight.

I amused myself by looking at the scandal sheets, which are laid out on a central table for everyone's perusal. Poor Prince George and Mrs Fitzherbert, their caricatures are most cruelly drawn. It is rumoured everywhere that they are secretly married, and Harriet says that they even have a love child! I do hope the royal couple will be in Brighton shortly; I long to see them.

A souvenir fan caught my eye, which I bought before I could be talked out of its purchase. It is very fine, made of ivory and parchment, painted with scenes showing the layout of the different camps around Brighton. There are many treasures in Donaldson's, which persuade one to part with money: jewellery, exquisite Chinese parasols, perfumery, and scented gloves. I have been sorely tempted by some sprigged muslin in a shop on the Steyne, which arrived this morning, reportedly smuggled in the cushions of a chaise brought all the way from Dieppe. So persuasive was the proprietor that Harriet marched me outside before I had a chance to reach for my pocket. We played the rattle traps next, staking a little money against the fall of dice—a very pretty nutmeg grater with a painting of the Marine Pavilion on its box was my prize after four throws! Fortune smiles on me in Brighton, though Harriet is inclined to think that I might not have been so fortunate if the boy in charge had not taken such a shine to me. C'est la vie!

Thursday, June 3rd

Harriet and I went bathing this morning. What a sight met our eyes! Some daring young men were exercising the horses that pull the machines into the water. We watched them as they sat straddled upon the great beasts, prancing in and out of the waves. Not only were they sitting bareback, but the "gentlemen" in question were wearing nothing but their breeches, and even they were rather too low slung for the close scrutiny of some ladies present who affected to be shocked and kept turning away. It must be noted, however, that despite calling for salts, none of the ladies were too distressed to return to their lodgings. Harriet and I are agreed that, despite the rough manner of the young men, they could not but help make a handsome exhibition. It was exceedingly difficult not to giggle, as they crashed through the water and their breeches became soaked through—there was nothing left to the imagination, especially when one of the riders jumped up onto the back of his animal. What a fine education for young women!

We stood thus, watching for half an hour until they tired of their sport, whence they departed, swimming in deft strokes to the other side of the groynes to dip any gentlemen bathers who might be up early enough to partake of the pleasure. It has to be said that the only gentlemen we saw on our walk to the beach this morning were on the cliff top, telescopes in hand, effectively perusing ships at sea but with their instruments trained in our direction!

Was knocked to the ground by Captain Trayton-Camfield's curricle—now there is a handsome man!

Chapter 5

THE FOLLOWING AFTERNOON FOUND Harriet and Lydia
taking a turn along the seafront. They were standing watching
some ladies riding on donkeys when Lydia was startled by a voice
in her ear which seemed to come from nowhere. "Mr Wickham,"
she cried as she turned to face him, "whatever do you mean by
pouncing on young women in such a manner?! You quite frightened the life out of me."

"Forgive me, Mrs Forster, Miss Bennet, but you were so
engrossed, I could not resist making you jump. I declare, Miss
Bennet, that I never saw you in such studied contemplation
since I saw you outside the milliner's in Meryton!"

Lydia could not help herself; she struck him on the arm for
his insolence. "As it happens, we are whiling away a pleasant
afternoon by watching the fashionables on horseback. It is
vastly entertaining. Look over there; that poor creature can
hardly stand for the two comely dames he has on his back."

"Ah, yes, that is most amusing, though for myself, there is
nothing so delightful as a horseback ride for two in my opinion,

especially if you can share a saddle. Now wouldn't that be a prospect, Miss Bennet? I am sure you would enjoy a ride with me above all else!" Mr Wickham twirled his cane with a flick of his wrist. "However," he went on, "press me not, I am unable to oblige today. I have important matters to attend, and in any case, I have promised Miss Westlake a turn in a donkey cart first."

Lydia regarded Mr Wickham's countenance, so smug and self-satisfied. He presumed too much if he thought that she would instantly say yes to his suggestion. She was most vexed to be considered only as an afterthought to Miss Westlake. He was full of his own importance, she decided, and determined right there and then that, if he ever should suggest they go out on horseback or in a donkey cart for two, she would refuse immediately. She was on the point of answering with a cutting retort when he started again, leaving her to gape with her mouth wide open.

"No, I must go," he announced, clicking his heels. "I can spend no longer standing here in idle chatter; our Colonel awaits me! I look forward to tomorrow evening, and Miss Bennet, if you stop scowling and smile pleasantly at me, I shall engage you for the first two dances. Good day, Mrs Forster." With a short bow he set off at a march along the promenade before Lydia had a chance to answer him. She left her friend in no doubt of what she thought of his behaviour.

"Well, of all the conceited, arrogant . . . good Lord! That man is the end! He thinks he has only to say the word and I shall jump. Well, I will not! I shall endeavour to dance all night with Denny and Chamberlayne or indeed anyone who might wish to partner me but Mr Wickham!"

Fortunately, by the evening, Lydia's spirits were restored at the prospect of some dancing, so for the moment, Mr Wickham was forgotten. By the time she was dressed in her new gown—a gift from her mama, the most heavenly, snow-white, spotted muslin that she had ever beheld—she was feeling thrilled with her appearance, especially when she considered that the Captain might be in attendance to see her look so well. To finish off, she had kid gloves and her new fan, her hair was all tumbled in curls around her head, interlaced with white beads and silver leaves, sent very kindly by her Aunt Gardiner from the shops in London. A pair of shoe roses, another treat from her mama, were stitched to her satin shoes—festoons of pink and white striped silk, edged in silver thread to match. Harriet, who looked a picture in Pomona satin, arrived at her door with Henry to set out for the promenade upon the Steyne at the fashionable hour. Their party was soon united with the officers, all looking most dashing in their evening clothes. Lydia was begged for half a dozen dances before they had even entered the Assembly Rooms, which were so magnificent in their splendour, she was forced to stop talking for two whole minutes as she stood enthralled before the majestic scene. Beautiful chandeliers sparkled above their heads, illuminating the spangles and silver trim on the ladies' gowns, adding a flicker of fairyland magic to their glittering flower-dressed tresses.

Lydia was pleased that Mr Denny first begged her to dance before anyone else had a chance to whisk her away, but then as they came off the floor, Mr Wickham appeared at her side to take her hand. "Miss Bennet, dear sweet creature, may I beg the second dance as Mr Denny appears to have got in before me. As you are Brighton's most popular partner, there may not be another chance, so please do not break my heart."

She had the awful feeling that he was laughing at her. As she opened her mouth to answer, she was halted by his arresting glance. He had stopped smirking to pause for a moment, before he steadily perused Lydia's form, from the top of her headdress to her satin slippers. His frank expression was of such marked desire that she was taken completely by surprise. She felt almost naked under his scrutiny and shifted uncomfortably from foot to foot, unable for once, to say a word. "I do hope you will forgive me this indulgence, Miss Lydia," he began again, "but I cannot let this moment pass without telling you what pleasure it gives a fellow to see such beauty and animation in one so young. Your complexion is so becomingly flushed, and those black eyes, which promise so much—why it does my heart good. I should say Brighton's air is suiting you already. It has put quite a bloom to your cheeks!"

Lydia knew he meant to discompose her. He clearly enjoyed mocking her and found it all very amusing, but she hardly knew what to make of it herself. Determined to ignore his behaviour and show him that she was not disturbed by his words in the least, she found her tongue at last. "Mr Wickham, I may reserve a dance for you later, though I see your teasing ways are unchanged. I warn you, it can have no effect. Come Denny." With that, she took Mr Denny's arm, slipping it through into hers and skipped onto the floor again, feeling rather cross that she had succumbed to Mr Wickham's charms so easily. As much as she wished to feel affronted, she found she could not stop thinking about what he had said and wondered if perhaps there might be a chance that his compliments were based in truth. But as they came down the set for the second time, she chanced to look up, only to observe him nudging Chamberlayne with a laugh and a nod in her direction. How she seethed! What could he be saying that was so amusing to Mr Chamberlayne? Well, if Mr Wickham expected to click his fingers and have her dance with him, he was very much mistaken.

As she and Denny were dancing, her partner was quick to point out a very distinguished looking person who stood at the side of the room, making himself known to Harriet and the Colonel.

"Who is that gentleman, Mr Denny? Are you acquainted with him?"

"I think it is Mr Wade, the Master of Ceremonies. I expect our friends will now be formally introduced to many of the fine company. I daresay you too will now be in the enviable position of meeting with many more acquaintances, which I am sure, if I know you, Miss Bennet, will be both to your taste and advantage!"

They came off the floor, and though Lydia did not wish to seek out Mr Wickham, she found herself scanning the room to see what he was about and whether he was coming to claim her. She was most surprised, therefore, when she was applied to by Mr Wade himself and it was soon evident why she had been particularly sought out. Standing a little way away and looking on with great anticipation was none other than Captain Trayton-Camfield, who as soon as the formalities were over, had ushered her onto the dance floor before she could refuse him, causing Lydia to thwart Mr Wickham who had just stepped up to take her hand. As she was whirled away, she looked back to see the reaction from her friend and was glad to see, if only for a second, that he was most put out. However, not to be outdone so readily, he quickly found another partner in Harriet. Lydia felt she had had the last laugh, although to tell the truth she was more than a little vexed that Mr Wickham had given up on her so quickly.

"Well, Miss Bennet, it is as I surmised," her partner began as he took her hand in the dance.

"And what, pray Captain, have you surmised?" Lydia had a suspicion that he was about to compliment her and was very ready to hear what he had to say. She only wished Mr Wickham was within hearing distance.

"I knew the very first time I set eyes on you that you would be a marvellous dancer; with such graceful movement and ease of action, you make the perfect partner!"

"Thank you, sir," she replied. "If I may be so bold, I would say you have a discerning eye. I flatter myself that my accomplishments on the dance floor have oft merited much attention and praise. But one must have the correct partner also," she added, "one whose strengths display the other's to great advantage."

"We make a pretty couple, I'll be bound," he said. "Look around; all eyes are upon us. They are all wondering who you are and how I managed to entice you onto the dance floor."

Indeed, it did seem as though everyone was looking in their direction, and it was true that she became a most consummate performer when she had an audience. She couldn't help but show off her skills, and to dance was all the more pleasant when one had a partner who was not only easy on the eye but an elegant exhibitor.

"You are here with the Derbyshire militia, is that correct, my dear?" asked the Captain as they came together in the dance.

"It is indeed," Lydia replied, "I am the guest of Colonel Forster and his wife. Harriet is my very best friend. It was her idea that I should come to Brighton, and I have to say I have not been disappointed. I have never been so far from home before, Captain. It is such an adventure, you cannot imagine."

"And your parents, are they here too?"

"Oh, Lord no! Though my mother would have liked it very much, my father would not be prevailed upon. He is not a very sociable person and will not stir out of his library from one week's end to the next, with his nose in a book and a bottle at his elbow. My poor mother is quite the opposite and, as you may imagine, suffers very much for it, though she does the best she can for company with our neighbours."

The Captain smiled at this last comment. "Has anyone thought to show you around the camp? I daresay Colonel Forster is very busy and his wife must have little time too. It would be my pleasure to be your escort and introduce you to some of the other fellows. They always enjoy the sight of a pretty girl they have not met before, and we cannot have you being on your own and lonesome in Brighton, now can we?"

Lydia's heart swelled. She could not think of a nicer invitation. "Thank you Captain Trayton-Camfield. I would be honoured to accept."

As soon as they walked off the dance floor Lydia could not believe the number of gentlemen who surrounded them, wishing to be introduced. Some she recognised as being officers of the Prince's regiment in their distinctive colours, and they were so entertaining, she could not think why Denny kept insisting that they were aloof and sneering in their manner. Lydia was quite delighted with them. Harriet and Colonel Forster were soon introduced and then she was overcome by the invitations to dance; indeed, she sat down not once during the entire evening. Such fine manners and such compliments flowed that, although she was sure she deserved every one, she almost had her head turned.

"I am so pleased with your handsome Captain, I think you have certainly captivated him with your charms," Harriet insisted. "You will see that I am never wrong when I say that I am sure it will not be long before you receive a declaration."

"I do not like to presume so much." Lydia smiled at her friend, bursting to tell her news. "As for a declaration, that might only be your fancy. But the Captain has expressed a desire to see me again and wanted to know if I would honour him with the pleasure of my company for a tour of the camp followed by a meeting at the Promenade Grove on Sunday!"

Saturday, June 5th

I have received several letters from home and at last Kitty is writing to me. I cannot be bothered to write such huge missives back, but I have managed to dash something off to mama before heading out to the camp, being very careful to withhold any information that I feel she does not need to know.

My most fanciful dreams could not have prepared me for such wondrous visions that were presented to me upon Sussex Downs. The camp stretches out forever; there are rows of tents and rows of soldiers wherever one casts the eye. What was most diverting was to hear my name uttered over and over again—oh, the nudges and winks and nods from those to whom introductions have already been made. I daresay there is not a soldier who does not know who I am now, and being in the Captain's company is such an advantage; I have never met so many officers in my life! I met some of their ladies, who were as elegantly dressed as any I have ever seen. When I expressed my heartfelt desire to be as fashionably attired, one of the officers said, "Well, I daresay if the Captain has his way, it won't be long before you will have the run of Mayfair's finest warehouses." He kissed my hand and added, "Could you enjoy life in a tent, Miss?"

This can only mean one thing! I will have to live in a tent if I am to be an officer's wife!

What would mama think if she only knew she had a daughter on the brink of matrimony with a Captain in the Prince's own regiment. I laugh to think on it!

We had such a wonderful ball this evening at the Castle Tavern, and our acquaintance grows ever larger. I have never seen such a sumptuous room for dancing; the ballroom, orna-mented in the Greek style, glittered with candles and company. The Captain immediately made himself known to me yet again and engaged me for the first three dances!!!

I do believe my dear friend Mr Wickham may be a little jealous of my suitor. He has not exchanged more than two words with the Captain and made some comment about him being a coxcomb and a new-moneyed dandy. I am very cross with him, and whilst I am very pleased with my new partners, I must still admit that nobody in the world dances like George Wickham. He did not ask me to dance; I do not think he looked my way all evening nor spoke to me despite my efforts to flirt a little with him. HE is a perfect example of the worst kind of coxcomb and sometimes I just HATE him. He thinks every woman is in love with him and what is most annoying is the fact that it is probably true.

Captain Trayton-Camfield flattered and adored me by turns. He is handsome and rich, and I think it will not be long before I fall in love with him.

Chapter 6

WITH MORE THAN USUAL enthusiasm did Lydia hurry to the Promenade Grove, certain that she would see the Captain. The little pleasure park situated next to the pavilion proved to be as wondrous as she had anticipated, fringed with an avenue of elm trees and beautifully illuminated with swags, garlands, and festoons of brilliantly coloured lamps. It was said to be like a miniature Vauxhall, decorated with flowers and bowers, and having a box for the minstrels. The crowds were great and, as the pathways were dimly lit and narrow, bumping into others was a constant hazard. Lydia admitted, it was quite diverting to be accidentally nudged by a handsome soldier or two in the dark and deemed it the most delightful exercise.

Captain Trayton-Camfield soon presented himself to the party and fell into step beside Lydia. She had not seen him since he had shown her round the camp; she believed he spent a lot of his time at Raggett's along with all the other fellows who preferred gambling to female company. She had overheard Mr Wickham boasting to Denny that Raggett's was as fine as any club in London and that he was enjoying a good run on the cards. Despite his good fortune, Mr Wickham appeared to be in great ill humour and seemed most preoccupied. Lydia could not account for his rude manners and was exceedingly displeased with his behaviour. She ignored him as much as she could and did not attempt to strike up a conversation. He soon left their party, vanishing into the night as though he had an appointment to be met. Lydia was pleased to see him disappear; she always felt awkward in the Captain's company when Mr Wickham was about.

The Captain was excessively companionable; indeed, she could not think when anyone had ever taken quite so much time and effort to secure her comfort. She wondered if she would ever get used to such behaviour. Every little attention that could be paid, any refreshment that could be offered, nothing was too much for her partner. "Miss Bennet, would you care for an ice or a lemonade? There may be a glass of wine to be had, of course, but lemonade is a ladies' drink I always think and perhaps if we see somewhere to have a glass, we will stop. I am a little peckish myself. Perhaps some cake and biscuits, or we could partake of some ham and thinly sliced bread and butter. We could sit in a booth and sup on a syllabub, now what do you say? But perhaps you are not hungry at all? We could look at the entertainments; the singers are second to none. Now do be careful here, the path is rather uneven. I would hate for you to meet with an accident in the dark. Do take my arm, Miss Bennet, I would not wish you to stumble. There now, I can see your pretty face so clearly now. Moonlight becomes your delicate features, my dear, in a most becoming manner."

Every now and again Harriet looked with great approval at her friend. She was clearly impressed by the Captain's behaviour, but Lydia had to admit, if only to herself, that she was beginning to find his manners quite wearisome. She had looked forward very much to seeing the Captain this evening, but there was something about his conduct that she did not quite like. She felt she was hardly allowed to make a decision for herself; as much as he appeared to be asking her to express her desires, she was not permitted to speak a word before he ran on again to something else or pointed her in another direction. She was not used to anyone taking over the conversation so completely or telling her what she must do, and she did not like it. Before she had a chance to say that she would enjoy both a meal and an ice, preferably washed down with a large glass of wine, they had moved on again without stopping for anything and all the while he did not pause for breath.

But he was so handsome and looked so well in his uniform that every lady in the Grove looked at her with envy, and she knew every one of them would swap places with her if they could. Her grumbles were soon forgotten. Lydia must admit she liked to be stared at as she walked at his side, and she began to feel happy once more.

At nine o'clock, they congregated in front of the box to hear the musicians, and although she heard the Captain suggest they might try the other side for a better view, she was so engrossed that she did not at first realise that he was propelling her towards the quieter, leafier side of the gardens. One moment they were in the thick of the throng and the next they were in the darkness of the avenue, with the leaves of the trees whispering above them.

"Please forgive me, my dear," he started as he guided her steps away from the path and towards the darkness of a roman temple, "but I have so longed to get you away on your own. We are constantly surrounded, are we not? Please permit me to tell you how earnestly I admire you, and although we have enjoyed but such a short acquaintance, I have to tell you that I am afraid I am falling in love with you."

Lydia did not know what to say. She was extremely flattered, and to be told by someone, especially a man as handsome and rich as the Captain, that he was falling in love with her was certainly a step towards matrimony, even if it was rather sudden. As she contemplated a suitable answer, for one did not immediately spring to mind, the Captain clutched her hand in the next instant and took a step towards her, his lips puckered as if in expectation of a kiss.

Lydia was astonished at the speed with which everything was proceeding, and when she felt his lips clamped on hers, she could not have been more shocked, though to tell the truth she was quite ready to appear willing. There had never been much opportunity for kissing young men, certainly not any handsome beaux, and here was a chance which had presented itself without any effort on her behalf. She had always hoped that some day she would be adored, loved, and cherished for herself alone, and here was the Captain proclaiming that his heart was hers! Closing her eyes and pouting her lips as seductively as she felt able, Lydia prepared to give herself up to rapturous feelings. However, whether it was because she had been caught by surprise she could not say, but try as she might, she could not return his ardent kiss. Indeed, she found the whole experience rather disappointing, despite her full attention to the matter in hand. He was a little too eager, and she thought her neck might snap, so wrenched back it had become as she tried to draw breath between his enthusiastic pecks.

She had not noticed it before, Lydia reflected, as he lunged at her a second time with quite as much vigour, but his aquiline nose, which she had previously thought rather noble, now seemed overlarge and kept getting in the way. Perhaps if she moved her head around she might have more success! But on doing so he moved his with great zeal and, not only did their heads clash with a huge blow to both parties, but she managed to catch the end of his nose between her teeth. To her horror she realised it had all gone terribly wrong. However, when the Captain pulled back to look longingly into her eyes, she knew that, as far as he was concerned, his experience had been more than pleasant. How she wished she could feel the same! Still, undaunted by the first attempt and resolute in her desire to improve, she was on the point of begging the Captain for another try when they were disturbed.

"Miss Bennet, Mrs Forster is looking for you everywhere," exclaimed a loud voice, which boomed out of the darkness. Lydia was as vexed as she could be at the interruption and turned to face the intruder as she defiantly took hold of the Captain's arm.

Chapter 7

MR WICKHAM HAD APPEARED out of nowhere with such an ill-tempered expression on his face that Lydia felt quite fearful.

"Forgive me, Mr Wickham, is it not?" Captain Trayton-Camfield asked as he steered her back into the light. "We seem to have lost the path; how fortunate that you have found us."

"Yes, I consider it very fortunate," said Mr Wickham, ignoring the Captain's proffered hand. "I was on my return to listen to the singing when I saw you both disappear and imagined that Miss Bennet might easily lose her way. The lady will now leave you and accompany me back to her friends. I hope you will excuse us; you may imagine that Mrs Forster will be most distressed."

"By all means, dear fellow," continued the Captain, "but do not imagine that your friend was in any danger. My intentions are entirely honourable towards Miss Bennet, and I hope there has been no misunderstanding."

"None whatsoever, sir," Lydia announced and shrugged away Mr Wickham's hand, which had caught her elbow and was propelling her towards the path.

The Captain started moving rapidly in the opposite direction. "I think perhaps it would be wise to return to your friends," he called. "If I may be permitted, I will call on you at your convenience on the morrow." He bowed with a great sweep before rushing off into the night, leaving a very cross Lydia on her own with Mr Wickham.

"How dare you," Lydia cried and slapped him hard across his face. Embarrassed and indignant, she had also been made to feel guilty. He had treated her like a child who needed a nursemaid, and a foolish child at that. To her great surprise, he slapped her hard in return, and she was so shocked that she could not immediately find the words she wanted to say.

Tears sprang to her eyes, though she did her best to blink them away. "I hate you," she cried. "You think you are such an exceptional man when you are not even esteemed as highly as those whom you despise. Captain Trayton-Camfield is an officer held in the highest regard and he will make me an offer before I leave Brighton: an offer of marriage. I daresay he would have declared himself tonight if it were not for your interference. He has told me he is falling in love with me and now you have probably ruined all my chances of happiness. Let me go, I hate the very touch of you. Leave me be!"

She ran, falling into a couple that had their arms wrapped around one another, knocking them over, and bruising her arm. Harriet and Henry were soon found, still standing in the same place, and were it not for her harried appearance, which slightly alarmed her friend, she guessed that they had not been at all concerned about her whereabouts and had presumed she was still close by. Her wretchedness was excused by declaring that she had a headache. Lydia could not tell them what had happened, she still felt so livid, and although she was convinced that Mr Wickham was entirely at fault in his behaviour, a persistent niggle at the back of her mind prevented her from confiding in her dearest friend. The truth was, Lydia was most unsure of her own feelings. Was she capable of returning the Captain's affections? Could she honestly believe that she was falling in love with him? She could not answer either question. Of one truth she was certain: how much she hated Mr Wickham. Why could he never leave her alone?

There was such excitement in the town on the following Saturday as word went quickly round that the royal party was due to arrive in the early evening. Every inch of the Steyne was swept, turf replaced, and fences whitewashed. The pagoda-like canopies and vast bow windows of the Marine Pavilion gleamed from the ministrations of many workers, not a blade of grass or flower was out of place, nor a bush or shrub which dared to display an untidy leaf. By midday, the Steyne was strung with ornamental lights and an area in front of the Pavilion roped off for the purposes of a grand firework display to take place as soon as the ball at the Castle Tavern was over. At five, the crowd had already started to congregate; Colonel Forster and the darling officers of the regiment, along with all the other regimental militia, including the Prince's own dragoons, had taken up positions to salute the royal party as it entered the Steyne. Lydia and Harriet joined the assembly just before six to fight for their place amongst the huge crowd.

"Have you ever seen such an enormous number of people? Everyone is so very eager to have the best view, and I have been pushed three times already," grumbled Harriet.

"But there are so many soldiers to gawp at and sigh over," said Lydia, standing on tiptoe, "that, if anyone told me that I had just died and had arrived at the gates of heaven, I would believe them. I would withstand any amount of pushing for this wondrous sight."

At half past six precisely, a trumpeter on horseback announced the Prince and his party, and a magnificent open barouche with postillions carried the royal presence into view. The Prince, accompanied by an Admiral and a Colonel, was conveyed in this first carriage, and a little while after the first tumults had died down, a second carriage appeared, to even greater applause, containing Mrs Fitzherbert and her friend Mrs Creevey.

"Such elegance," shouted Harriet above the din. "She is far prettier than I would have expected."

"And he more handsome, if a little stouter than his portraits allow," Lydia laughed. The Prince stepped down to greet the troops, several speeches were made, the military band struck up playing "Brighton Camp" or "The Girl I Left Behind Me," and the royal party processed about the crowd, greeting old friends and retainers. There was much shaking of hands, curtseying, and scraping as the crowd cheered and Lydia huzzahed with the rest of them.

All too soon the spectacle was over and the honoured few were swept into the inner sanctum of the Pavilion to refresh themselves before an evening of entertainment. The atmosphere was quietened, the groups of people thronged about were soon broken up and headed off to their various destinations, but the huge majority swarmed like bees over to the Castle Assembly rooms, where they pushed and shoved, intent on securing a position at the head of the queue, fearful that to miss this evening's ball might result in failing to witness sight of the Prince and Mrs Fitzherbert, who, it was rumoured, were likely to attend the dance later in the evening.

"We will wait here for Henry and the officers or I fear we may lose our lives in the confusion," said Harriet.

"I wish they would hurry up," Lydia implored. "I am so afraid we will be turned away."

They caught sight of them amongst a sea of redcoats and were soon scrambling with everyone else into the Assembly Rooms. Their party was the last to be allowed in before the doors were shut, leaving an angry mob outside. Then they were at liberty to join the dance; Denny begged the first two, Pratt engaged Lydia for the two after, and then she lost count as the requests came from every officer, except the very one with whom she had had cross words. She could not help noticing that Mr Wickham seemed to enjoy Miss Westlake's company very much this evening. Lydia owned, even if she hated the very sight of him, that they made a handsome couple, despite his partner's insipid, fragile beauty.

At half past nine, the same frisson of excitement that they had witnessed in the town that morning seemed to gather momentum amongst the crowd, and the news gradually spread of the imminent arrival of the Prince, Mrs Fitzherbert, and some of their guests. The splendidly attired party made their appearance;

Mrs Fitzherbert swathed in white muslin and rubies with her partner sparkling quite as much, his dark coat encrusted with jewels and decorations. Amongst the entourage, dawdling about at the back, deep in conversation with a gentleman was Lydia's friend, Captain Trayton-Camfield. As they passed, she could not help calling out to him, and she was instantly rewarded with a smile, a bow, and an introduction to his friend.

"Sir John Lade, may I have the pleasure of introducing you to Miss Lydia Bennet of Hertfordshire?"

"It is my honour to meet you, sir," said Lydia, smiling and curtseying as deeply as she knew how. She had heard of the gentleman's legendary fondness for fast driving and felt exceedingly honoured that her friend held her in high enough regard to introduce her to so illustrious a figure. She promised to keep herself available for a dance as soon as the Captain could be excused and was overwhelmed by Harriet's reaction as the party moved on.

"I hope you have told your mother about your conquest, Lydia," she said hugging her and fair squeezing the breath out of her. "If you are not promised to be married before we leave Brighton, then I do not know my own mind!" she declared.

"Oh, Harriet," cried Lydia, "you cannot make such assumptions. It is too early, though I must confess he does seem rather keen. I would love to tell mama, but you know as well as I that any hint of a romance will have her down here before I have written the letter. I am having such a lovely time, and I do not want the wonder of it spoiled, as surely it would be with one breath of a mention to my mother. And . . . " Before she had a chance to finish her speech or even hint at her misgivings, her beau presented himself and proffered his arm. He was a very fine partner, and once more the whole room attended to their dance. Lydia was sure they came under the scrutiny of the Prince himself, whose eyes followed her about the room, and she was certain she did not imagine his smile or the enquiry made to Sir John as he gazed in their direction.

"Miss Bennet," the Captain started, "I must admit that I do not feel at all comfortable about the incident that took place at the Promenade Grove. May I be so bold as to ask if there is any prior claim on your affections? Mr Wickham is no more than an interested party in your welfare is he, my dear?"

"Let me assure you, Captain Trayton-Camfield," Lydia declared forcefully, "that there is no claim whatsoever on my affections. Mr Wickham is merely a close friend of my family and has been like an uncle to me, though lately he has taken more liberties than I can describe."

"If that is the case, my dear, say the word and I will make sure he does not overstep his mark again. I will have it done straight away. Let me speak with my friends."

"Oh no, there is no need, I beg you," she pleaded. She might be cross with her sparring partner, but she did not wish him to come to any harm and there was something in the Captain's way of speaking that made her fear for her old friend. "I know how to deal with Mr Wickham, I promise you." She turned the subject of their conversation at once and they spoke of happier affairs. The Captain told her that there was to be a race meeting on White Hawk Down on Saturday, and he said it would give him great pleasure if they should meet. It did sound as though it would be immense fun; there were to be all sorts of entertainments and a huge ox would be roasted. The royal party would also be in attendance and, as a number of the Prince's horses had been reared by the Captain, it would be especially interesting to see how they went on. The Captain was in the mood for conversation, and as they left the dance floor, he began to ask about her family, wanted to know where she came from, and all about Longbourn, which seemed to particularly engage his concern. She may have exaggerated the truth about the size of their manor, but this seemed to make him attend to her all the more, and she found embroidery of the truth, where it would not harm, a delightful and most diverting exercise.

"And your mother and father have no plans to join you?"

"Good Lord, no! Thank heavens for it too; my mother would never leave me be and would spend all her time fussing round me if she were here. I would hardly have a chance to escape and do anything on my own. My friends are quite different. They allow me all the freedoms I want, which includes being able to talk and dance with you as often as I like!"

"I am glad to hear it, my dear. Perhaps we may enjoy another walk on our own later if you think your friends can spare you. I have a little something for you."

Lydia wondered what he could possibly mean, but as he took her hand in the dance again, she had no more time to think on it. They danced four times in a row and the Captain was more attentive than ever, complimenting her looks and grace at every opportunity.

The ball was over too soon, and the crowd made its way out onto the Steyne with the same abandon with which it had entered it; slippers were mislaid, muslins torn, and flowers lost. As they made their exit, the scene before them had been transformed; the Steyne was lit up with chains of coloured lanterns and everyone was gathered to witness the grand firework display. The Prince stepped forward to ignite the first, and then gunpowder and beauty erupted against the night sky. Sparkling diamond showers and flower bursts lit up the black velvet, followed by thunderous reports that shook the ground, reverberating through the bones of the spectators and deafening their ears.

As the crowds cheered in wonder, the Captain drew Lydia to one side and presented her with a small velvet box, which he insisted she open immediately.

"Miss Bennet, it is just a small token of my adoration. I hope it pleases."

"You are too kind, Captain. I cannot thank you enough," she said, quite overwhelmed by his generosity.

With trembling fingers she opened his gift to discover the loveliest heart-shaped locket she had ever seen, fashioned from gold, suspended on a thick chain. The Captain removed his gloves to assist in placing it around her neck and made a great fuss about arranging it in just the right way, his fingers lingering about her throat.

"You have quite captivated me, Miss Bennet," he whispered, taking her hand and leading her round the corner of the library into the darkness. "We were interrupted last night, just as I was getting to know you better. Now, where were we, my dear?" He enveloped her in his arms in a moment, and Lydia braced herself as his face loomed once more towards her. His mouth enclosed hers so much so that she could scarcely draw breath. His kisses came rapidly, urgent and demanding. "You are exactly formed to please a man," he gasped as his eyes swept down over her figure, "and it gladdens me to feel your responses, my dear."

Lydia had not realised she was responding in any particular fashion but was joining in as well as she might. She was certainly delighted by the effect she had on her friend, even if she was not experiencing such ecstasies of sensation herself. She kissed him back, but she could not honestly say she was enjoying herself. Perhaps if she returned his attentions with as much ardour, she would be transported too. She tried again with more vigour.

The Captain immediately took her enthusiasm to mean more than it did. "I knew from the moment I set eyes on you that you would be as eager as I for love," he whispered, as he grasped a handful of softness through diaphanous muslin.

Lydia stepped back, the Captain was getting quite carried away, and she could not bear his fervent expressions of love a minute longer. "I must find Harriet," she cried, "she will be looking for me, and Colonel Forster hates anyone to be late."

"Surely you tease me, Miss Bennet," he murmured in reply, as he drew her closer to kiss her again. "You are as reluctant as I to rejoin your friends, I can tell. Your wish is to inflame me. How you have succeeded. Is it your desire to torment me?"

"It is not my wish to distress you in any way, Captain," said Lydia, who wanted to get away from his unyielding grip as quickly as she could, "but I really must go." His kisses repulsed her, but at the same time she was delighted by his apparent admiration. As she could not remember a single instance when anyone had ever shown her such open adoration she was reluctant to displease him. She did not know what to think.

"Very well, my beautiful Lydia. Another time will present itself and I would not wish you to be late," he whispered, drawing her ever closer to peck at her cheek. "You will promise to keep our appointment at the races, will you not? My heart might break if you fail me and the day promises to be such fun. We will win a little money for you on the horses. If I say so myself, I am the finest trainer the Prince of Wales has ever had. Orville won't let us down. He'll come through for the cup! You'll soon be shopping to your heart's content, my dear. Could you be tempted to a new bonnet?"

How could she refuse him? Lydia walked back to the inn with her friends, full of the splendours of the evening, but for all her gaiety she was troubled. Once in her room, she stood before the glass to examine her new locket in the candlelight. She could not help but admire her reflection, and she knew there would be more from Captain Trayton-Camfield if she played along. He was one of the most handsome men she had ever met; why was it so difficult to return his affections? Surely it should be easy to fall in love with a rich man who seemed so eager to please her. And the locket was very beautiful. She carefully removed it, placing it on the little cupboard next to her bed where she could be sure of seeing the necklace as soon as she awoke in the morning.

Monday, June 14th

I am at a loss as to describe my feelings for the Captain. Whilst it has to be said that I am flattered by his attentions and declarations for the most part, I cannot say the same for his caresses. It is all so disappointing. Far from being transported like a romantic heroine to the very brink of ecstasy, every encounter with my ardent beau leaves me feeling sick! His kisses have less charm than if I was slobbered over by a codfish! His very touch makes me shiver like Hill's jellies on the pantry shelf! It does not make any sense—he is a well looking fellow; why do I hate it when he comes anywhere near me?

I had the most awful trouble concealing the Captain's love token from prying eyes and removed it from my neck as soon as I could. Hiding it was my first thought and a most delicate operation, but it is now secreted amongst my linens. I do not want Harriet to see it and have all the attention that such a discovery might make. There will be talk of engagements and wedding plans, and I cannot endure such teasing.

I do not know how to proceed and am unable to imagine what ails me! I would be a simpleton if I did not encourage him. If I can only ignore my feelings and think about the prize, a chance to be married to a rich man, I am sure it will work out for the best. He admires me very much, I am certain. He has told me he loves me and no one has ever said that, except perhaps mama. Papa shows me little affection and he has never been demonstrative; at least the Captain can't wait to kiss me! That he is within a hair's breadth of proposing I have no doubt and, with a little more encouragement, I am convinced of my efforts to secure him! Oh, I am sure I can fancy myself in love if I can just believe it. More effort is required—I recall papa's constant entreaties—but I never thought I should take such notice!

Saturday, June 19th

A day which held so much promise and started out so well has turned out to be so horrid I hardly know where to begin.

The whole of Brighton turned out for the races; there was such a spectacle, so many red and bluecoats, and the Royal party in their boxes. Before the races began, there were all sorts of hilarious diversions, pony racing, donkey racing, and even running races. Many handsome ladies were applied to for joining in the fun and I was one of them! I chose to ride like a man, while the prissy misses struggled along, sitting side saddle, which had them constantly falling down. I have never ridden so fast in my life, and I swear the entire race ground cheered my name, urging me on. My pretty little donkey brought me home victorious, and at the finish, the Captain was there to rein in my four-legged friend. He and his handsome friends carried me about on their shoulders up to the Royal Box; I was so admired and everyone applauded. The Prince, who clutched my hand for such a time I declare he forgot he was holding it, told me how much the sight of my vigorous riding had cheered him. He is such a kind gentleman, and Mrs Fitzherbert is elegance itself.

The horses then made their appearance on the horseshoe track, bets were placed, fortunes won and lost, wine and porter flowed, and the entire company was all very merry. As the last races were running, the Captain bade me join him to cheer on the Prince's horses he had trained. He placed several bets on my behalf, and we watched his geldings win each race with great excitement. At once a crowd surrounded us, he was taken, lifted high above everyone's heads, and carried off. Just as I was enjoying the moment, aware that everyone's eyes were employed in the direction of the Captain's curricle and hence on myself, my attention was caught by the vision of one who was not attending me, one whom I know well, who was engaged in what appeared to be outrageous flirtation. Anyone could see that the recipient of his attentions was observing him with what I can only describe as a look of pure adoration. Mr Wickham was gazing into the eyes of Miss Westlake; he had her hand in his and was raising it to his lips. He kissed her fingertips then leaned forward to whisper something into her hair.

The day was very hot, and suddenly, I felt quite overwhelmed by the heat, though I cannot account for why I felt so unexpectedly out of sorts. A tiresome headache plagued me, throbbing in my temples, to put me quite out of humour. The Captain was entirely taken up with his friends, Harriet and her Colonel had disappeared, there was no one for me to even sit or have a conversation with; everyone was occupied with their own amusements.

The evening was no better; the Captain declared that I owed him more than a little civility for being so generous with his money, and when he turned his attentions to another young lady, I can only say I was relieved to see him go! I cannot ever remember such a tedious day and I am sorely vexed!

Sunday, June 27th

I am still unable to rally—nothing and nobody can amuse me. Everyone and everything is intolerably dull and stupid. Captain Trayton-Camfield bored me senseless at Promenade Grove this evening; his behaviour, though attentive, is lacklustre and dreary.

Mr Wickham seemed diverted enough in the company of Miss Westlake, who gazes at him with complete admiration and unerring devotion. Thankfully, they disappeared before the evening was over; I could not bear to watch them staring into one another's eyes a moment longer. Mr Wickham seems completely unaware of anything or anyone else; he has no manners and hers are even worse. I should hate to have him fawning over me like a lovesick puppy. Lord! If I should ever carry on in such a way, I would be ashamed of myself. Ugh! I am reminded of a certain pawing Captain who I wish would go to the other ends of the earth and take his curricle with him!

It is my birthday tomorrow, and we shall be attending the assembly ball at the Castle Tavern. I have a mind to dance with Denny all night. Mr Wickham will have to beg if he wishes to step out with me!

Tuesday, June 29th

I gloried in my popularity last night, as all my favoured beaux and many more besides declared a wish to dance with the birthday girl. I received good wishes and tokens from all my friends but one. Mr Wickham was not in attendance at the ball. He sent no excuses or pardons, no birthday greetings or felicitations.

There is to be a dreary card party tomorrow evening, but I do not know if I shall go—I grow weary of my devoted beau who appears to find the society of others as interesting as my own company. I declare I have quite given up on young men. Gallants of old, such as one reads of in Miss Burney's books, are knights of the past. Indeed, my sister Kitty and I are of the same opinion: True gentlemen are becoming such a rarity that, *if Catherine and I were ever to be solicited for our hands in marriage, I daresay we would refuse outright unless the intended could prove his undying love and proffer a book full of gentlemanly accomplishments.*

Chapter 8

BY THE END OF the week Lydia's humour had improved enough to enjoy some shopping in St James's Street with Harriet. She was determined to spend her winnings on some well-chosen purchases, and so she set off with a light heart.

Their first port of call was the pastry cook's on the corner, where they stopped for a cup of chocolate and a delicious pastry. They sat in the window, which afforded a wonderful spot for observation of the passing world in the shape of the citizens of Brighton, young and old, rich and poor. They laughed at the poor wretches who struggled up the street against the wind, which whipped in off the sea, exposing pretty ankles and gouty legs alike.

Clutching their bonnets tightly, they made a tour of the shops. At the linendraper's they found some lovely silk, just fit for a ball gown, and a coloured muslin with a small red spot at three shillings and sixpence, which considered a great bargain. Lydia bought stockings, three pairs for twelve shillings, but Harriet bought silk stockings at twelve shillings for a single pair—extravagance indeed! Lydia was expressing a desire to look at some gloves when a familiar voice declared he would like to be of assistance in her choice of a new pair.

"Good afternoon, Mr Wickham," Harriet greeted him. "May I ask what brings you to town?"

"It would seem we are in pursuit of the same objects of desire. A pair of new gloves is my requirement."

Lydia refused to meet his eyes, though she felt them observing her closely. The memory of him encountering her with the Captain in the dim grove came rushing forth and all she wanted to do was run away.

"Come, Miss Bennet," Mr Wickham said, "let us see if we may find our heart's fancy."

Taking her arm, he marched her into the shop before she had a chance to protest and stood at her side, calling to the shopkeeper who laid out several pairs for their perusal. The sight of such achingly beautiful gloves was wholly engrossing, and though Lydia would have liked to remain feeling cross with Mr Wickham, she soon forgot quite how vexed she was with her attentive companion. Despite herself, she was very pleased to see him again.

"I will leave you a moment, Lydia. I am badly in need of evening gloves and I think I see just what I want," said Harriet, before she moved to the counter opposite.

"They are all so fine," Lydia sighed, hardly attending to her friend who had already left them, "but I cannot help admiring the York tan which are heavenly. What do you think, Mr Wickham?" She picked them up and sighed over the soft leather, which was the perfect hue and so fashionable.

George Wickham glanced over his shoulder, and seeing that her friend was occupied on the other side of the shop with kid gloves for the ballroom, he turned to whisper in her ear. "Let it be my treat, Miss Bennet. I had a good run on the cards last night, and besides, I would wish you and I to be friends once more," he said, taking her tiny hand and unbuttoning her old, worn glove before he carefully and deliberately removed each leather finger, as she looked on aghast. He held her fingers between his own large palms, turning them one way and then the other, as if to gauge their size, before picking up the most expensive pair and instructing her to try them on. His hands were cold, and the touch of his long tapered fingers interlaced with hers, quickened her breath and rendered her quite insensible.

"Oh, Mr Wickham, it is too generous; I cannot accept your money. It would be quite wrong," she stammered as she fumbled to try them on, relieved to be out of his grasp, which had such a disturbing effect on her senses. The exquisite gloves were so irresistible, perhaps she would just see how they fitted; after all, she could purchase them herself if need be. She did not have to accept his money.

"They fit perfectly," he said, taking both of her hands in his own. He held them and stroked the leather across her palms with his strong thumbs, making Lydia jump before she snatched her fingers away from his firm hold. She was bewildered by his behaviour and found herself to be uncharacteristically speechless. Before she had a chance to remove them, Wickham had reached for his purse and paid for the gloves. Lydia knew she should have stopped him, but they were so lovely; she wanted them to be hers so much, and she felt a certain thrill that he had wanted to pay for them.

"Mr Wickham, I cannot thank you enough," she exclaimed. "They are beautiful!"

"Yes," he said, staring at her with an earnest expression.

She could not look into his eyes, which seemed to see into her very soul, and so stared down at her hands, which were trembling.

He lifted her chin with his finger, so that she was forced to meet his gaze once more, and looking at her intently whispered, "Beautiful!"

Lydia blushed, her cheeks burning as red as the lobsters they had seen in the fish shop that afternoon. "I do not know what to say, 'thank you' seems such an inadequate expression," she faltered.

"It is enough to see your face and the pleasure they so clearly give you." He lowered his voice. "You need not say anything to Harriet; this will be our little secret."

The gloves were boxed and beribboned, he presented them with a bow and was on the point of addressing her again when Harriet returned, having selected her evening gloves. Thus satisfied with their purchases, they left the shop. They stood outside for a moment. Lydia asked if he would like to accompany them some more but was instantly disappointed. Mr Wickham immediately took his leave, saying he was to meet a friend down by the seashore. Harriet suggested a walk in the other direction much to Lydia's frustration, as she was longing to know exactly whom he might be meeting. She wondered if it could be Miss Westlake and imagined what they might do to amuse themselves. No doubt Miss Westlake would contrive some opportunity for them to be thrown together—in a donkey carriage perhaps? As Lydia mused on the possibilities and half attended to her companion's conversation, she reflected on what had just passed at the glove-makers. She was thrilled with her purchase, but she was most disturbed by Mr Wickham's manners. Thinking on it, she had been rather pleased to see him leave them; she could not explain it, but whenever she saw that gentleman lately, she did not quite know how to act or behave and it was a most unsettling feeling.

Wednesday, July 7th

Much to my relief, the Captain has not called. I happened to hear Mr Denny say that he had seen him driving out of Brighton very fast in his curricle this afternoon and had overheard his friends say he has gone to London on important business. I cannot say I feel at all anxious for his return!

Friday, July 9th

Mr Wickham has made me a present of the most exquisite pair of gloves I have ever owned. I tried to stop him, but he would have it no other way. How could I resist? No one ever treated me to such a thoughtful present in my life, and it was all done in such a discreet and gentleman-like manner. It is a secret, however, and I am not to tell. Harriet, it is true, would disapprove. She does not yet know that the Captain has gone away, and I do not want to enlighten her. She will only ask too many questions that I have not the answers for. I cannot help comparing Mr Wickham's delicious gift with the vulgar trinket, which lies forgotten in my chest of drawers. I know which I would rather possess.

Mr Wickham has the most beautiful hands of anyone I have ever known. They are very strong and encased mine completely when he held them in his grasp. His touch was as gentle as if he held a tiny bird. I hope I shall see him soon—I think we are friends again!

Chapter 9

THE PARTY OF FRIENDS was sat in the Ship Inn gathered around the fire, for though the month was July, the last few days had been chilly. The ladies, shivering in their muslin gowns, felt particularly cheered by the sight of the flames. The Colonel was anxious to raise their spirits and was telling them he had arranged a little excursion out near Worthing for them all to enjoy a pic-nic and look over an old ruinous folly that he was sure would be to the young ladies' tastes. "For I know what tales of horror you enjoy, Miss Bennet," he said. "The grotto was built by an eccentric nobleman; it is a vast place with deep underground passages and subterranean chambers. They say that deep within a gloomy chamber there is evidence still to be seen of his undying love for the poor girl who was found dead in mysterious circumstances."

The Colonel paused for dramatic effect and Harriet screamed. "Not a skeleton, Henry, please do not tell me there are bones in that horrid place. I must say, I am not at all sure that I like the idea of rambling over ruins where maids are murdered and their ghosts are seen roaming the grounds."

"Please be easy, Mrs Forster," Mr Wickham interjected. "The only evidence—if indeed it may be described as such—is a name picked out in tiny pink shells as small as Miss Lydia Bennet's fingernails," he said, raising her hand and examining her fingertips closely, before planting a tender kiss to her utter discomposure.

She snatched away her fingers. "And what name in this cavernous grotto is fashioned out of shells, pray?"

He answered looking directly into her eyes. "I believe it is a name shared by someone in this very room," he whispered, "Can you guess it?"

Lydia felt her cheeks redden and a flush swept over her in so swift a fashion there was nothing she could do to disguise her confusion.

"Now I consider the matter," he continued, "I do not think I shall reveal the name after all. I propose there should be a search conducted, a game of 'Hunt the Name.' Do you not agree, Colonel?"

"I love to play hunting games," Harriet exclaimed, "and if you have not given us too many clues," she added, glancing across at Lydia, "I should be happy to search amongst the shells. Will it not be a terrible, dark, and gloomy place though, Mr Wickham? Is there sufficient air?"

"Alas, I cannot answer, Mrs Forster, but I would imagine there to be brackets for torches and some moving air down the shafts, unless the rumour that the farmer's daughter met her death in the airless passages waiting for her lover is true!"

"Mr Wickham, you are truly vexing," Lydia protested, "and now you are teasing us with fairy tales, you troublesome man. I do not believe there ever was such a girl, murdered or not. You are a horrid tease!"

"If I am, it is in retribution and only fair," he replied in a whisper. "You tease me constantly and in ways which I am sure you are not even aware."

She could not listen to him any longer for fear of displaying her blushes, so she turned away to ask the Colonel how soon they should be making this delightful outing. It was agreed that they should meet on the following afternoon, and Lydia felt quite excited at the prospect. At least she would not have to entertain the Captain, whose company she could not bear at present. She was becoming more than a little tired by his constant flattery and attempts at seduction, which had at first been so pleasing to her. She decided she might have given up on him sooner if not for Harriet's encouragement, though she knew she might yet secure him and had to admit the thought of going home with a rich and handsome husband, to the envy of all her sisters, was a tempting thought indeed.

Lydia and Harriet were late setting off for the Steyne the next day and were flustered by the time they reached the Castle Tavern, where they had agreed to meet their friends. The Colonel had been with his men all the morning and was due to meet them at eleven. They were relieved to see no one waiting, but as they approached, they were met with an unfamiliar sight. Mr Wickham was perched, reins in hand, upon a whisky gig (which he had no doubt hired at great expense for the day), and at his side was seated Miss Westlake.

"Good morning, Miss Westlake, Mr Wickham," Harriet called out as they approached, but Lydia could not find her tongue. She could not help being surprised to see Miss Westlake sitting in such an intimate way with Mr Wickham. Why, Lydia thought, if she sat any closer she would fair be on his knee!

Miss Westlake smiled and muttered pleasantly enough, but Wickham barely nodded in their direction, let alone addressed them. He seemed only interested in his partner and was, therefore, most attentive to the beauty that sat beside him, as was she in her turn. Lydia was so cross she could not even be civil to Harriet and stood in sulky spirits as they waited for everyone else. Out of the corner of her eye she could see them whispering, and although she attempted to appear in absorbed contemplation of her surroundings, she could not help glancing up at them on occasion. They ignored her, so totally engrossed were they in each other. Lydia grew quieter and more vexed by the moment.

Fortunately, she did not have to wait long before the Colonel and Mr Denny arrived in the Colonel's coach and waved at the sight of them. Mr Pratt and Mr Chamberlayne soon joined them on horseback and then they were off on their way, travelling with speed out of Brighton, following the coastal path, Lydia urging on their coachman to overtake Mr Wickham if he could.

"Some people will never know what it is to have good manners and, for all their lofty perspective, needn't think they are so far above me as to have the right to ignore me," Lydia complained.

Harriet was intrigued. "Who has been so rude as to slight you, Lydia?"

"Mr Wickham and his lady barely had a word to say," she replied. "He did not utter a word nor acknowledge us in any way, did you not notice?" Lydia cried. "I am most put out!"

"That is most unlike him," said Harriet. "He is usually such an affable young man. I cannot say I noticed anything particularly, I was too busy looking out for Henry."

"His friend was almost as bad, twittering away to him without once including us in her conversation," Lydia continued. "I've never witnessed such rudeness. She is certainly throwing herself at him. Did you see the way she was looking at him? I was almost sick at the sight of such fawning!"

"Forgive me for saying so, and perhaps I shouldn't repeat this," admitted Harriet, "but Mr Chamberlayne has intimated that Mr Wickham is very keen on Miss Westlake. Lovers never do have eyes for anyone else."

"Well, from my observation," said Lydia, "I did not see any partiality on his side. Do you truly think he has feelings for her?"

"Well, they have certainly been spending a lot of time in each other's company," admitted Harriet. "I would think it likely!"

Lydia was quite taken aback. She did not know why she felt quite so vexed, but as the others mused over the possibilities of the lovers' constancy, she could not help thinking that his attentions towards herself mattered far more than she ever would profess aloud.

After a pleasant ride through open countryside, they arrived within the hour, coming to a halt at the edge of a large park with wooded grounds. They glimpsed a single track leading to its heart, which begged them to follow its course. Colonel Forster handed the ladies down from the coach; they were all vastly pleased to be able to stretch their legs at last, and Lydia was anxious to discover the delights within. The Colonel led the way, Harriet clutching onto his hand with grim determination, convinced that she was going to meet with her death before the afternoon was over.

"Are you quite sure it is safe, Henry dear? There could be footpads lurking and any number of murderers in these woods. I don't like it!"

"Oh, it's thrilling," shouted Lydia, her excitement at the prospect of any kind of adventure raising her spirits. "I hear not all footpads are murderers and some are quite handsome. Are you sure you would not enjoy an episode in a darkened grotto with a masked man, Harriet?" she whispered before laughing out loud at her friend's screams of terror and delight.

They had been walking three or four abreast until the path narrowed; the trees became denser, their gnarled branches vaulting over their heads in gothic style. Everyone fell into single file, each becoming lost in their own thoughts, and, apart from the calling of a bird in the branches above and the snap of twigs underfoot, the entire company was quiet. Although the sun had decided to come out at last, the woods were deep in shadow. The scent of cool ferns and moss assailed the senses, a perfume to awaken the spirits. The cold green tunnel threatened to engulf them, tree roots clawed across the damp earth to trip the unwary, and Lydia twice caught her muslin on brambles which snagged and snapped back, scratching her bare arms.

"Do be careful, Miss Bennet," called Mr Denny and Lydia turned to smile at him. Dawdling along at the back, she could see, were Mr Wickham with Miss Westlake, who was crying out for him to take her hand, lest she fall over. He seemed only too eager to comply. Lydia was so busy observing their antics that she did not see the tree root which caught her foot, sending her sprawling. She could only hear the muffled titters of laughter behind her as Denny helped her to her feet, and she knew that Mr Wickham and his friend were laughing at her clumsiness. How wretched she felt. Why had she not been more careful? They must think her a blundering oaf. She brushed the leaves from her gown, feeling overwhelmingly subdued and rather vexed with herself. Why did she mind so much what Mr Wickham thought about her? She determined on the spot not to mind what he did or said; she would not be so easily upset.

Everyone sighed in admiration as they came out of the woodland walk, at last into the open, and were faced with the grotto entrance a few feet away, set into towering rocks, which formed part of the bank before them. It was fashioned like a Grecian temple; the ivy covered door stood invitingly open.

"May we explore?" Lydia begged. The full-length windows of the porch entrance gave a tantalising foretaste of what lay within, and she longed to take a look.

"There are lanterns, candles, and a tinder box kept in a recess in the porch if anyone is brave enough to explore further," said the Colonel, "but do take care; there have been tales of sheep losing their way along the passages, only to be found later . . . a pile of bones." He laughed, enjoying the effect his commentary was having upon an avid audience, and then added, "I'll give a bottle of my best wine to the first person to find the name in shells."

The Colonel, Denny, Pratt, and Chamberlayne entered first, leaving Lydia, Harriet, Miss Westlake, and Mr Wickham to bring up the rear. Lydia tried to engage Mr Wickham in conversation and was in mid sentence before she realised that he was not listening to a single word she was saying. As soon as he could release himself, he was off at Miss Westlake's side, and by the time Lydia had sorted out a lantern with all the trouble of lighting it, he and the rest of the party had disappeared. She began to feel very cross again with George Wickham, who it seemed only enjoyed her company when it suited him.

The porch entrance was very beautiful, the walls being inlaid with hundreds of pieces of shell, flint, and glass, all put there by many hours of work, a labour of love indeed. There were three passages, one directly in front and two side passages, leading to various chambers and tunnels.

"Which way did Henry go, Lydia? I cannot see him anywhere. So intent is he on being the intrepid explorer, he and all those other so-called gentleman have left us quite behind."

"Well, they are not far away," Lydia answered, leading Harriet to the right, down a dark passageway where they found themselves in a large round chamber with stone seats set back into the walls. They searched as well as they could in the dim light but could not find anything that looked like a name amongst the shells. Harriet admitted that she had begun to find the whole idea rather tiresome when Lydia persuaded her to venture into the connecting passage, suggesting that they might find Henry. "I think I hear them, don't you?" Lydia declared, cupping her hand to her ear and striding on ahead.

"No, I think you are mistaken," Harriet cried in response. "Wait for me, Lydia, you are going too fast!" Harriet was becoming increasingly anxious, and her companion was starting to feel she was rather spoiling her fun.

Lydia ignored her and hurried along, the lantern lighting up the narrow tunnel, which ran along in a straight line. The air was thinner, the walls slimy to the touch, and there was a pervading smell of damp.

"Ooh, I don't like it, Lydia. Where have they got to?" Harriet ran to catch up, trying to cling onto her friend's arm for reassurance; unfortunately, Lydia was becoming quite out of patience.

"There is nothing to worry about, Harriet. We have a lantern, we can always retrace our steps, and I am sure I heard Henry's voice just now," she lied.

They had entered a smaller chamber, exquisitely decorated, where the walls were pierced with mother-of-pearl and pieces of silvered glass that twinkled, displaying a thousand reflections that illuminated their lanterns' candle flames.

"We have discovered a treasure cave," Lydia cried. "Just look, Harriet. Have you ever seen anything so lovely?"

"It is beautiful," Harriet exclaimed, "but where is everyone? I should have thought we must meet someone by now. I confess this place is starting to unnerve me a little."

"Nonsense, Harriet," Lydia cried. "They must have all taken the left fork, that's all. We will run into them at any moment, I am sure."

No sooner did she speak than they heard the boom of a man's voice a little way off. Before Harriet had a chance to call out, Lydia snuffed the lantern.

"There, what did I tell you. Let's keep quiet and jump out on them; what a good joke we will have," she whispered.

"Do you not know that I am afraid of the dark?" Harriet cried at once. "I am quite terrified! Oh, Lydia, why did you do that? It is so black; there is not a chink of light!"

"Harriet, we are perfectly fine," Lydia assured her. "We are not in any danger!"

"How do we know that the voice belongs to someone we know?" Harriet whispered in terror. "It could be anyone, even a murderer! It does not sound like Henry to me!"

"Of course it must be someone we know," Lydia moaned. "Stand still and be quiet or they will realize we are here!"

"Well, I am not going to stay here to be frightened or starved to death, I am going back," Harriet retorted. "Henry will be worrying where I am."

"Suit yourself," Lydia told her, "but you would be much better off waiting here with me for the lantern to be lighted again."

She would not be told, and feeling her way along the craggy walls, Harriet set off in the direction they had come, complaining of ill usage as she went.

The voices grew nearer and were heard more loudly. They belonged to Miss Westlake and Mr Wickham. Lydia strained her ears, but she found it almost impossible to hear what they were saying. They were in the next chamber and it was plain they were in dispute over something.

"I will not listen any longer to your foolish plans, it is hopeless," she heard Miss Westlake say. Wickham answered, but his voice was so deep and low, she only caught the words "love" and "money."

"It will only make matters worse; I never heard of a scheme more doomed to failure," his agitated partner replied. "I am going now, are you coming?"

Without waiting for his reply, Miss Westlake left him without speaking another word and scuttled down the passageway in the opposite direction. After a moment or two of listening to him cursing the world and every female in it, Lydia called out his name before she knew what she had done.

Chapter 10

"WHERE ARE YOU, MISS Bennet? What has happened to your lantern?" called Mr Wickham. As she lied and told him the candle had blown out by itself, Lydia heard his steps come closer until at last he reached out to touch her. She stumbled backwards in the dark; his touch, though gentle, made her heart hammer.

"Where is your lantern?" she asked, recovering herself enough to speak, knowing that Miss Westlake must have taken the one they shared. "I suppose you have given it to your cross companion."

Wickham sighed deeply.

"I must admit I overheard you both talking," Lydia continued. "At least, I gathered you were in disagreement with one another. I didn't hear all that was said, but one thing seemed very clear."

"And what might that be, Miss Bennet? Pray tell, for I have never found dealing with any lady to be clear cut."

"You are in love with Miss Westlake, are you not?"

There was a silence, and Lydia wished she had not spoken. How could she have said such a thing? How would it sound to him? She wished she had kept her tongue.

"No, I am not," he replied eventually, his voice very low. "I am not in love, you must know I am not." He paused and she heard him sigh again. "I have never been in love in my life," he continued. "Indeed, Miss Lydia, I do not know if I am capable of ever loving anyone. I confess I do not know what will become of me." He took a step towards her, and though she was inclined to move back, her legs seemed to have lost their power to take any action at all. "Who will teach me of love, Miss Bennet?" he asked. "Will you?"

"Please stop being silly, Mr Wickham," Lydia replied as firmly as she could. She did not know how to answer him. He unnerved her and left her feeling completely defenceless. "You have made sport enough of me today; I declare I quite hate you for your teasing ways."

There was no space left between them. Lydia could feel the damp of the wall penetrating the thin fabric of her gown.

He clutched and held her hand. "Forgive me?" he asked. "I cannot bear to think of you hating me."

"I think we should go back, Mr Wickham," she said, shaking her hand free. She still felt cross at the manner in which he and Miss Westlake had snubbed her, laughed at her, and there was something in his soft voice which made her feel uneasy. She felt helpless and unable to think as she should.

"Let us not be enemies, Miss Bennet," he implored. "I so dislike being at odds with you, my little friend. I much prefer to see you when you are happy with me, and I can recall many occasions when you have been more than delighted with my behaviour. To name but one instance, I can never forget the expression on your face when you accepted my gift of gloves in town the other afternoon. I avow it was not one of reproof."

He pulled her towards him, grasping her upper arms tight, kneading his fingers into her tender skin. Goose pimples tingled at his touch.

"Whatever do you mean?" she demanded, hating him for having seen the truth of her feelings. "I was very grateful for your kindness to me on that day."

"I am sure I cannot describe it," he said, "but it is my dearest wish to see that look on your countenance again one day."

He slipped his hands under her arms, his thumbs brushing the flesh liberated by a wanton fichu that had fallen to the floor. She caught her breath. He leaned in towards her, forcing her hard against the damp wall before he caressed her cheek with his lips. She gasped; he was pressed so close she could feel the ivory buttons on his waistcoat and the fob within the pocket of his buckskin breeches leaving their rigid impression. His lips sought hers, and she allowed him to kiss her with greater urgency.

"There!" he declared as he pulled away. "I am sure that must be something like it. If only there was light enough to see your beautiful eyes with their knowing expression."

Her feelings were in such confusion she could not breathe and did not know what to do. "How dare you," she cried at last, with as much feeling as she could, and tried to push him away.

Wickham laughed and pressed himself against her. "How I love a challenge; are you taunting me, Miss Bennet? Do you dare me to kiss you again?"

The truth was that a part of her longed for him to kiss her again. She did not think she could refuse him. "I am not . . ." were the only words she managed to utter before he had his mouth enclosed on hers again. She could not resist and found that, not only was she letting him embrace her, but she was kissing him back; that is, she kissed him until the recollection that he was there with Miss Westlake floated across her mind's eye and she pushed him away with some force. Lydia was so vexed with him for making her feel so completely in his power that she could not find the words to express her emotions. She did not know what to say; she just knew she should leave.

"I think we should go back," she said. "I suddenly feel very cold."

"If that is what you want," he said catching hold of her hand again and suppressing a laugh, "but you are not cold, Miss Bennet; you are a flaming arrow, my sweet little girl, burning a way through my heart. Please tell me that you are my friend before we return and that you forgive me for stealing a kiss. I could not help myself; your eyes have been begging it of me since we came to Brighton."

"I will forgive you, Mr Wickham, but I beg you will not take such liberties again," she cried. "We must go back or they will send out a search party."

"You are quite right, come along, Miss Bennet. Everyone will think we have got lost or that you have seduced me." He took her hand and pulled her along in the darkness, laughing as he went. "Come along, my sweet Lydia, my dear little friend."

"Oh, Mr Wickham!" she shouted as they set off into the passage. "You make me quite despair!"

They were out again in the sunshine soon enough and everyone was congratulating Mr Denny on finding the name they had been seeking. He declared he would have found "Harriet" pricked out in seashells much sooner but had been labouring under the misapprehension that the name he had been looking for was someone else's. Lydia looked across at her friend to see if she was still cross about the lantern but a grin from Harriet was enough to let her know that there were no hard feelings. Harriet was happy now she had found her Henry, and she sat holding his hand as if her life depended on it. Large rugs and cushions had been fetched and spread out on the grass so they could enjoy their pic-nic, and Pratt and Chamberlayne were happily engaged in arranging platters of cold chicken and meat pasties, polishing crystal glasses, and popping corks from bottles. Mr Wickham made no attempt to catch Lydia's eye and soon joined Miss Westlake; they sat quite apart from the others, and he was as attentive to that lady as ever. How Lydia fumed. She could not believe that she had let her guard down quite so badly. How dare he take such advantage of the situation! She was adamant that she would not give him the satisfaction of seeing just how discomposed she was and endeavoured to be as light-hearted and flirtatious as ever. Before long she had drawn an admiring audience of his fellow officers around. Anyone observing her would have imagined she was in love with everyone.

Miss Westlake seemed to tire of her admirer rather quickly. Lydia could see that relations between the pair, though civil, were tense. When Miss Westlake turned her attention to Mr Denny for the rest of the afternoon, Lydia felt a certain satisfaction that Mr Wickham had failed to have everything his own way.

Sunday, July 18th

I was resolved to forget my experience as quickly as I could, but to my utter dismay I have found that such a task is not that simple. Mr Wickham will NOT be forgiven for his behaviour, though I can think of nothing else, playing over the scene in my head with a different ending each time. I now know just how I should have behaved and what I should have said which is vexing in the extreme. However, I am inclined to add that it is not my fault if an ardent young man finds he is attracted to me and cannot keep his hands off me. I cannot be held responsible!

It did not escape Harriet's notice that I was unusually quiet on the journey home, and she repeatedly asked if I were quite well. I was unable to answer; I could still feel Mr Wickham's lips on mine, his gentle hands upon my arms, and his smell, which exuded from my thin dress, scenting the air around me. Despite appealing to Harriet to lower the window in order to get the air, I could not resist drawing my fichu, redolent with his fragrance, across my shoulders once again. I do not want to admit it, but against all my efforts to feel otherwise, I think I am falling in love with him.

Tuesday, July 20th

I do not know if it is my imagination, but whenever I have been in company with Mr Wickham these last two days, he has not spoken a word to me, yet at the same time, his behaviour towards me is most brazen. I can scarcely describe the shocking way he looks at me. I have found him staring at me on occasion, and it seems to me that when our eyes meet they lock with such intensity that I feel everyone must be aware of it.

However, Harriet has made no comment, and she surely would if she suspected aught. I do not know what to make of it. He appears to ignore me and does not attempt a single conversation on the one hand, but on the other, his actions, his eyes, which bespeak so much more, leave me in utter confusion. I have not forgiven his behaviour on the day of the pic-nic, but I feel myself relenting. He looked so very fetching this morning in a blue coat; there is something about the cut of his breeches which makes me swoon at the very thought! His black eyes are most provoking and profligate in their way of glancing at me. I think him one of the most handsome men I have ever set eyes on!

Chapter 11

WITH A MIND EXCITED by the promise of an entertaining afternoon, Lydia set forth with her friends on the following Wednesday to attend a review given by the Prince to celebrate the magnificence of the encampment. Barouches, landaus, and gigs paraded into the grounds with military precision, each one filled with laughing girls in sheer muslin, decorously draped to best advantage, displaying new bonnets with fluttering ribbons, all determined to catch the eye of a handsome soldier. Every regiment was involved in some way, every soldier out swaggered the last, and it was impossible to know where to look; Lydia's eye wished to be in every direction at once so as not to miss a single treat. They witnessed the Prince's inspection of the parade ground and there were several mock fights and displays of sword fighting. Lydia watched in awe as Mr Wickham, whose execution in wielding a sabre was as superior as any of the royal dragoons, showed them all how it should be done with dash and flair.

"Mr Wickham is in such good looks today, is he not?" Harriet said, as she stood up out of the Colonel's landau to make a closer study. "Where is Miss Westlake? I daresay she is enjoying his performance."

"I have not seen her; indeed, I do not think she is here," said Lydia, well aware that Miss Westlake had not been seen at any function since the day of the pic-nic and that she was not in attendance at the review either. Lydia had her own idea that Miss Westlake was out of humour with Mr Wickham and was keeping her distance. There had obviously been some falling out between them on that last occasion, and though Lydia had no idea what it had all been about, she felt certain that neither of them were in a hurry to make up.

The man in question chose to ride past their carriage at that moment, doff his hat, and blow a kiss in her direction.

Lydia glowed as she looked out at the scene, and though her bonnet afforded some protection, she shaded her eyes with both hands, thus obscuring her reddened face. She watched him gallop away on his horse, resolute in her desire not to completely forgive him. She had not forgotten how badly he had behaved, and she kept these thoughts uppermost in her mind.

"Would you like a drink, Harriet? It's so very hot, I've a terrible thirst."

"Yes, please," answered Harriet turning to face her. "Are you quite sure you wish to go? You look awfully pink you know."

Lydia nodded furiously, opening the carriage door and skipping off to find the refreshment tent before her friend could witness her agitation.

In the sweltering heat, a mock battle of epic proportions was taking place next, with the Prince leading his dragoons against the other regiments. Lydia kept one eye on the proceedings as the two opposing armies lined up facing one another. All was quiet but for the clink of swords and stirrups, the creak of leather, the flap of flags snapping in the breeze. Horses stamped, twitching with impatience to be on the move. George Wickham, groomed to perfection, looked steadily ahead, waiting for the signal.

It was so hot Lydia felt she might faint as she hurried along under the blistering sun, and she wondered how it was that the soldiers did not collapse in the heat. She appeared to be the only person moving amongst the quiet crowds, who watched intently in expectation. Then the silent tranquillity of the day was broken. A flag waved, a pistol fired, the Prince's troops advanced with lightning speed. The battle began with such bloodthirsty vigour that, within minutes, it got completely out of hand, and it soon became impossible to separate the spectators from the combatants. The defending army was forced back into the crowd. Soldiers on horseback became entangled with carriages and laundelettes, phaetons and tilburies. Horses reared and bolted, ladies screamed and fainted, blood was spilled by overzealous swordsmen, and the air was thick from pistol fire, sending all into confusion.

Lydia found herself in the middle of the battle scene through no fault of her own. Officers on horseback charged towards her, shouting to get out of their way as they let pistol shots fire into the air to warn others of their proximity. She ran as hard as she could, but there was nowhere to go but further into the ensuing battlefield, and she missed being trampled underfoot by mere seconds. A young officer of the Prince's regiment grabbed Lydia's arm as she stood looking about her helplessly. "Come along my pretty girl, I will look after you," he said, taking her hand and leading her away at a trot.

She snatched her hand from his firm grasp and ran towards the place she thought she had left Harriet, but she could not see the Colonel's carriage. Everyone was running in every direction, horses panicked and brayed, and gunpowder smoke from the cannons filled the air, making it impossible to see or decide on the best course. As she started to feel more than a little hysterical at the worsening scene and had become like a young rabbit rooted to the spot, too frightened to move, a horse galloped alongside her and a hand was thrust in her direction. She looked up but hesitated as she identified her rescuer. She was overcome to see him but wanted him to know that she had not fully forgiven him.

"Do you want to stay here and be killed? Give me your hand for God's sake!" shouted George Wickham. He leapt down from the horse to help her mount before she could utter another word, and as he settled into the saddle behind her, she felt his arm snake around her waist, his fingers pressing through the fabric of her gown as he held her close. She was enjoying the sensation so much she quite forgot to be vexed. All she could do was smile.

"I have you safe, Miss Bennet," he whispered into her hair. "Hold tight, lean into me; I will not let you fall."

Mr Wickham is rescuing me, she thought as they left the horrific scene, galloping away with speed, weaving their way through the mayhem. It was all quite delightful. She giggled and saluted as they passed Harriet, who was safe at the Colonel's side, and waved at everyone she encountered, whether she knew them or not. She held tight onto Wickham's arm, unable to believe her good fortune. He did not utter a word to her for the entire journey back to the inn, but she was content to savour the pleasure in the moment, enjoying the strength of his arm holding her tight and the touch of his thighs against hers like a caress. She wished the ride would last forever.

He was to set her down at the door of the inn, but as they approached, he seemed to change his mind and turned into an alleyway where he said he should be able to tie up his horse more easily. He jumped down and held up his arms towards her, catching her by the waist, as she fell against him, which caused such a worm of excitement within her she knew she had only one course. She boldly caught hold of his hands and fixed him with her dark eyes.

"Do you note the expression on my countenance, Mr Wickham? Is it not the look you expressed a wish to see?"

"It is quite delightful, Miss Bennet," he said as she stepped up and kissed him on his cheek.

"There," she giggled, "a kiss for my hero. Thank you for coming to my rescue."

"Miss Lydia, you have no need to thank me, although . . ." he touched his cheek where she had planted her kiss, "to thank me like this could never be unpleasant to me."

"If that is the case, Mr Wickham," she whispered softly, "may I be so bold as to thank you again?"

She looked back at him, with an expression that told of her earnest desire to please, and knew that he would not refuse her. Lydia did not wait for his reply, and this time he bent his head towards hers, so that she only had to pull just a little on his lapel to bring his mouth into line with hers.

"You are cold standing here in the shadows," he said, after that first, sweet kiss. Lydia felt his fingertips stroke the back of her bare arms. "Will you allow me to put my jacket about your shoulders, Miss Bennet?"

"I will," she replied, wishing that he would just hold her in his arms and kiss her again. Mr Wickham deftly removed his jacket, placed it about her shoulders, and then took hold of both her hands. "No, it will not do," he whispered, kissing her fingertips. "I am afraid, Miss Bennet, there is nothing else to be done, I must insist that you come a little closer." He pulled her towards him, and she did not resist. She stood on tiptoe to caress his lips, draping her arms around his neck, entwining her fingers in his curls. Their hearts beat together through his thin chemise; he cradled her face in his hands, and this time he kissed her with a passion that left her reeling. Lydia felt she had left her own body and was floating some-where in the heavens, enveloped in Wickham's arms. She could not help but compare George's kisses with those of the Captain and was glad once more that he had chosen to leave Brighton for the present. An enormous feeling of relief lifted from her; indeed, she hoped he might never return. Nevertheless, she spent the next five minutes in delicious reverie, as she submitted to George's kisses, imagining what might happen if he did come back to claim her, convinced her suitors would fight for her favours.

"But what of Miss Westlake?" she asked eventually, pulling away from him. "Does she not engage your affections?" She hardly wanted to hear his answer, she was so afraid it might be what she did not want to hear.

"Miss Westlake is a fine girl, but there is only one who engages my affections at this moment, Miss Bennet," he replied.

Lydia did not wait to hear confirmation of her name but gave herself up with abandon to George's slow and sweet kisses, which put her in such a state of delirium that she swooned in his arms.

Thursday, July 22nd

I do not want Harriet to know of my new amour just yet, as I know she will not approve. As far as she is concerned, I am practically a married lady—what would she think if she only guessed half the truth?!!!

I think I might just burst with the excitement of it all and I cannot think what I am to do. I have written to Kitty, whom I know I can trust implicitly. I have described for her in the most minute detail every feeling in my body, every sentiment of my soul, not omitting that she must either set to with the scissors as soon as she has read the letter or burn the evidence, whichever she feels most prudent! I have a feeling that she is not going to be wholly surprised by my news and will also be congratulating herself on the fact that she declared in a letter to me more than a fortnight ago that Wickham and I were in love. In love!—Oh, yes indeed!

Friday, July 23rd

I declare that George Wickham has bewitched me and all I can think of is him, his face, his mouth, his kisses, and how I want him to hold me once more. I cannot imagine how we will ever be alone again, and I might just die if a moment does not soon present itself!

Tonight I danced four times with my Georgie, three with Denny, two with Pratt, and various odd ones with others of my acquaintance. I near fainted away with Georgie in my arms as we danced and looked longingly into each other's eyes whenever we dared. During the third, he whispered to meet him outside just after tea, and I could hardly contain my excitement. I managed to slip away and ran into the night air, turning into the darkened alley by the side of the inn. A hand grabbed me from the shadows, and I was engulfed in Mr Wickham's arms. He embraced me so tightly that he took my breath away. I declare George's slow and sweet kisses put me in such a state of frenzy, from the curls on the crown of my head to the lace edge of my fichu, that I nearly succumbed to a fainting fit. Indeed, he was so worried about my pallid countenance and shallow breathing as I lay motionless in his arms that he was obliged to lay his head on my heart to determine if I still breathed. Thankfully, I was soon revived by his thoughtful actions and could gasp once more, although George insisted on counting my heartbeats for a full five minutes, soothing each quickened pulse with the balm of a tender kiss, before he was completely satisfied. Those kisses still burned at the close of the evening, and I felt that anyone looking at me could see the impression of his lips, like red scars scorched into my flesh as though he had branded me as his own. George Wickham has left his imperceptible mark on me, and I am enslaved! Oh, happy state!

Once in the ballroom again, I was grieved to see that George took great pains to avoid me, preferring to dance with anyone who smiled in his direction and claiming three dances with Miss Westlake (how I have come to detest her), and I thought I should die until I received a sign to let me know I was still his chosen one. It was not until we were going home and were standing at the cloakroom that George surprised me by taking it upon himself to collect my cloak, which he carefully placed about my shoulders and then tied under my chin, brushing his fingers against my throat and behind my ears. I looked wildly about me, for although I was enjoying every sensation far more than I could ever describe, I did not want us to be discovered. Thankfully, his actions seemed to pass unnoticed. I long to caress him again. I cannot wait for tomorrow!

Chapter 12

THE NEXT DAY, THE usual party was to be found promenading along the cliff top; Harriet and Henry were leading the
way in front, Mr Denny, Mr Pratt, and Mr Chamberlayne
followed, leaving Lydia and Mr Wickham to bring up the rear.
They had been in Donaldson's all morning, and as the sun came
out from behind a cloud, Lydia remembered that she had left
her parasol behind.

"Miss Bennet, will you do anything to get me away from your
friends?" he whispered.

"Indeed, Mr Wickham, it is no falsehood," she answered. "I
do not know what has happened to my mind lately; I have
turned into more of a scatterbrain than ever I was in my life
before. Indeed, my thoughts seem to be preoccupied on other
matters and not on those which are necessarily of the moment."

"Are these other matters or other people, Miss Bennet? In
particular, do your thoughts tend to favour many individuals or
just one person?"

"Oh," she cried unable to resist striking him on the arm, "you delight in vexing me, Mr Wickham. I do not understand you."

"I will escort you to Donaldson's, Miss Bennet, to retrieve your parasol; you cannot go alone," he announced loudly in the next breath, for all the company to hear.

"Why, thank you, Mr Wickham. That is most kind," she answered with as demure an expression as she could.

"Don't be long," called Harriet. "We will wait for you at Dr Awsiter's Baths."

They rushed away, Lydia heady in Mr Wickham's company, yet being careful not to gaze into his eyes too often for fear of giving all her feelings away. The parasol was soon found, and they were on the point of leaving when George espied a pair of the most exquisitely carved cameo earrings in a glass topped cabinet, insisted that they should be hers, and bought and paid for them before she had a chance to object to his wild generosity.

"Oh, George, I long to be on our own," she whispered. "Yet, I feel the chances for us to be alone are so few and far between that I will go distracted before much longer. Thank you for my beautiful earrings, but how will I be able to wear them? I cannot be seen in them whilst I am in Brighton; however would I explain where they came from? Harriet would be sure to notice them for she has been exclaiming after a pair for several weeks without any success from her dear Colonel."

"I have a plan," said Mr Wickham when she would allow him to speak. "Will you promise to meet me tomorrow morning, down on the beach at dawn?"

"I cannot think of anything I would like better than to be washed up on the shore with you," she cried, wanting to catch hold of his hand.

"Will you promise to wear your earrings for me? A mermaid must wear shells in her ears."

"I do not believe in mermaids, Mr Wickham," she replied with a smile, "but you should be careful. There may be such a creature by the sea in the morn, one who wishes to entrap you with her charms!"

When he replied, she thought she would faint dead away. "I am yours to entrap, Miss Bennet. Please say that you will meet me tomorrow."

She nodded in affirmation, too tortured with emotion to speak, and could only find her tongue as they caught up with their friends, who very fortunately regarded them with no more curiosity than was the norm. For this she felt sincerely grateful, yet she felt every look in his direction and every conversation that passed between them must betray her feelings.

Such was her excitement at the prospect of meeting Mr Wickham that Lydia did not sleep at all well and, therefore, it presented no great difficulty for her to rise at dawn, dress, and leave the inn at the appointed hour, after first admiring her reflection in the glass. Her new earrings, screwed onto her ears with care, looked stunningly beautiful, and she thought how pleased George would be to see them.

As she descended the steps, it suddenly occurred to her that, although they had agreed to meet on the beach, they had not suggested any particular place, and as she looked anxiously about her, she realised there was not anyone in sight except for one of the dippers who was opening the door of a bathing machine. Lydia looked out over the sea, as calm as a millpond in the pearly light, and pulled her cloak closer against the chill of the early morning air.

"Have you come for a dip, my love?" the old crone asked. "The water's lovely today, my dear, just like a bath." Lydia smiled indulgently at the old lady and looked around for any sign of Mr Wickham but there was not a soul to be seen. "Come, come, my dear, I insist," the dipper entreated, "just step this way. I must have known you were coming, my dear. Why I've just opened the machine."

Lydia shook her head, but as she did so the old woman stepped forward and, taking her hand, started to pull her up the steps. She felt most frightened and tried to snatch her hand away but then, as the old woman's voice broke into a laugh, Lydia recognised she could hardly stop from laughing herself. The old crone was none other than her handsome Georgie, dressed in a ragged gown and stout shoes with a shawl wrapped round his head. Before another moment passed, she resisted no longer and allowed herself to be taken up the steps, falling with laughter as she went, tripping herself up and bruising her shins.

As soon as the door was shut, Wickham revealed himself, shedding his old woman's clothes and they fell into each other's arms. He showered her with kisses and she would not let him stop despite his poor head being bumped up against the low pitch of the roof.

"Come here," said Wickham, sitting down on the low bench that ran along one side. "There is not much room. We will have to share the seat, Miss Bennet, and perhaps you could sit on my knee."

"Thank you, Mr Wickham, you are most kind," she giggled, removing her cloak before he pulled her gently onto his lap. Then, as he watched, quite clearly bemused by her behaviour, she untied the ribbons of her bonnet with trembling fingers and

let it fall to the floor. It felt terribly wicked but completely delicious to be sitting with him in such a manner, feeling the
muscles in his legs twitching beneath her, in an effort to keep
her from toppling, and she flung her arms round his neck to
steady herself.

"There, now you may admire my earrings," she said and
moved her head slowly from side to side, giving him a chance to
inspect his gift, knowing that his eyes were captivated by more
than the shells in her ears.

"They are the most bewitching picture," he said and kissed
her until she gasped with pleasure. "Miss Bennet, I believe you
might just steal my heart." He stroked her curls and took the
pins from her hair, letting her raven tresses tumble through his
fingers. "Now you look more like the mermaid of my dreams,
quite the most delicious little fish I ever caught."

She could hardly breathe and was unable to move; he covered
her mouth and face with the sweetest kisses, exclaiming after her
beauty, as he pecked his way down her soft throat. Lydia felt transfixed with delight, but all was happening so quickly, she thought
she might faint dead away. She giggled with sheer pleasure, especially when she thought how diverted Kitty would be when she
wrote to tell her all about her escapade. Mr Wickham paused to
fix her with a look that took her breath away before he caught the
top edge of her muslin sleeve, pulling it down to reveal the creamy
white flesh of her shoulder. His lips brushed the bare skin, and she
knew she did not want him to stop.

Lydia had not appreciated how much of a natural propensity
for shameful conduct and wanton fancy she possessed until she
fell in love with George Wickham. She owned she had become

a capricious creature, reckless in her habits, and driven quite mad with passion. She was as addicted as a poor soul who craved a draught of laudanum or a bottle of gin. She knew he would lead her to the very devil before he was done with her, but she could only embrace this reflection with an open heart and mind. Her only desire was to inflame him all the more. Lydia laughed out loud at the expression on his face when she declared a wish to go swimming. Abandoning her gown and kicking off her slippers, she jumped into the azure water, like a Venus from the waves, begging him to follow her as he stared in astonishment. She swam as hard as she could and was amused to see him pull off his white shirt and dive in, clad only in his buckskin breeches. The little mermaid was soon caught in his arms, wriggling against him like a little fish, protesting vehemently to be let go but begging him to take hold whenever he threatened to release her. He swam back with her in his arms, mounting the steps two at a time, before he let her go and sprawled across the seat to sit back and observe. Although he scolded her for her depravity, affecting to behave like the perfect gentleman with a stern and disapproving countenance, she quickly observed that he did not turn his back or avert his eyes as she twisted her long mane into a cloth before slowly mopping and drying every last trace of the sea from every iridescent scale and translucent fin. Indeed, when she proffered her damp linen, he was all attention to the task of patting her softly dry, whilst soothing her salt-stung, oyster-soft lips with his own.

A sudden pounding on the door made them both jump and then Lydia heard a voice she recognised, a voice clearly in distress.

"Lydia, is that you? Are you in there? Oh, please say that you are!"

As George quickly threw a shawl over his head, Lydia opened the door a tiny crack and discovered Harriet, looking for all the world as though she had lost a fortune. Her face broke into smiles of relief when she saw Lydia, as she explained that she had become worried when she went to call on her at the breakfast hour and had not been able to discover her where-abouts or anyone who knew where she had gone.

"I have just been for an early morning bathe," Lydia assured her as well as she could, though she was sure she looked flustered and breathless. "I couldn't sleep; I do not know why I feel so anxious, I declare!"

Harriet expressed her surprise at seeing the old dipper, but Lydia explained that the woman had been assisting her in the lacing of her stays and prayed that Harriet had only just come upon them. It seemed that she had and, after persuading Harriet not to go for a bathe nor to engage the help of the old crone, who made a hasty retreat as soon as "she" could, Lydia insisted that they take a walk along the seashore before returning to the Ship for breakfast.

Inevitably, the lovers' secret trysts were halted for the present. Lydia was not able to speak to George again that day, nor see him, but she became increasingly concerned when he did not call at all. When she had not seen anything of him for three days together, she was distraught.

Wednesday, July 28th

George has gone! I am so distressed and do not know what to imagine. Though I have walked as far as the encampment, I cannot discover his whereabouts, and indeed, no one has seen Mr Wickham for some days, though there has been a suggestion by some uncouth louts that, if he is not to be found in Ragget's, I might try the moneylenders. If only I could go to his club, but no woman is allowed admittance in that establishment. I am hoping desperately that he will make an appearance this evening.

Is it my fault that he has taken himself off? I am convinced that I alone must be responsible for his disappearance, that somehow I must have displeased him, and I do not think I can carry on. What shall I do if he does not return?

Harriet has no comprehension of the truth of my situation and imagines I am pining for another, reassuring me that my spirits will be restored as soon as the Captain returns, which she is certain must be imminent. "And then I think we might all guess what happy event might take place next, Lydia," she said this morning, with a glint in her eye and a merry laugh. "He must have gone to town in search of a betrothal ring. Yes, I am sure that must be what has taken him away. Patience, my dear friend, and you will see he has been working on your behalf. Good things come to those who wait!"

Fortunately, Harriet quite missed the expression on my countenance after she made this very suggestion. If she had witnessed it, she would have been far more troubled.

Chapter 13

LYDIA, HARRIET, AND THE Colonel entered the Rooms the following evening and found the usual crowd, but there was no sign of Mr Wickham. Trying to appear unconcerned, Lydia was sure her face was betraying every emotion. She could not remember ever feeling so low. Perhaps George had met with an accident. What if he was lying in a ditch, thrown from a curricle, and she was not there to nurse him?

Mr Denny asked her outright why she appeared to be so downhearted. "Miss Bennet, are you quite well? You are very quiet this evening, and if I may say so, you are looking a trifle ill."

"I am quite well. I am just a little tired that is all. I am sure I will improve with an offer of a dance."

Mr Denny took the hint and whirled her away. She tried her best to be the light-hearted partner he knew, but there was still no sign of George and she thought her heart might break. They came off the floor and Denny offered to fetch them some drinks. She sat on a chair in the corner, hoping that no one would see her and make further enquiries or ask her to dance. Everybody seemed to be in high spirits, in great contrast to her own. What if Wickham had gone away, never to return? She could not bear to think of it and realised that her life would be unbearable without him. It had been coming on so slowly she could not think when she had first truly fallen for him, but she supposed in her heart it must have been from the moment she set eyes on him in Meryton High Street.

Then she saw him, George Wickham, the love of her life, moving with great rapidity towards her across the floor. Fortunately, Harriet and the Colonel were dancing and quite missed catching the expression of relief on Lydia's countenance or the agitated entreaties whispered into her ear. Anyone watching would have immediately guessed their intimacy, their bodies naturally curving in towards the other, and Lydia's expression of sheer adoration as her love begged her to step outside.

Once in the moonlit alley, she threw herself into his arms, covering him with kisses. But although he returned her caresses, she felt something wanting. He was not the passionate suitor she had known; there was a reserve about him and she felt unnerved.

Lydia broke away; she was all concern, knowing something was not right. "What is it, my love? You do not look yourself. Indeed, you are suffering truly, are you not?"

George Wickham was pacing the alleyway, his head in his hands. "Lydia, can I trust you?"

"Of course, with your life!"

"I am in trouble. I cannot go into the particulars, but believe me when I say that I have no choice but to leave Brighton, to go away for a while until I have sorted out some money matters which are most pressing."

"Leave Brighton? Leave me? But, George, you cannot leave. Say it isn't true."

"I must go; it cannot be avoided. Indeed, if I am not gone by tomorrow, I will surely be in fear of losing my life."

"George, you are alarming me now," she cried, grabbing his arm and searching his face. "How can you say such a thing? Surely you do not mean it."

"I have no choice."

"But there must be a way of solving your problems. You have many friends who will help you. Let us talk to Denny; he will think of a way I'm sure."

"I cannot ask him. He has already done what he can and it is not enough." He took her in his arms, looked beseechingly into her eyes and then down the length of the alleyway, as though he might find the answer in the darkness. Lydia felt she had never seen him so handsome and her heart lurched. She wanted to help him so much.

"If only Mr Darcy had seen fit to give me the living I had been promised by his most generous and kind-hearted father, I should not be in such dire circumstances. No, indeed, I would not be suffering such distress," he said, shaking his head in a sorrowful way.

Lydia felt so sorry for him. It was common knowledge that Mr Wickham, who had grown up with Mr Darcy on his Pemberley estate, had been denied the clergyman's living which had been promised to him on the old squire's death. He had been forced to make his own way and become a soldier. If only she were rich enough, she would have given him every penny to see him smile again.

He turned, grabbing her arms as though suddenly excited by an idea, which had not struck him before. "What about your winnings from the horses and your allowance? You must still have a lot of money left. I am right in thinking you had quite a sum, my dear?"

"I did have, but it is all but spent, you must know that. Lord! There have been so many wonderful reasons to be a spendthrift, and I own I have never been a girl who saves very much."

He let her go and leered at her in the darkness. "How much? How much have you got?"

For one moment, it put her in mind of being interviewed by her father. "I do not know exact amounts, but yes, I have my allowance and there is a little left from the racing."

"Will you lend me what you have, Lydia? I promise I will repay you as soon as I can. My money is all tied up at present."

Lydia hesitated. "And will you stay if I do?" She searched Wickham's face. He had drawn back into the shadows, and though she could not make out his expression, she knew she was about to lose him. She knew very well that he would not stay with her if she gave him her money, but she also realised that without it he was lost. "Please don't leave me," she begged. "I will give you all my money, but there is one small condition. I insist that you take me with you." She threw her arms around him once more. "We are only just becoming truly acquainted. We have so much to give one another. Indeed, George, I wish to give you everything I have."

"You do, don't you?" He looked down at her as though he was trying to make up his mind.

She peppered his face with kisses. "It would be an adventure, George. You know we can never be completely on our own in

Brighton. I am quite sure I have enough money for two. And it is all yours, I promise, as I am myself."

"Very well," he said at last, sighing. "There is nothing else to be done. I will take you with me. We will leave tomorrow evening as everyone is dancing at the Ship Assembly."

Lydia was ecstatic. All her fears about having upset him vanished in a moment. "George, are you asking me to elope with you? How romantic! We could go to Gretna Green! I shall be married before any of my sisters! Oh, they will be so very jealous, especially Lizzy who can have no idea how attached we have become."

"All that matters is that we leave without anyone's knowledge and with the money. Do you hear? You must not forget to bring the money!"

"There is no need to shout," Lydia scolded. "But surely you have some money?"

"I have explained to you that it is tied up. Listen, can you borrow some from Harriet?"

"I could not ask such a thing. Besides, she would wish to know why I need it. I cannot abuse her friendship. Oh, George, this is horrid. You are spoiling everything for want of wretched money."

"And you must not breathe a word of this to anyone, especially Harriet. Swear to me that you will keep quiet."

"Of course I will, George, but why are you being so unkind? I will do anything you say, you know I will."

Lydia was bursting to confide in Harriet. She was certain that her friend would not really be so very cross with her; being married was the important thing. All that mattered to her was that she was to be with George. She suspected the Prince's

129

dragoons had tricked Wickham out of his money and that was why he was a little short at present, though why he could not use the Brighton Bank to withdraw more funds she could not think. He said she must not worry her pretty head about it. Indeed, she gave it not a thought. All she could think of was the romantic image that presented itself in her head—being wed over the anvil and how she would be the envy of all her friends. How she loved George Wickham!

Friday, July 30th

I am so beside myself with excitement that I cannot think, speak, or behave in a rational manner! My darling Georgie, whom I love most in the whole world, has asked me to marry him!!!!!!!!!! I cannot believe what a fortunate girl I am. He declared his undying love for me and said he was so wild with passion for me that he could not wait a minute longer, saying that we should elope. I can think of nothing more romantic! Despite what George says about keeping our secret, I have just penned a letter to my sister Kitty, telling her all my plans. I pray it will not be intercepted and that Kitty will not give away my surprise as a result of her excitement. I cannot wait for the day to tell my family that I am married and see the astounded expressions on their countenances. To have my beloved's name as my own is a dream come true. Mrs George Wickham! How good that looks and sounds!

I am so afraid that my face will give away all my thoughts and am so aware that I cannot remove the smile that plays about my lips that I have taken to practising expressions of melancholia.

Oh, to be married in Scotland, at Gretna Green, like so many lovers before us. I would love to see my dear Wickham kitted out in tartan on our wedding day, and I could quite fancy myself in a green Tam with heather adornments!

We are to run away tomorrow night at midnight!!

Chapter 14

LYDIA DRESSED HERSELF WITH great care for the ball, her very last in Brighton. She stood before the looking glass and could not help giggling at the thought that she was to run away in her white satin and organza with orange blossoms in her hair. All she lacked was a piece of French lace to complete the picture. She gazed at her face; her large dark eyes were brimming with secrets, and she could not stop the smile that played about her lips from betraying her thoughts.

"I will never again look quite as I do this evening," she mused and could not help laughing out loud. "For though I may not yet wear George's ring, in my heart, I will surely be as good as wed tonight. Sweet Georgie Wickham, you will be mine at last."

She turned to stuff another dress into the bundle she had prepared to take on her adventure and added an assortment of combs, her hairbrush, her precious cameos, and anything else that would fit. The rest she would have to leave behind for the present, but no matter; she was sure George would buy her new things when they reached Scotland. Mindful of the time, she hastened to call on her friends at last. Lydia could hardly contain herself and hoped her feelings, which kept bubbling to the surface to erupt in a surfeit of giggles, would not give her away.

"Lydia, you have such sparkling looks tonight and there is a bloom on your cheeks so becoming to your complexion," remarked Harriet as the Colonel escorted them downstairs to the Assembly Rooms. "I think a girl in love often has a look of something indefinable, and you certainly have it tonight, my dear."

Lydia looked horrified for a second until she realised Harriet was referring to her being in love with the Captain. She thanked her friend for her compliments, ignoring her comments on being in love, before she scanned the place in search of George. She found him in the card room and, as soon as she could, gained his attention. She was more than a little pleased by his appraising stare. He looked her up and down in so brazen a manner it was all she could do to stay on her feet. In the next second, however, he was ignoring her once more as he attended to his game, and Lydia was left to find her friends in the ballroom before she aroused any hint of suspicion.

She was more than a little surprised, therefore, when just two minutes later, as she was considering with whom she might like to dance first, she felt her elbow caught by a strong grip as she was steered into the darkened alcove behind her by the man she most wanted to see. "Mr Wickham!" she cried, feigning shock, "What is the meaning of this?"

"You look quite edible tonight, Miss Bennet," he whispered into her curls, drawing her close, "like a plump, ripe cherry, begging to be taken for a bite."

"And just as succulent," she giggled, "though one bite will not satisfy, Mr Wickham, I fear on either side."

"No, indeed. A cherry taken whole and nipped with measured deliberation to prolong the pleasure is the best way to devour a ready fruit," he murmured, tracing a finger along the lace edge of her gown.

"It is not long now, my love," she whispered. "Oh, George, I cannot wait to be your wife."

"Remember, as soon as the supper bell rings, you are to fetch your things and leave by the alley door where I will have a carriage waiting, though by God, I have had to pay the fellow over the odds for it."

"But George, we will be together, alone at last."

"Do not forget the money, Lydia. Do you hear?"

"It is all in hand, George, do not scold me so."

"And now you must return. Do not speak to me again nor look in my direction. Is that clear?"

"I do not like it when you shout so, George, do not be so cross. I will not . . ."

Her words were quickly stifled as he covered her mouth with his, kissing her hungrily, leaving her begging for more.

Mr Chamberlayne stepped up on her reappearance to claim the first dance. As he took her hand, she glanced at him and could not help but wonder what he would think if he only knew that she was on the verge of an elopement. She had to laugh at the idea; she could not keep it in. Imagining his shock if he could read her mind only had the effect of making her laugh again.

"Miss Bennet, you are in a very teasing mood this evening. Pray, what are you about? Is something amiss? Do I have a hair out of place or mud on my breeches?"

"No, dear Chamberlayne, nothing is amiss," she said, chortling all the more. "You've never looked more dapper, and if this was the occasion on which I should flirt my last with you, I would take away a handsome vision, truly!"

"Then why do you still smirk, you saucy girl? You are up to something, I have no doubt, and I have not forgotten any of your tricks, miss. What merry jape are you planning now?"

"Mr Chamberlayne, I would not tease you again for all the world; it is enough to have the memory of your appearance as 'Miss Lucy.' No, indeed, it is not at you I laugh, but at myself."

"But why should you laugh at yourself, Miss Bennet?"

"Suffice to say, all will be revealed in time; it is a very big secret and you are all in for a big surprise!"

"You think you are very clever, Miss Bennet, but alas, I am not such a dolt as you think. I daresay I have guessed your secret!"

Lydia looked at him with alarm in her eyes. He drew her attention to a figure fast approaching them. "Aha, here is the Captain returned; he looks all set to claim you."

Lydia noted with increasing horror that Captain Trayton-Camfield had indeed returned and was pursuing his object with determination. He was at her side in moments, before the dance had even finished, begging her hand for the next two and demanding he be allowed to step in. "I have not finished dancing with Mr Chamberlayne," Lydia hissed, feeling the utmost alarm at seeing him again. "Please go away."

"I must speak with you privately, my dear," he was saying as he ran round after them, making a comical sight; Lydia did her best to ignore him, though he was colliding with the rest of the dancers in the set and making a thorough nuisance of himself.

To her great concern, her partner chose that moment to back away with a bow, allowing the Captain to take her hand. "I need to discuss a matter of great importance with you, Miss Bennet," he declared. "Will you allow an interview with me after the dance?"

"Captain, it is very pleasant to see you and I would wish for nothing else than some fine conversation, but unfortunately I am otherwise engaged. I have pledged the next dance to Mr Pratt, the next after that to Mr Denny, then Colonel Forster and then . . . I've promised Mr Wickham a jig too!" she declared, before she fell about laughing at the very thought.

Just then the supper bell sounded and Lydia looked about her in despair. She knew time was of the essence; if she was late George would be so cross, and she did not want anything to spoil this long-awaited evening. The Captain was still holding onto her hand, though the music had stopped, and it was evident he was not going to let go. She knew she would have to think quickly and use all her guile if he was to release her.

"Will you give me ten minutes, Captain, to slip away unnoticed into the crowd? I have a plan. A private audience would be delightful, but let us be completely alone. Let us meet down on the shore, at the bottom of the steps opposite this very inn."

"My dear, what a splendid idea. I see you have anticipated me. Yes, go my love, I will await you."

"Goodbye, my sweet," she returned, winking at him. This produced a huge smirk and a wink back, and she hastened as fast as she could across the dance floor and through the gathered throng.

Chapter 15

SHE RAN TO HER room, retrieved her bundle, and was about to go when she was taken by the idea that she could not disappear without leaving Harriet with a hint of where she had gone. She sat down at the desk in front of the window to compose her letter. As she reached for her pen and dipped the quill in the black ink, she was overwhelmed by a desire for mirth. She tried to steady her nerves, breathing the salt tang coming in off the sea, but her laughter rose inside her to erupt into the silence of the room. The muslin at the bow window, caught by a sudden gust, snapped and flapped back, rattling the curtain rings, shaking the blinds. Lydia paused to look out through the glass at the grey clouds massing over the sea and heard the sound made by the waves as they crashed and churned, water sucking up the stones and dashing them down again on the beach below. A summer storm was brewing, but it did nothing to dampen her excitement. She could hardly believe that the time to depart had arrived.

She started to write:

Dear Harriet,

You will laugh when you know where I am gone, and I cannot help laughing myself at your surprise tomorrow morning, as soon as I am missed . . .

She hesitated as a resounding clap like a cracking whip tore across the heavens, lighting up the sky in sulphurous tones before a roll of thunder crashed overhead. At once the rain began, blowing large, fat droplets across her missive, smudging and dissolving the ink, extinguishing the candle she had lit to provide more light against the dim evening. She stood up and lowered the window, taking in the scene below as figures dashed for cover from the tumultuous downpour. Carriages were arriving, bringing their pretty passengers to dance at the Assembly Rooms below. A girl, shivering in sheer muslin, alighted from a phaeton with her beau and was buffeted along by the wind, which whipped at her legs and threatened to snatch her bonnet. Some high-spirited young men leered enthusiastically at a trio of females who left them in no doubt of their mutual interest as they passed by. Coachmen turned up their collars, pulling down their hats and fastening close their carriage hoods against the unseasonable squall. Satin slippers were soaked through in seconds and shawls clutched tightly in an effort to stay dry as another coach-load of ladies ran from the streaming gutters, shrieking and hopping through the puddles.

"Lord, what fun! What delights have been mine whilst here," mused Lydia. "I will never forget my time in this pleasure haven. I could never have imagined, when I begged mama to let me go dancing with my sisters all those months ago, that my life would change so much, that I would not only be in love but with the dearest and most handsome man in the whole world." She felt another wave of sheer joy, mixed with the hope that her dreams were at last to be realised, and she laughed again to relieve the feelings bubbling inside.

But there was no time to stand and ponder, especially when her eye caught sight of a certain young Captain she wished to avoid running out across the road. She quickly drew back behind the curtain, returning to the desk to resume her letter.

I am going to Gretna Green, and if you cannot guess with whom I shall think you a simpleton, for there is but one man in the world I love, and he is an angel. I should never be happy without him so think it no harm to be off. You need not send them word at Longbourn of my going if you do not like it, for it will make the surprise the greater when I write to them and sign my name Lydia Wickham. What a good joke it will be! I can hardly write for laughing. Pray, make my excuses to Pratt for not keeping my engagement and dancing with him tonight. Tell him I hope he will excuse me when he knows all, and tell him when we next meet at a ball I will dance with him with great pleasure. I shall send for my clothes when I get to Longbourn, but I wish you would tell Sally to mend a great slit in my worked muslin gown before they are packed up. Goodbye. Give my love to Colonel Forster. I hope you will drink to our good journey.

Your affectionate friend,
Lydia Bennet

"La, what a good joke," she said to herself laughing and putting down her pen with a flourish. "She will be vastly surprised when she reads with whom I have run away!"

Lydia slid the missive to Harriet under her door, in the hope she should find it by the end of the evening, before running down the back stairs as fast as her legs would take her. Her flight was nimble, marred only by twisting her ankle on the last step, but as she limped through the back door, her heart leapt with joy to see that Wickham and the carriage were waiting.

So it was that Miss Lydia Bennet and Mr George Wickham did leave all their friends in the middle of a dance and run away together. Miss Bennet had no sooner stepped out of the rain and into the carriage before she had drawn the blinds and asked her beloved to remove her slipper, for her foot ached so much from the wrench it had endured.

"Lord, I am in such agony! Blast those stairs if I haven't sprained my ankle," she cried. "And my slippers are so wet, they are ruined!" She sprawled across the leather buttoned seat and stretched out her foot towards him.

"Georgie, take off my shoe, rub my toes better. I cannot wait any longer," she murmured.

"You're late, Lydia. I told you we have no time to mess about." He took her foot in his hands and eased off her satin slipper, moving his fingers so gently as to make Lydia swoon with anticipation. "Do you have the money?"

"Yes, it is all here and yours for the taking, as is everything I have, George," she declared, tossing over her reticule. He swiftly released her foot and emptied the money into his pockets. He shouted to the driver, banging on the roof with impatience. "We're in a hurry man, can your horses not go any faster?"

"Lord, it's hot and stuffy in an airless carriage," Lydia cried, tossing aside the lace from her bodice and unbuttoning the top of her gown. She could see George was more than a little agitated and hoped she could distract him. "Where is my fan? I hope it is not lost nor dropped on the dirty floor," she exclaimed, falling onto one elbow to look down, well aware that Wickham's eyes would be drawn to the tumble of ivory flesh which strained against white satin and pillowed over her gown.

"Do you like the clocks on my new stockings, George?" she asked him, as she sat up making no attempt to adjust her déshabillé and pulling up her gown to show him the pretty embroidery. "They're real silk you know; don't they feel exquisitely expensive?"

"Exquisite," he murmured, as he stroked her calf with deft fingers, but she could not help noticing that his attention was not entirely her own. He looked out through a chink in the blind.

"I have new garters, too," she added, arching in delight at his touch, "but I fear in my haste, they have come undone. Will you look, George? I am all thumbs!"

Lydia hitched her skirts higher and was pleased to have gained his attention at last. As a lightning flash seared through a chink in the blind illuminating the dark interior, she saw him smile. His eyes greedily followed the line of her leg to come to rest on her dainty garters tied just over her knees with a silky pink rosette.

"Do you like them, George? They are without doubt the most wonderful confections of ribbon and lace, do you not think? Come closer; do look at this flower! Have you ever seen such a pretty bud?" But just as she thought she had arrested his notice completely, her companion became distracted and did not attend her, peering anxiously through the window of the chaise, drawing back behind the blind as a horseman thundered by. Lydia was vexed; she could not bear to be ignored and decided to amuse herself by waving at any likely passerby and banging on the glass, until Mr Wickham growled at her that, if she persisted, he would have the horses turn back to deposit her at the Ship Inn once more. He only turned his attention when they were some distance out of Brighton, but Lydia was too cross and tired to wish to comply with his desires and grumbled at him about how dreadful it was to make a long journey in the most uncomfortable chaise she had ever known.

"Well, in that case, you will be pleased to hear that we are not to travel such a distance after all," ventured her companion who chose this moment to pull Lydia onto his lap to caress and cajole her back into good humour. "I am afraid we are not able to head for Scotland after all."

Lydia was all attention, sitting up at once. "What do you mean? Where are we going?"

"We do not have enough money to get to Gretna Green; we shall be lucky if we manage to get to Cheapside in a Hackney coach from Clapham."

"Cheapside! London! Are we to go to London?"

"I have a friend who will help us find lodgings, I am sure."

Lydia clapped her hands. "George, I have always longed to go to London and to be going with you, my darling, is more than I could ask. Who cares if we have little money now. I am sure we shall have soon, and we can go to Scotland some other time. How I love you!" she declared throwing her arms around his neck.

George allowed himself to be petted, fondled, kissed, and adored. "Now, where were we, my love?" he whispered as the storm thundered above their heads. "I believe you had a pretty flower to show me."

Saturday, August 7th

The days run into one another with such immense gratification that I am hardly aware of time and live in perfect rapture, drunk on love and the fulfilment that my Lord and Master brings me. We have not stirred for days, and I do not think we will ever rise again—though for dear Mr Wickham rising often is never a problem!!!

Dear me! How Harriet would laugh if she could see me! How I wish I had seen her face when she discovered my note to tell her of my elopement—I bet she split her sides!!!

I did feel a little anxious when we first arrived in Edward Street to see Mrs Younge for we had nowhere to stay, and with little money, we did not know at first what was to become of us. However, Georgie had soon secured us lodgings in Candlewick Street with the help of his dear friend, and though we have but two rooms and the furnishings are a little shabby, I have contented myself with playing house and find happy employment in buffing the gate-leg, polishing the candlestick, and turning down the bed covers on innumerable occasions throughout the day.

For the first time in my life, I find I am entirely given up to the task of pleasing one person; I am utterly and completely compliant, and submit wholly to dear George's every whim. He is such a patient tutor, and I am a very willing pupil. Papa would be most astonished!

I have but one regret and concern. We have very little money left, and my disappointment in having to part with my beautiful cameo earrings is truly breaking my heart. Georgie has gone to raise some money against them while he sorts out his affairs; he promises me faithfully that they will be returned very soon. I do not remember anyone ever showing such affection for me with such a thoughtful gift. I feel their loss greatly.

I do not know how we will ever manage to reach Scotland without any money. I feel sure that we will marry sooner or later, but I couldn't care two straws about that at present; all that matters to me is that we are together and in love. George is an angel, and he is the only man for me. I cannot think why it took me so long to realize that he was my true amour, my partner for life! But then, papa always did say I was one of the silliest girls in England. However, he shall not be able to say that now, and when we go home, man and wife, I will make my father proud of me at last!

I do wish we could go out to the theatre or entertainments a little. I am longing to be seen out with my darling Mr Wickham and to be recognised as a couple, so that all the world can know he is mine, but George says we cannot possibly go out and about until his affairs are all in order. I declared I should just like to look at the shops this morning, only to view some pretty baubles, and promised to wear my veil over my bonnet, but Mr Wickham had other ideas. He has taken lately to kissing me whilst I am in the midst of *conversation, and then I completely forget what I am saying and am forced to surrender. I cannot say no to him and am required so often to assuage his zealous appetites that there is little time for anything else. Indeed, as far as I am able, I have taken to anticipating these demands and have entirely dispensed with the necessity of formal attire. Idling the days away in languid recreation is more diverting than I ever dreamed possible, and I find I am able to bear all most cheerfully. Can Charlotte Collins know of such bliss? I declare mama would be quite shocked at the hours I am abed and at my willing obedience to retire. Lord, how the very idea makes me roar with laughter!!! I love dear Mr Wickham with all my heart, my body, and my soul!!!*

Chapter 16

AFTER A WEEK OF connubial-style bliss, however, Lydia was restless and bored. Her mood was peevish and her requests to go out into the town remained unchanged. Whilst sitting at the window one evening, watching the bustle of humanity going about its business, she decided she would have another try at bringing her lover round, convinced that she could persuade him to change his mind.

"I am sure you would like to go to Astley's, my love, to see the horses; it is just the sort of place we would both enjoy. Isabella declares it is her favourite haunt in all of London. She says she has seen a man stand on the back of a horse and jump through hoops as he is galloped around."

"We cannot afford to go to Astley's, my dear," said Mr Wickham gravely. "Perhaps if you had been more prudent, we might well be sampling its delights this very moment."

"Oh, George, how can you be so cruel? We must have a little money now you have pawned my earrings. Let us skip supper and go out. I long to meet your friends. There must be somewhere you can take me."

Mr Wickham finally acquiesced, his patience at its end. In truth, he craved some male company, and he knew Lydia, not biddable enough to stay in on her own, would insist on accompanying him. "Very well then," he announced, "get your cloak and bonnet, come along, and let us go out."

Lydia did not wait to be told twice, appearing moments later in her only other muslin gown, her hair dressed and topped with the only bonnet she had. "George, I was just rummaging amongst my things for a comb and I found this florin, it must have fallen out of my reticule. We will be able to eat too!" she declared.

"Are you sure you haven't any more hiding in that voluminous bundle of yours, my sweet?" said Wickham.

"It was not hid; I have only just found it. Search my belongings if you care to, but please let us not quarrel. I do hate it when you are displeased with me," she answered. "Let us be merry, and when we return, your little mermaid will play with you. What game shall it be? Hide the soldier's swordstick? I declare that is your favourite!" She laughed, unlatched the door, and ran down the staircase into the night air before he had a chance to change his mind.

They kept to the side paths and the dark crooked alleyways, not venturing far. Though she was pleased to be out and about, Lydia did not like the London streets. "It is so dirty and smelly, not in the least what I expected."

"Well, it ain't Mayfair, that's for sure," he said, as he turned into a passage where the flare of lamps lit up the courtyard of an inn. Lydia sidestepped the steaming piles left by the horses as well as she could. Her satin slippers were already looking past their best, and in her haste to leave Brighton, she had not thought to bring any more.

A woman in a low cut gown leered drunkenly out of the shadows and grabbed Wickham's arm. "Want some company, handsome?" she slurred. Wickham shook off the woman's arm and led Lydia under the swinging sign that proclaimed the establishment to be "The Boar's Head." They entered the hostelry and found themselves in a dim, narrow room, filled to the brim with customers who either sat in partitioned booths at tables eating their supper or jostled one another at the bar. At one end of the tavern, a fire flickered, burnishing the range of pewter mugs and candlesticks along the mantelpiece to a golden glow, and at the other, an old clock ticked away the hours. In the space between, the patrons were high in liquor and in jovial mood. Lydia was fascinated by the ribald company, made up mostly of men whose eyes were all upon her as she clung to Wickham's arm.

As they searched for the impossible, an empty table, a voice called out, "Wickham, by gad. What are you doing in this neck of the woods?" Its owner was a good-looking young man who stood up from the table he was sharing with a group of his fellow sailors as they approached.

"Edward Draper, is that you?" Wickham laughed and clapped the man on the back. Lydia looked on, aware that Mr Draper's companions were staring at her approvingly.

"Come, sit yourselves down," entreated Mr Draper. "Introduce me, you old charmer. Who is this pretty girl you have on your arm? Sit next to me, miss, and I will tell you some tales about your friend that will have your hair standing on end." He took her gently by the hand, easing her past his knees. For a moment she fell onto his lap; the snug space, much to her assistant's delight, did not permit her to pass easily. Lydia giggled, Mr Draper feigned embarrassment, with a thousand apologies and a squeeze of her waist, before helping her to a seat in the corner of the alcove where she sat in intimate proximity to her newfound friend, bemused by the attention she was getting. Mr Wickham did not seem perturbed in the slightest; he was already ignoring her, swapping stories, catching up with other old friends who plied him with porter, and ordering a large dinner for them all.

"Do you believe in love at first sight, Miss Bennet?" Mr Draper asked, taking her hand in his own and kissing her fingertips.

"I do, Mr Draper," she returned, easing her hand from his grasp but giving him the benefit of a long stare, which told him in no uncertain terms that she found him most attractive. "I declare I fell in love with my George at once, though I tried to deny it for many months. My sister was in love with him, you know, and he, naughty man, seemed unaware of my existence at first."

"That I find hard to believe, though George Wickham wouldn't recognise a likely gal if she fell over him. Your sister liked him you say. Do you mean to tell me there are more like you at home?"

"I am one of five sisters, 'tis true, though they are not at all like me. They would never follow their heart and run away as I have," she added, joining in with his laughter as he threw his head back and guffawed.

"So, is it an elopement?" he whispered. "Trust George to never leave things to chance."

"It is an elopement of sorts," she answered, "but I'm afraid we have run out of money, so we can't get wed. Still, I daresay we will get to Gretna Green sooner or later."

"I daresay you will; I always thought Wickham was the marrying kind," he announced loudly enough for the company to hear, who all fell about with laughter as though he had made some huge joke. Wickham shifted in his seat and declared that they must be going soon, though Lydia's pleas to be allowed to finish her roast beef soon quieted him. After all, he was not sure their next meal would be such an excellent one; the porter was good and he was glad to see Edward, though his tongue was still loose, he observed. Lydia was at her most flirtatious. She declared she liked a naval uniform as much as a redcoat and thought, if it were not for Mr Wickham, she could quite easily fall for Mr Draper's charm. London was fun after all, even if she hadn't yet been to Astley's, but now they had been out once, perhaps George would change his mind and take her shopping. She needed new shoes and a new bonnet, and she knew she could procure them with the help of a visit to the pawnshop. The Captain's locket still lay in its box at the bottom of her bag, and she was determined to find a means of disposal to suit herself on the morrow!

The day started well, and they rose late. Whilst lying abed, taking care to choose her time carefully, she confessed that she had the locket in the bottom of her bag and claimed she had forgotten she had such a thing in her possession. She had known that, at such a moment, George would only be half attending to what she was saying and, indeed, at first he did not express either interest or amazement. "Why did you not tell me of this before?" he said, as a dawning realisation had him sitting up and paying attention.

"I forgot it, George, I swear on my life, but now I have remembered we can make the best of it. Let us pawn it or sell it if you like, and then I thought we might do a little shopping. Oh, can we, George? Please let me have new shoes. My satin slippers are in shreds, and you know how I like a new bonnet. And you shall have new shoes, too, if you like."

"I am not inclined to think that we should spend it, Lydia. We have to live, you know."

"Please, Georgie," she whispered, as she caressed him. "Just some new shoes would do. I don't have to have a bonnet too, though I truly need one."

He had given in at last, and she had got her way; let out alone in the street at the shops for a few hours, she had spent a large sum of money on a new pair of shoes, some satin ribbon, and a bonnet with a veil, which she could not be without.

She was just turning in from St Nicholas Lane, to cross the street to their lodgings, and was considering what a fine thing it was to spend a morning employed with a little shopping, when she was astonished to see someone she recognised too well outside their door, which closed behind him before he walked off with an air of superior purpose on the other side of the street. She had never been so surprised to see anyone in her life!

Chapter 17

MR DARCY! WHAT COULD he be doing there? Lydia thought as she crossed the street with a sense of foreboding and ran up the staircase, demanding to know what he had wanted. She soon discovered that the odious man had been there for some time, upsetting her beloved boy, making him all cross and exceedingly gloomy. Even worse was the news that he was to call later on in the day in order to speak with Lydia.

"Why didn't you send him away with a flea in his ear?" she remonstrated. "I do not want to speak to him. How dare he interfere!"

"Do not be so hasty, my dear," Wickham answered, trying to calm her down. "He may be able to assist me. Proud and arrogant he may be, but he is rich, and if I could just extract a little money out of him, money that is due to me, my problems might well be resolved."

"I do not want his money," Lydia insisted.

"You will listen to what he has to say."

"But if he is uncivil, as I expect, I will not suffer his company any longer than I must."

Wickham roared. "Listen you silly girl, you will be polite to Mr Darcy and help me if you can. He owes me a living, and you might well be the person to help me get it, but you must heed my advice and ignore his requests. He may ask you to go with him. Above all, if he demands that you leave me, be firm and refuse."

"Of course I will, George. Do you think it likely I would run off with him? But I do not see how he will give you any money on my account. Who am I to him?"

"You do not need to worry about that, just tell Darcy you are staying put and that you will not be removed. Leave the rest to me."

Lydia was instantly thrown into a temper, though she did her best to keep her feelings from Wickham. She hated to see him so cross and wished only to make him happy. However, she was determined she would speak to Mr Darcy on her own terms, and though she wished to stay with George, she decided she would be as civil as she cared. George was not going to tell her how she must behave.

She could not say that she was left feeling any more cheerful by the interview that she was forced to endure with Mr Darcy in private. He dismissed Wickham as soon as he arrived and took a seat opposite her, staring at her a good deal before he chose to speak. Lydia looked back at him with as much intent. She noted his immaculate appearance: his dark coat moulded to his figure in the very best cloth, the starched, crisp folds at his neck and his dark eyes, which penetrated hers.

"Madam, I am at a loss as to understand the willful and wanton manner in which you have lately conducted yourself," he began, looking about the place with an expression of contempt, "without any redress, thought, or consideration not only for your good parents but for yourself. Your total want of propriety, which I have often observed in your behaviour since first I was introduced to you, has been of the gravest concern to me and to your family, who are now beside themselves with worry for your welfare. But in the first instance, I must satisfy myself that Wickham has told me the truth about your willingness to follow him here. In short, I must ask you, Miss Bennet— for I would like to assure myself that you are not the selfish, licentious creature that at this moment you appear to be—to explain yourself. Did Mr Wickham force his attentions upon you and take you against your will? Or must I conclude, as I see your expression bears no symptom of unease, that you came with him willingly to this den of iniquity?"

"I came most willingly, Mr Darcy. It was my idea as much as dear George's," she professed, daring to meet his stern gaze.

"Have you not considered your position, madam? Look around you. Are you not sensible of the condition in which you find yourself?"

"I am wholly sensible of my condition, Mr Darcy, and it is one with which I am perfectly happy; indeed, I have never been more content with a situation in my life!"

"Mr Wickham is in most serious trouble, Miss Bennet. He has taken a young girl away from her friends and placed her in the most compromising, discreditable predicament. He is a libertine and seducer of the worst kind. It is neither safe nor seemly for you to remain here any longer under his roof, and immediate steps must be taken to remove you from his influence."

"I will not be removed, whatever you say. I hate the very sight of you, Mr Darcy," she declared, standing up to confront him. "You do not frighten me with your sour looks or your threats. How dare you accuse my darling George of seduction, when it should be plain that, not only have I encouraged our liaison, but have been instrumental in it taking place at all. I should be accused of seduction if anyone is to be blamed. Indeed, George did not stand a chance. I was determined to have him, and I would do it all over again. We would be married now if we had been rich enough, but you would have no idea what it is to be at the mercy of others for your fortunes!"

"Miss Bennet, you do not know what you are saying," he replied in earnest. "Think of your mother if you cannot think of yourself. You must leave this place immediately and go home. I have a carriage waiting outside, and I can assist you in any way you wish. Do you have a friend you would like to stay with and visit? Please be sensible and consider what I can do for you."

"No, I will not, Mr Darcy, and you cannot make me!"

"Well then, Miss Bennet, let me put this to you. I have money for you to buy new gowns, bonnets, and all manner of luxuries that I will put at your disposal if you will do as I ask and leave Mr Wickham this instant."

"Well, I think you have a nerve, Mr Darcy, and I will tell you now, I do not care for you to interfere. I do not want your money. Mr Wickham and I will marry sooner or later without your help. I am not about to go and stay with any friends at your suggestion whilst I am having the time of my life with the man I love best in the whole world. Nothing you say or do will change my mind about him."

"You cannot know the danger you face from him. You would be much better off staying with your friends."

They sat in silence; Lydia could feel his temper rising, though he had all the appearance of a calm countenance. Lydia folded her arms and looked away as though she were regarding something of great interest through the window.

At last he spoke. "I will return tomorrow," he said, standing to glower at her with his dark, brooding eyes. "I wish you would consider very carefully my offers of assistance to you. If you cannot oblige me, Miss Bennet, I beg you would think of your family, especially your parents and your sisters."

He departed without giving George his compliments, leaving Lydia feeling quite triumphant, though her account of the interview did not improve her lover's temper one jot.

Saturday, August 14th

Georgie is in better humour today, despite being closeted with Mr Darcy for half the morning. That man is the rudest I know; he scarcely nodded in my direction on his arrival before banishing me to the bedchamber, which, although the scene of many happy hours, is now beginning to pall. I declare I could recount each and every cobweb and spider on the tented canopy of our bed if I was called upon to do so!

I daresay we have not seen the last of Mr Darcy, but this afternoon we did not give him a thought. With George's good spirits returned and his request to see me dance for him again, we might have been the only two people in the world. 'Tis surprising what effect an exhibition with two or three classically draped bed sheets can have on a young man, though it has to be said my efforts were slightly impeded by the vase which I held for authenticity. Afterwards, George pulled me onto his lap, and I fed him cherries as I sat on his knee, twirling his black curls through my fingers in rapturous elation.

I wonder if Lady Hamilton's exhibitions for a certain Naval intimate command such euphoric encores? I would lay bets that they do not!!!

Chapter 18

MR WICKHAM'S GOOD SPIRITS continued. Lydia
suggested he must have a secret by the smile that played about
his face, but it seemed he was not prepared to share it however
much she pleaded with him. He insisted that, if all went
according to plan, he would very likely have some good news
for her on the morrow. Lydia did not think she could wait but
wondered if all depended on Mr Darcy, who she surmised they
would soon see again. By the very next day it was all settled. Mr
Darcy appeared but did not stay for long. As soon as Lydia heard
the door shut behind him, she emerged from the bedchamber,
demanding a full report.

"Well, Miss Bennet, it seems you are to make my fortune
after all," Wickham declared mysteriously, a broad smile on his
countenance. "I always did admire you, but this afternoon, I
declare, I never felt more in love."

"Whatever do you mean, George? Is Mr Darcy to give you
some money? Is it because of me? I confess, I am astonished."

"Do not flatter yourself, my love. It is, after all, quite what he owes me, you know. If everything continues as well as it might, all will be to our satisfaction, I am certain. You will be pleased to be addressed as Mrs Wickham, I think, will you not?"

"Whatever do you mean, George? Why do you tease me so?"

"We are to be married, my dear."

"Married, George?! Are you asking me to marry you?"

"Why yes, I suppose I am. In any case, it is all arranged."

"George, you are so clever! I knew you would find a way and to do it without me knowing a thing. But what did you mean by saying you only admired me before this afternoon? If I recall, you were the one desperate to have me run away with you. I never should have if I didn't think you loved me."

"Quite so, Lydia, as you say. But I have important matters to occupy me. Now, where is my account book? Let me attend to my finances."

It appeared that his money worries had been resolved, yet she could hardly believe it had anything to do with Mr Darcy. He was intent on revealing their whereabouts to her uncle, and it transpired that her father had been in London searching the streets for days. She certainly did not want either of them turning up at their lodgings. Why they were making so much fuss she could not understand; she and George would have gone home sooner or later. Why could they not wait a bit longer? However, she could not be cross for long. She was to be married by the end of the month. Lydia thought they must be the happiest couple in the kingdom.

Mr Darcy soon made another appearance, telling her she must pack her bag and be ready to leave for her Aunt and Uncle Gardiner's house first thing on the following morning.

"I will not go, Mr Darcy, and you cannot make me!" Lydia protested.

"Let me assure you, Miss Bennet," Mr Darcy declared, "there will be no wedding unless you do strictly as you are told. If you comply with these wishes, Mr Wickham will be allowed to visit you at your aunt's house whenever you please, although to tell the truth that is a privilege I would have denied you!"

Again she protested and appealed to Wickham.

"My dear, I think on this occasion," he answered, "it would be well to do as Mr Darcy requests. We do not want to upset your aunt, do we?"

She was not looking forward to seeing either her aunt or her uncle, and only the thought that she and Wickham were soon to be married could make her visit there bearable.

George was unusually quiet during the whole interview with Mr Darcy. Lydia thought he was such a ninny around him. How could he let Darcy dictate what his behaviour and actions should be? When there was a pause in the conversation between the two men, Lydia asked, "Mr Darcy, have you happened to have seen my papa?"

"No, Miss Bennet, I have not had that pleasure," he replied, "and I think you will understand when I say I am grateful that I have not had to witness his distress at this time."

She was sorely relieved. Her father had never thrashed her in her life, but she owned that she had been terrified at each knock upon the door, for she was sure he would not have held back with either herself or her amour on this occasion.

"Your uncle will be acquainting your family with the particulars of the engagement in a letter, and I must add, Miss Bennet, that I think you are most fortunate to have such kind relatives to take in such an ungrateful girl and have the trouble of seeing to all the arrangements of your wedding. I hope you will be sensible and make yourself as pleasant and useful to your aunt as you can whilst you are under her care."

Lydia was incensed. Who did he think he was? He scolded her as a brother might, and she was affronted! No wonder her sister Lizzy was so revolted by him; Lydia could see exactly what she meant now.

With great reluctance did she take leave of her dear Wickham and set forth to her aunt and uncle's house on Gracechurch Street. Their welcome, although civil, was not exactly effusive and warm. She had just been relieved of her pelisse and shown to her room when her Aunt Gardiner appeared at her door, there to tell her exactly what she thought of her behaviour.

"Well, Lydia," she said, "I have often thought that your behaviour was not always seemly and that perhaps a little less overindulgence would have curbed the worst excesses, but I was prepared to think that, because you had been spoiled in your youth, you could not entirely be blamed for your impetuous ways. But I am at a loss as to know what I can say to you on this occasion. How could you be so selfish? You did not consider anyone else but yourself before you acted so rashly. Did you never once think of your poor mama, your papa, or indeed your sisters, on whom your sins would blight? Do you realise what such a scandal will do for the reputations of your sisters as well as your own? What sort of alliances they will be able to make now, when this gets out, I do not know. I only hope your marriage may stem the worst of the gossip, although people will talk. Your imprudent and dissipated ways have cost your sisters dearly. Folly and frivolity have been your undoing, and I hope you will now consider the damage you have very nearly brought to your reputation!"

Lydia had never been told off quite like it before in her life; she was sure her mother would have been disgusted with her aunt if only she had known. Mindful of Mr Darcy's dire warnings about upsetting her aunt, she managed to endure the worst by engaging her thoughts on last night's passionate embraces, the memory of which had her blushing with blissful recall. Her aunt instantly took her reddened cheeks and downcast eyes to show contrition, so for the time being, she was left alone to consider how fortunate she was that the disgrace she had brought upon her family would be slightly lessened by the fact that she was to become a respectable married woman.

George called that evening and dined with them all. It was very strange to have to say goodnight to him, but Lydia was glad they were at least left alone for ten minutes in the hallway. How she would ever sleep that night without him to alleviate her rest-less spirits she did not know. He did his best in the confines of the cramped corridor, but all was totally unsatisfactory as his kisses only left her longing for more.

Friday, August 20th

I was allowed to go shopping for wedding clothes today and have made some good purchases, despite being forced to comply with every one of my aunt's wishes. She gave instructions to the dressmaker for gowns with such a high décolletage that I shall look like an old matron. Every style she chose for me was at least two years out of date. My only comfort is that the dress-

*maker seemed to see my point of view, and I hope that my whis-
pered entreaties will win the day. I am to wear cream silk on my
wedding day with a blue bonnet and accessories, but I long to
know which coat George is to wear. I favour his blue, and I
declare no one ever saw a more handsome picture than him in it.*

*The days drag along so slowly. I am scolded on a daily basis.
Nothing I do or say seems to please my aunt, who is as bad-
tempered as ever, making no attempt to understand me. Nobody
seems to realise how much in love I am with George and that we
didn't have a choice about running away together. I am sure my
aunt has forgotten what it is to be young and smitten with a young
man, and I daresay she never loved Mr Gardiner with half the
passion I have for my Georgie. Uncle Edward, it has to be said,
whilst being a very affable kind of fellow, is not the sort to inspire
passion in anyone, least of all my aunt. But then, it is very difficult trying to imagine one's elders submitting to their feelings. I
cannot begin to think about mama and papa being in love, and as
for fervent ardour . . . well, perhaps the less said or thought about
that the better.*

*I only live for George's visits, but even he does not please me
today. When I first came here, he would visit all day and sit with
me, but lately he has taken to disappearing for hours at a time and
only turns up for his dinner. I have told him how lonely I am, but
it is as if he does not hear me. I cannot wait until we are married
and then we shall be in company with one another as much as I
please! I love my darling angel so much and long for the day we
are united as man and wife!*

Chapter 19

LYDIA WAS SITTING WITH her aunt the next day, wishing that she did not have to endure yet another reprimand nor hear her aunt cluck once more in dismay, when the door opened and in stepped Mr Wickham with a jaunty air and a grin on his face. "Good morning, ladies, is it not a wonderful day? I have good news! It is all arranged, my love," he said, turning to Lydia. "We are shortly to be removing to Newcastle!"

"Newcastle, Mr Wickham!" Lydia shouted. "Lord above! Where on earth is that?"

"Lydia!" admonished her aunt. "There is no need for such blasphemy!"

"How can we leave all our friends, Georgie?" Lydia persisted. "I do not know that I care to go to this Newcastle place, and in any case, what on earth will we do there?"

"I am to go into the regulars. I have an ensigncy in General Turnbull's regiment. You will soon make new friends, have new favourites, my dear."

"Oh, a new regiment, you should have said so at once, my dear. How thrilling! Now that puts quite a different light on the matter. How envious Kitty will be; a whole new regiment of soldiers to be discovered and courted," she shouted, leaping up to hug her fiancé. "Though to be sure, Mr Wickham will always have first place in my heart," she added, glancing at her aunt whose eyebrows were raised to the heavens.

"George, shall we have a large house in Newcastle? My sisters will be able to visit us and see for themselves how well you have done."

"I am sure we shall be very comfortable, my love. We will soon find some lodgings to suit us."

"Lodgings! Tush, George! We must have our own house. I can see it now, just on the edge of town, with ten windows either side of a large front door and a gravel sweep! I long to see to everything. We must have new furniture, and we mustn't leave London without going to Wedgwood's for a new dinner service. You know we can afford it now that Mr Darcy has given you some money."

"Lydia, I do not think it at all prudent to be spending money in such an ill-advised fashion," interrupted her aunt. "You must learn to live within your means. I know some more reasonable warehouses where you may purchase china that will be more than adequate for your requirements. You will not be expected to entertain very often, and an expensive dinner service will only be a waste of money. If you are careful, and Mr Wickham works hard and is promoted, well, then you may have the cause and the funds for fancy things in Newcastle, but mark my words, Lydia, spend unwisely now and you will live to regret it." Lydia did not listen. She did not care. Soon she would be gone and she would no longer have to listen to her aunt's rantings.

They were to travel to Newcastle immediately after they were married! But Lydia longed to see her mama and sisters before they went, and she was quite prepared to meet with her papa if he would be kind to her. How she would love to see all their faces and show off her ring. Married before any of the other Bennet girls; as her mama had always said, how jealous of her they would be. She did hope Elizabeth would not be too upset with her for stealing her beau. Lydia had thought her sister had had very high hopes of securing his affections once upon a time. Poor Lizzy and Jane—to be old maids and not know anything of the joy of married life. How Lydia felt for them.

She was a little sad at not being able to see Harriet or Isabella, but she was sure they would meet from time to time. Her mother and poor sisters would not be able to see her for many years, but they would just have to get used to the dullness and silence, which would inevitably ensue when she was gone to the North. Poor wretched souls!

Monday morning dawned at last; Lydia had hardly slept a wink during the night for all the nightmares she had, dreaming she was late to the church, dreaming that Wickham could not wait for her and that she was forced to marry Mr Darcy instead. She was so tired by the time she sat to her breakfast at ten that her aunt reprimanded her a dozen times for insolence and a host of other crimes because she was too tired to open her mouth.

"Civility costs nothing, Lydia. I would have thought you could have wished your aunt good morning at the very least on this, your wedding day. All the trouble you have put your family to and you cannot find the tongue you were born with."

"I didn't sleep well, and I am so fagged I couldn't care if I had upset the King of England, let alone my family. I can hardly keep my eyes open."

"Lydia, you must learn to speak in a more ladylike fashion and have a little more respect for your relatives, as well as the monarchy, though I am not so sure they deserve it. Still, I do not know what your mother would think if she could hear you running on so."

Lydia's poor nerves were quite torn to shreds before they had even arrived at St. Clement's. Aunt Gardiner continued to abuse her and preach at her all the morning whilst she tried her hardest to dress. She could not understand why everyone was so vexed with her. Perhaps she had been unwise to run away, but she was so in love with George that she was not answerable for her actions. Could they not see that she had acted with the very best of intentions? George had needed her, she was in love with him, and that was all there was to the matter. She pulled on her gloves and stood in front of the glass. On the whole, she was pleased with her appearance. She wore a new cream silk dress with a short pelisse over, a hat of blue satin with a cream lace veil, decorated with sprigs of convolvulus—quite the latest accessory.

At the last minute, her uncle was called away by his business associate, Mr Stone, just as the carriage was arriving, and Lydia was thrown once more into the throes of anxiety, fearing that they would be late and that Wickham would think she was not coming. At last he appeared and off they set, her aunt's scolding resounding in her ears and only the thought of seeing her darling Georgie and knowing that she was to be united with him in holy matrimony prevented her from having a fainting fit or running away.

Lydia thought Mr Wickham looked as handsome as the devil in his blue coat and cut such a dash that Mr Darcy, who stood gravely beside him, paled into insignificance. Why he had to be there Lydia could not understand. She thought he had interfered quite enough already and suspected that her lack of wedding clothes had been a result of his all too frequent conversations with her aunt. She wished she could have been married from home with all her friends to see her and was sure her mama would have preferred it. Longbourn church would have been filled with people and posies. There was scarce a creature to be seen near St Clement's: hardly a soul inside it nor a flower in sight! There was no music, and she knew there would be no peal of bells on the way out. Nevertheless, as she hung onto her uncle's arm and walked up the aisle, she smiled to herself at the thought that this was, after all, her wedding day; she was to be married before any of her sisters!

The bride was all beaming smiles and could not stop giggling at Wickham, who looked the very picture of solemnity, his face the same ashen shade as the statues who guarded their loved ones out in the graveyard. Lydia let go her uncle's arm as soon as she could to stand at George's side. She smiled up at him. "I shall laugh out loud, Georgie, if you wear that expression much longer. Do not tease me so on my wedding day," she whispered before giggling into her prayer book. He bit his lip, his brow furrowing as though the weight of the world had been laid upon him.

The ceremony passed off exceedingly well, Lydia decided, despite Mr Wickham's voice being so quiet as to be hardly heard and for Lydia's unfortunate trip up the aisle on the way out which scuffed her new shoes. "You should learn to keep a tighter hold on my arm," she scolded. "Indeed, you are a little tardy in these matters, Mr Wickham. If only you would attend more."

"You should look where you are going," he responded in a surly tone, letting go of her arm. "If your mouth were still for long enough, instead of being engaged in gabbing to anyone who will listen for two half seconds together, you might have been aware of the uneven paving and the direction in which you were walking!"

Mr Darcy spoke only two words to her all morning and neither was an expression of congratulation for either of them. George held out his hand to him, but Lydia noticed that a moment or two passed before the other proffered his to shake, and then it was done in such a paltry manner she did not know why he bothered. To tell the truth, everyone seemed out of sorts, and why they could not be happy for her was a mystery. However, Lydia was determined to enjoy the day, even if she had to do it on her own! She smirked and smiled as though her life depended on it, and even when George left her on the steps of the church to take his seat in the carriage without first handing her in, she was able to forgive him and remain cheerful. She imagined he had merely forgotten her in his haste to escape from Mr Darcy!

At last they were able to take leave of her relatives, and she imagined their regard for one another to be mutual, in that, were their paths never to cross again, no feelings on either side would be injured. They set off in the chaise and were to meet Mr Bennet's carriage at Hoddesdon. Mr Wickham was very quiet throughout the entire journey; indeed Lydia declared he looked most ill.

"You are very quiet today, Mr Wickham, I declare I never saw you such a ninny. Are you feeling quite well?" She put her hand on his forehead. "You do feel awfully clammy. I know what must ail you; Mr Darcy took you out last night to celebrate your impending nuptials and you had a bad oyster, am I right?" Mr Wickham stared out through the window, his expression remaining impassive.

"La, you cannot even laugh at my jokes, you must be sickening for something. What is it George? I hope you are not going to be ill for our wedding night. George, I have an awful foreboding. Tell me I am wrong. Will it truly be as fun, now it is legal and aboveboard?" She laughed at her questions, but George Wickham would not be cajoled out of his silent inclination until they reached the inn, and he would not speak to his wife other than to say that she must not divulge the fact that Mr Darcy was at their wedding to anyone at home.

"It is a secret which must be kept strictly between ourselves, do you understand, Lydia? You must not breathe a word of it to a single soul."

"I shouldn't think there is a creature who could care less whether Mr Darcy was there or not," Lydia scoffed, "but why does it have to be such a secret? I should have thought you would want everyone to know that, finally, he has paid his dues to you. I will certainly want people to know that he has at last seen the error of his ways."

Wickham roared at her in such a fashion, and with no explanation, that she was forced to consider the prudence of holding her tongue. "Do not speak of it, do you hear?" he shouted. "You are to tell no one, not a soul, have you got it? If I hear you have breathed a word of it to anyone, Lydia, I shall thrash you with my bare hands."

"Not even my father has ever shouted at me like that before, and if you think you are going to make a habit of it now we are married, you had best think again," she shouted back. "I am so shocked, I shall burst into tears!"

If George had a weakness where women were concerned it was that he hated to see them cry. Indeed, he took great pleasure in helping any lady in distress, often using the situation to his own advantage. There was nothing he enjoyed better than drying a young lady's tears, especially if he could take her in his arms to alleviate her suffering. Knowing how much her Georgie would wish to comfort her, she put a little extra effort into her performance, which achieved the desired effect. He soon had his arm round her, and although she resisted for a full five minutes, she then let him kiss all his favourite places.

He certainly cheered up after a drink to their health, in the very dining room where she had met her sisters all those months ago. They had a fine nuncheon; pink ham, roast beef, and a dressed salad, washed down with as much wine as they wished. After all, it was their wedding day, and they both knew that the most gruelling part of the day was yet to come.

"I am not afraid of my father," Lydia professed, "but I know his reception is not going to be the same as the rapturous welcome we shall certainly have from my mother." She took her seat in the carriage. "Small wonder that you have been so quiet at the start of our journey, Mr Wickham. What a silly girl I am! For a moment, I had begun to think you might have regretted marrying me after all." No, she thought, it was clear he had been thinking of her papa, and so she assured him that all would be well; her mama would not let her papa misbehave and she would see that everything would be affability itself.

Tuesday, August 31st

I am married today to dear Georgie. Mrs Lydia Wickham— how droll to see my name so! We arrived at Longbourn just in time for dinner, to an ecstatic reception from mama, a chilly one from papa, and a diffident response from my sisters, who are such perfect ninnies at times that anyone would imagine that they did not know me, except Kitty of course. It took a full fifteen minutes before they could be roused to congratulate me on my marriage, and as usual, I had to do all the talking. Mama and I held sway, which is the norm, but even my poor husband had to struggle to make Lizzy have any conversation. I have not noticed it before, but there is something in my sisters' manners which sets them quite apart as old maids, and I fear their lack of spirit will not endear them to the neighbourhood beaux. I certainly think the fact of their impending spinsterhood was brought home to my sister Jane, who needed a gentle reminder as we passed through into the dining room that, as a married woman, I must now take her place next to mama. Poor mama, how is she ever to get rid of them?

I have received two letters of congratulation from those dear friends Harriet and Isabella. They, at least, are very happy for me and eager to hear news of my new life. They seem very pleased, though Harriet is by all accounts a little vexed that she had not been let into my secret earlier. She implied her husband, the Colonel, had been put out by the worry that I had caused, but said she was sure everything would blow over in due course and that I am not to concern myself. Dear me! I must say it had not occurred to me to be too troubled, but I will make amends to Harriet; indeed, I will see that she is invited to Newcastle. What fun we will have!

Mrs Hill, Rebecca, and Mary were so pleased to see me downstairs in the kitchen and wanted to hear all about Brighton and have all the particulars of my wedding. I showed them my ring, and it has to be said they were far more interested to see it than any of my sisters. I suspect a little of the green-eyed monster is behind my sisters' reticence to hear all about my wedding, and they do not seem to admire Wickham at all, especially Lizzy, but then I daresay he did break her heart and it must be difficult for her to see how much he is in love with me.

Friday, September 3rd

How I long to be in Newcastle! We have less than a fortnight to moulder here and the thought of leaving is sweet rapture!!!!

I cannot wait to be gone, and though it has been pleasant to be the centre of attention, in the warmth of family love, and the envy of all the maids in Meryton, I feel a desperate need to be away and to be setting up my own home. I have related all the details of my nuptials to everyone I know, and though Lizzy has not seemed to be so interested in listening to any account of my wedding, I felt obliged to relate it all to her as she was the

only person who had not heard all the fine details and arrangements. It has to be said she remained completely disinterested
until I happened to let slip that Mr Darcy had been there and
then she had such a look of amazement on her countenance that
I knew I had a captive audience in her and Jane at last. Of
course, I told them I was sworn to secrecy and could not tell
them how Darcy had owed Wickham lots of money—at least I
think that was what Georgie said. I forget the particulars, but it
was something to do with money to which he was entitled.

Anyway, Mr Darcy has finally decided to make amends
for the living promised by his father to my dear Wickham. It is
little wonder George cannot abide him; and to think they were
brought up together like brothers!

I do not care. All I know is that we were very poor and
now we are quite well off. I am sure dear Georgie will soon be
promoted and I will see him as a Colonel of the regiment yet.

I do think him the most handsome man I ever set eyes on!!!

Part Two

Chapter 20

LYDIA KNEW VERY WELL that the written accounts of her new life, penned in the only proper letter her mama was to receive for a month after her marriage, would be read by half the neighbourhood, and if not read, then its contents would be relayed by word of mouth or written and passed on again in missives to her sisters in their new homes: Jane at Netherfield and Lizzy at Pemberley. She was careful not to make any reference to her thoughts on her sisters' recent marriages. She could not help but envy their good fortune. Jane had got her Mr Bingley at last, and Lizzy had surprised them all by marrying Mr Darcy, though Lydia would not have swapped her husband for that gentleman, despite all his money. She had never got to the bottom of how exactly her sister had come to fall in love with Mr Darcy, but according to Kitty, she had not been persuaded by his fortune and huge house alone. Shortly after they had arrived in Newcastle, Lizzy had acquainted Lydia by letter of the news of both sisters' engagements, along with a detailed account of the extent of Mr Darcy's involvement in securing Lydia's marriage to George Wickham. Lizzy's object had not been to set out to upset her sister, she wrote, but she could not suffer to hear Lydia abuse her fiancé any longer when, indeed, she should have been grateful to Mr Darcy for his thoughtful actions. Whilst Lydia did not want to believe the accuracy of it, her more intimate knowledge of her husband's character had eventually led her to surmise that it must, in part, be true. Mr Wickham, it seemed, had been bought, made to marry her in an effort to save her reputation, and Mr Darcy had paid for it all. Still, on the whole, she was convinced that, though her husband might not be as enamoured of her as she was of him, his affection for her was something near enough and she would make the best of it. She would love him so much that he wouldn't be able to resist loving her back. In a letter, therefore, she had to ensure that her family had something on which to cogitate and converse. She was determined to show them all how happy she was with her new situation, how in love she was with her husband, and how there had not been a more lively nor likeable town to live in than Newcastle, a rival for Brighton with all its diversions.

Pilgrim's Buildings, Tuesday, October 12th
Dearest Mama,

    You will be wondering why it has been so long since you have heard from me, but I am sure you understand that being a married woman makes many demands and, as such, letter writing has lamentably had to remain at the bottom of my list of impending and important duties.

    Wickham and I are settled for the present in lodgings in the town, and whilst we wish for a house of our own, dear

George has so many commitments and is called away so frequently by his regiment that we have had little time to attend to house hunting. George assures me that it will not be long before we will have an abode to call our own, but to tell the truth, we are so happy, it would not matter to me if I were living in a hovel on High Friar Street!

I have been shopping for some items of furniture, as it all desperately required updating, and I have filled our sitting room with a new sofa and chairs, some small occasional tables, and have green blinds at the window. Everyone who calls comments on my style, and all say I have the most exquisite taste. Was it not always so, mama? My talent for trimming a new bonnet has held me in good stead for decorating a new home.

I have made many friends already; Lucy Fenwick has been very kind, though I am not so partial to her particular friend Evelina Armstrong. Quite frankly, this lady sees me as a threat to her position as leader in all matters of fashion and society soirées; though to speak plainly, while it had been my intention to entertain frequently, our current expenditure forbids it. Still, it does not seem to deter others from inviting us, and despite our lack of returning hospitality, we remain as popular as ever. I have written to Lizzy and Jane, but you might hint that it would be a kindness to their younger sister if they were to think of her whilst her husband is still making his way in the world. I have never been of a proud disposition and, therefore, they should not hesitate to send me money. They need not worry that it will be insulting to me in any way. Indeed, if I could clear a few bills, I might be able to buy the bonnet of lilac crape with a shade and puffing of white muslin and grey feather to match that I spied yesterday in the milliners. We are not so hard up for the necessities of life, you understand, but a few luxuries help to pass the days more pleasantly, I know you will agree. In any case, I shall see Jane at Christmas, and she is always generous. Wickham and I have been invited to Netherfield; at least one dear sister does not ignore my fond requests to visit. I daresay I shall see Pemberley one day, though later than I should like.

As I have already intimated, I have been received with great cordiality by the officers' wives and even more so by the officers themselves. Mama, I am sure you are not surprised to hear that I have several favourites already. Mr Gascoigne is so attentive and so like dear Denny, whom I am sure I shall miss to the end of my days. Captain Welby is the most handsome man I ever set eyes on, and Mr Lambert is so sweet, he blushes like a girl whenever I look his way. Needless to say, I could fill two sides writing of just these lovely fellows and their antics to present. Other notables include Annesley, Bostock, and Herbert, so you see, I neither lack for company nor friendship! The society may not be quite so refined as in Hertfordshire but does not suffer for it in my eyes; I am as happy to befriend a milliner's daughter as anyone of higher standing. Indeed, there are many more people here made wealthy by trade, the ship industry, and coal than are what we would call gentry. The ladies certainly spend a lot of money on their appearance and are as fashionable as any I saw in Brighton, if not more so. I can almost understand what they are saying now, for their way of talking takes getting used to, and for the first week, I thought

I was in a foreign country and asked dear George what language they were speaking. Quite frankly, it is not unpleasant to the ear, and I am sure I have picked it up in the few weeks I have been here; certainly, if Mr Gascoigne spends any longer whispering in my ear, I shall be a true proficient! I expect to see the latter and all his comrades at the Assembly Ball this week. There are many dances and occasions for socialising; how you would love it here! Everyone is vastly pleasant and great fun. Please rest assured, dearest mama, that I am happy, hale, and hearty, and if in my next letter I do not write with "increasing news," if you take my meaning, I assure you it will not be for want of trying; George and I are meticulous in that endeavour! Do not worry if you do not hear from me for a while; believe me to be living my life to the fullest.

Your loving daughter,
Lydia Wickham

That Lydia was prone to flights of fancy was well known, and with the exception of her doting mama, the others of her family received her news with more than a liberal sprinkling of salt. Lydia was very pleased with her composition, which she felt evinced just the right tone, giving both an impression of marital bliss and domestic felicity, which would surely strike a note of envy in her siblings whom she was sure would receive a suitably embellished account from their mama.

The truth of the situation was that, on reaching Newcastle, Lydia had been delighted and disappointed in equal measures. "Is this what all of Newcastle is like, my love? Grand and ramshackle buildings sat side by side? I confess, I did think there would be a little more grandeur; and everywhere is so dirty, even more so than in the country. There's coal dust everywhere. The entire town seems black with it!"

"I am sure when we have been all over the town, we shall find cleanliness and grandeur enough to satisfy even your sensibilities, my dear," was her husband's answer. "For now, we must make haste to our modest lodgings and remember this is only the start. We will soon be moving on."

"Oh, I do hope Mr Darcy can help you to obtain a higher commission soon," Lydia cried. "Lizzy has promised that she will speak to him and then we shall have a house of our own."

Lucy Fenwick was the first to call with her friend Mrs Armstrong. Lucy was engaged to Captain Bostock, on the point of getting married herself, and so they soon found they had a lot in common, though when pressed for particulars of her own wedding, Lydia had glossed over all the parts that she felt might not withstand close scrutiny. Lucy was amiable enough, but Lydia did not like Evelina Armstrong at all. She was one of those women who were always ready to be vindictive or spread some malicious falsehood. She enjoyed sniffing out any hint of gossip and was forever telling tales about errant husbands in the regiment. It was a well-known fact that her own husband had more than a roving eye, and Lydia presumed that being spiteful at everyone else's expense was the only way Mrs Armstrong could divert unwanted attention from the Major.

"Mr Wickham called in to see me with one or two of the officers yesterday morning," she said, addressing Lydia as they sat in her best parlour, a fortnight after Lydia's arrival. "There was quite a little party. Mr Gascoigne's cousin Miss Arabella was with them, and a very lively young lady she is too. I hope you do not mind me passing this on, Mrs Wickham, but I do not think I would be letting my husband enjoy the company of such a forward miss."

"Oh, Wickham has always been a terrible flirt if that is what you mean, Mrs Armstrong. He cannot help himself; he means nothing by it, you know," Lydia replied as brightly as she could.

"He may not, but there was no one in the room could have mistook her motives, I am telling you. She could not keep her hands to herself; she touched his arm, his hand, whispered in his ear, and when she put her arm in his to march him out of the door, I thought, 'Evelina, you have a duty to your dear friend, Mrs Wickham, who can have no idea what Miss Arabella is about.' I am sure you understand, my dear, I only wish to be helpful."

"Yes, of course," Lydia smiled. "I shall certainly take note of what you say, but I am sure Mr Wickham is aware of her wiles and wishes to be friendly in the most commonplace sense."

The following week Mrs Armstrong had reported at least three more sightings of young girls in the company of her husband. Though Lydia was not prepared to challenge him outright and was convinced of his innocence, she was feeling a little unnerved and regarded all females under the age of twenty-five with suspicion, especially if they had any dealings with George. Even Bessie, her maid, seemed to colour when he came into the room, and on more than one occasion she had found Wickham alone in the sitting room with her at some very odd hours. There had always seemed to be a perfectly good reason for this, however; if he was not helping her to poke the fire or jiggle a key in a cabinet, he was insisting on carrying her heavy pails of water upstairs to the bedchamber, though this very act of kindness seemed to tire him more than anything.

Thursday, October 14th

To be a married lady is almost enough in itself to warrant ecstatic effusions. I simply adore the look of my wedding ring and have at last got used to the strange sensation upon my finger. To be addressed as Mrs Wickham is my greatest pleasure and making a new home comes a very close second, though it has taken several weeks to become accustomed to the smallness of the place. What I would really like is a house on the higher slopes of town where the wealthy are settling, not timbered lodg-ings in the old part of town. Mr Wickham is at pains to point out some of the imposing public buildings nearby, which he suggests are equally comparable to those of London, but I am not impressed. Still, my darling Georgie has promised me an exciting new life and I feel sure all will come to us in time. In the meantime, I do the best I can with the rooms we share and fill every corner with purchases from the warehouses and craftsmen nearby until my husband quite despairs. "There will be no room to take a turn before you are finished, Lydia. There is not a table or a chair left in the carpenter's window that you haven't purloined, or a Chinese trinket in the warehouses, and I will never understand your obsession with cushions, pads, and bolsters of every description, which grace every seat. 'Tis fortu-nate I have a slender behind!"

I have inherited my mother's ability to disregard a husband's complaints, for which I am very grateful!

Sunday, October 24th

There is an Assembly Ball tomorrow evening. Everyone who is anybody in Newcastle attends and turns out without fail.

I am thankful for the fact that the weather is still warm, as I still have to wear my summer gowns, part of my wedding trousseau; but how I long for something new to wear to the ball. There is no money left for luxuries at present, especially now as the rent must be paid and as Wickham spends what is left going out on the town. Going to the Rooms is a treat and one of the few times I share an evening out with my husband. I try not to complain, but it is very difficult when he is out every night of the week and spends all day with the regiment. I would never confide to a soul that I am lonely, but there are times when I feel downright miserable. The officers' wives are not as friendly as I had hoped, and certainly nothing compared to dearest Harriet and Isabella. Still, I look forward to the balls, and I am determined to make the most of every occasion.

Mr Wickham and I are toasted and complimented on our dancing by all. We make the most elegant couple, and whether we are feeling particularly pleased or vexed with one another, we are sure to put on a good show. The ball cannot come soon enough!

Chapter 21

MAJOR ARMSTRONG AND HIS wife greeted Lydia and her husband at the close of the first dance, stopping them as they crossed the room. Lydia's heart sank, though she was pleased to see that Evelina's exertions on the dance floor had rendered her complexion the same shade of puce as the velvet hangings at the windows.

"Mr and Mrs Wickham, here we are again, how charming to see you both," Mrs Armstrong proclaimed. "So, Mrs Wickham, that dress is all the mode in Hertfordshire is it? Southern style, bless me, and here I was thinking long sleeves were quite the thing. I daresay you are wearing quite the latest fashion, but one wonders how some of these designs can be entertained. Lucy and I must look to Hertfordshire in future if we are not to appear perfect frights."

Lydia fumed inside. It was not the first time her clothes had been commented on by this woman, and she could not think of an immediate reply. If only Wickham had not been gambling again this last week, there might have been enough for a new gown. She would write to her sister Lizzy in the morning; she could not possibly go out and about in the same gown much longer, and she silently cursed her Aunt Gardiner for her choice of wedding clothes once more.

"And, Mr Wickham, you are delighting us all with your dancing."

"Why, thank you, Mrs Armstrong. If your husband will allow, I hope it will be your pleasure to step out with me for the next."

"I would be delighted if your dear wife does not mind. How very gallant."

Lydia maintained her smile, though she knew in the next breath Major Armstrong would be leading her out onto the dance floor, gazing too often on her décolletage and squeezing her hand. She knew if she were to give him any encouragement he was the type of man that would declare his all, despite his wife, and she was extremely careful never to be anywhere alone with that gentleman. She had met the type too many times in her short life. Before the dance was over, her fingers, her waist, and her toes had all been violated in more ways than she could number, he had undressed her with his eyes and made several none-too-subtle suggestions about needing to take the air, begging her to accompany him outside.

As soon as she could make her escape, she sought out the officers of her acquaintance who made life in Newcastle such a joy. It was not long before a little group surrounded her. George sought out his next partner; he would not attempt to remove Lydia from Captain Welby's side, and in any case, there was that pretty milliner, Miss Skinner, standing all alone and forlorn, in want of a partner. He would be the man to step in and whirl her round for the next one, secure in the knowledge that his wife was otherwise engaged and oblivious to his own activities.

"Mrs Wickham, the lady formed to break all our hearts, would you not agree, gentlemen?" Captain Welby addressed the party who stood admiringly in a circle around her.

Lydia laughed and patted her curls. "Captain Welby, you flatterer. I am sure I could not inspire such heartache, though I am also sure I have affection enough to bestow on you all."

"The lady underestimates the depths of our torture, does she not, my friends?" the Captain quipped.

"Mrs Wickham, promise to dance with us all," begged Mr Gascoigne, taking her hand and kissing her fingers.

"Yes, who will be the lucky man, Mrs Wickham?" shouted Mr Herbert, blushing crimson at his courage for speaking up at all.

"Why, I will dance with each one of you," she pronounced loudly as Captain Welby stepped up to take her hand first. Now, there was a handsome man, Lydia reflected; he was as good a dancer as her dear husband and so eager in his compliments.

The Captain would have needed little encouragement if Lydia had chosen to pursue him; that he found her attractive he let her know at every opportunity, but beyond a little harmless flirtation, she was not interested. George Wickham was the only man for her, and she loved him with a true heart. That the Captain made a gallant partner there was no doubt, but as soon as the dance was over, Lydia thanked her partner and went in search of her husband. She was feeling hot and disquieted; she needed a drink and would ask George to fetch her one. However, after scanning the ballroom and perusing the card room, he did not appear. She couldn't find him anywhere and no one seemed to know of his whereabouts either. She could not imagine where he could be, but in desperate need of some fresh air, she passed through the doors leading out into the gardens beyond. It was very dark but for the pale wash of moonlight that highlighted the gravel walk and lit up the cold stone statues as the clouds passed overhead. She felt better out of doors and breathed in the sweet autumnal air, watching her feet as her slippers crunched on the path. Everywhere was quiet and still, the smell of newly cut grass and the fragrance of late blooming roses lifted her spirits. Her head was full of thoughts of George. When she found him, she would do her utmost not to be cross, she decided. George's temper was so easily lost; at the slightest provocation, it would flare. Without meaning to plague him, she knew that he would accuse her of nagging and pestering him. Lydia sighed. Although she was sure she was not the easiest person in the world to live with, she knew George Wickham must be the most difficult. She stepped beyond a hedge of yew trees where she spied a bench and was making her way along with a view to having a rest on the seat when her attention was caught by the sounds of low voices approaching—the unmistakable resonance of sweethearts' talk and lovers' exertions. They stopped and kissed passionately. Lydia froze.

"We cannot keep meeting like this," a lady said quietly giggling. "Someone is bound to see us. I really think I ought to go, although I hate to leave you."

"Dear sweet creature," he answered, "I believe you might just steal my heart. Please stay a little longer, I beg you. Step into the gazebo, my dear; we will not be long."

Lydia could only just hear what was being said. She knew she should not listen, but she was caught. If she moved, they would hear her. She stopped, waiting for a moment when she could return to the safety of the Rooms. It was too quiet, as were the activities of those in the gazebo. She sat down on the bench, her ears straining and her heart hammering.

The voices were heard again. From the safety of the sheltered spot, their guard was let down, their voices ringing across the quiet of the gardens audibly. "But what of your wife? You always look so perfect a couple, I cannot hope to compete for your affections," the lady was heard to say.

"We are not here to discuss my wife," he answered forcefully. "There is only one who engages my affections at this moment and that is you, my dear. Come, it is a little too cramped to share the seat in comfort. Perhaps you could sit on my knee." Lydia gasped in disbelief. She clamped her hand over her mouth as quickly as she could, but she had been heard. As she rose from her seat to withdraw out of sight behind a hedge, the courting couple she had disturbed emerged from the shadows, arranging their dress, picking the fallen leaves out of their hair as they ran laughing back in the direction of the Rooms. Lydia did not recognise the lady, but she could not fail to distinguish the gentleman. She would have recognised him—his profile, his infectious laugh, and especially his heartfelt protestations—even in the pitch black of a night with no moon, for it was her very own husband George Wickham.

Lydia did not want to cause a scene, always mindful that she was forever under the scrutiny of her vindictive acquaintances. How she kept her tongue until they were going home before telling him exactly what she had seen, she could not tell. Instead, she took revenge by flirting wildly with every man who came in sight and even made a play for Major Armstrong, to his great gratification and much to the annoyance of his wife. She drank copious amounts of wine, draining glass after glass, until the visions and noises that haunted her were distorted into faded recollection.

She became aware that her husband was watching her with increasing anguish. Finally, after witnessing her throwing her arms around Captain Welby, he marched her off the dance floor and into a carriage, which they could ill afford, where the combination of too much wine and the swaying motion of the vehicle resulted in the ultimate remedy of relieving her stomach all over Wickham's lap, causing him to scold and abuse her vehemently.

"Good Lord, Lydia! Are you drunk? Now look! These are my best breeches, damn you. Have a care!"

"Indeed, sir, I would apologise but I am not sorry in the least. You have got off lightly for your misdemeanours!"

One look at her face told him all he needed to know, and at once he identified the intruder who had shortened such an exhilarating interlude in the garden. "What are you talking about, Mrs Wickham? I do not understand you."

"I saw you, George, making vile love with that woman, whoever she might be. I saw and heard everything!" She sat looking out of the window at the dark streets, her eyes purposefully averted from those of her husband, and waited for him to speak. Unable to cry, she acknowledged the truth she had suspected for so long. She had been betrayed.

"And what of your disgraceful behaviour, Mrs Wickham?" he began. "Yes, the woman who bears my name, the greatest flirt in all Newcastle. Do you consider your actions to be so very different from mine?"

Lydia could not believe her ears. Far from receiving the contrite explanation and apology she had expected, he was red faced and agitated, staring straight into her eyes, and telling her that she was the one to have behaved badly.

"And I might ask you," she said as calmly as she could, "why you felt it necessary to risk humiliating me in front of all my friends and neighbours. Can you deny that you are carrying on with that hussy?"

"Lydia, listen to me, my girl. A man must have a little sport now and again. It was just a little kiss; no one saw us, only you, my dear. You know she is nothing to me; you are my partner in life, you have my ring on your finger, and I married you. Nothing can change that, and if I have been a little indiscreet, well my dear, I shall see to it that I am more careful in future."

"More careful in future? More careful in future!" Lydia was incensed and, rising out of her seat, pummelled her fists on his chest in frustration. "Do you not repent your heinous behaviour? Are you not sorry for what you have done?"

"Come, come, calm down, dear," he soothed, firmly removing her and forcing her to sit back down on the opposite seat. "Do not upset yourself. You must know I am a man of the world. You are making more of this trifling affair than is necessary. Why, there isn't a soldier in the regiment who doesn't have a wife and a girl besides. That is the way of life. You are being unreasonable, my dear. I am a good husband; I have provided you with a comfortable home, have I not? All I ask in return is that you do your duty as a wife should and turn a blind eye to certain necessary circumstances."

"So you can carry on gambling, drinking, and womanizing to your heart's content?" she shouted, unable to keep her composure any longer. "A comfortable home has been my creation alone, and if not for my generous sisters, I would be miserable indeed!"

"As far as I am concerned, I have kept my side of the bargain," her husband answered quietly. "I might ask exactly what it is you feel you have been denied. You have had everything money can buy. You, in your turn, do little except sit about the place laughing with your friends. If I enjoy a little drink, a game of cards, and the young flesh of a filly now and again, as your husband, that is my right and the sooner you understand that, the better off you will be."

They arrived home, but Lydia was not to be quieted so easily. She paced up and down the pavement as Wickham searched for the key in his soggy pockets and, aware that she felt inclined to scream at him, did her best to lower her voice to a rant. "And what is it that you expect me to do now?"

"Come now, let's have no more of this nonsense. You will certainly set tongues wagging if our neighbours hear you shouting like that. Be a dutiful wife and I will see you get a new hat. Nay, I'll go so far as to promise a new gown! Now, what could be more handsome than that?"

"Mr Wickham," came his wife's reply, "I warn you, if I ever find out you have betrayed me again, I shall run away with Captain Welby!"

She ran into the house, pushing past him as the door opened, barely managing to keep from crying. Wickham was left standing, at first with an expression of bewilderment on his face as though he could not possibly conceive what had occurred to upset her so, but then a look of mirth spread swiftly across his countenance and he gave in to huge guffaws.

Wednesday, October 27th

I feel so wretched I think I might die. All my hopes of making George love me have been completely dashed. In my heart I know this is not the only time I have been deceived; the rumours I have heard are more than just gossip. Misery engulfs me. All my anxiety and sorrows of the last couple of months well up inside, along with the tears that come relentlessly. Happiness seems so elusive; I had imagined that life would be so perfect with George, but I now know that my marriage is as tarnished as the copper pans in my kitchen. I cannot think what to do; there is no one I can talk to, and even if I were to write home, I have a feeling they would all take great pleasure in telling me that they had expected nothing else.

No, there is only one way to deal with this problem. There is nothing I can do but forgive him. I am far too proud to have anyone catch even a sniff of scandal and am determined to carry on as though nothing has happened. After all, surely most young men are tempted at one time or another. The risk of sending him running off into his lover's arms again is great, and I do not want that above anything else. My heart might be broken, but it is not irreparable. I will be everything he desires and more. And he will fall in love with me all over again, so much so that he will never think about straying again.

Chapter 22

THE NEXT DAY LYDIA set off for the milliner's in Percy Street; the afternoon was mild, the sun was shining, and she felt happier for being out of doors, though her object in strolling out was not to enjoy the weather. Nothing improved her disposition more than the purchase of a new bonnet, and she was determined to buy one. Indeed, she had decided she would spend the entire afternoon on a shopping expedition. Never was there a happier way of raising her spirits, and she was exceedingly excited at the prospect of a whole new wardrobe. After all, was that not what Wickham had promised? He would not dare refuse her! Let Mrs Armstrong abuse her fashion sense now. By the time she had finished, there would not be a more elegant creature in all of Newcastle. George would not be able to resist her. She would look so well, he would never look at another woman again.

When she reached the milliner's, she stopped and stared in at the window before going in to see what might be of particular interest. Beyond the exquisite pokes, shakos, tams, and turbans, she could see that the shop was surprisingly busy for a Thursday afternoon. She could see Miss Skinner, holding court behind the counter, surrounded by half a dozen or more of her particular friends who were there, not in any pursuit of headdresses for themselves, but to hear what she was saying. She looked most adamant, and Lydia wondered what could be so entertaining to the other misses intent on cooing like doves at her animated discourse or laughing out loud. Lydia was intrigued, and hoping to hear a little of the gossip that engaged them all so fervently, she walked in through the open door unobserved by anyone. There was such an atmosphere of charged excitement and hilarity in the little room, it would have caught the interest of the least curious person.

"And what did he do after that?" exclaimed a young lady leaning on the counter, eagerly gazing up at Miss Skinner as though she were a story book heroine. There were hoots of laughter as Miss Skinner ran her fingers passionately over her torso. "He asked if he could warm his hands!"

"And what did you say?"

"I said I had the very place and then I puckered my lips and . . . . "

Lydia could not move, and though she was intent on listening to a conversation not meant for her ears, she was certain that she did not want to hear its conclusion.

" . . . Mr Wickham kissed me!"

The bell above the door clanged loudly as Lydia grabbed the handle for support. Miss Skinner's emboldened discourse was instantly quieted as she took in the presence of the person who stood in the shop's doorway. She became quite mute. No one ever looked more embarrassed; her cheeks flared in a most unbecoming way against the fairness of her porcelain complexion, contrasting greatly with her auburn ringlets, which curled about her countenance. Her audience turned as one and stared at poor Lydia, who was rooted to the spot. Someone gasped with concern and another giggled as she tried to suppress her amusement. Lydia was mortified. She turned on her heel and flounced out of the shop. The only thing to do was get away.

In haste, she turned the corner into Moseley Street and ran as fast as she could. She was aware that people were staring at her as she flew by, but she did not care. How could she have been so stupid? She should have realised that Miss Skinner had been the hussy to have so engaged Wickham. Oh, it was too cruel! And to find her entertaining half the town with lurid reports of his behaviour was the worst outcome of all. Lydia knew it would not be long before the news had circulated around the town and was anxious to get home as quickly as she could.

Unfortunately, she had not anticipated quite how rapidly the gossip would spread, or how speedily it would come to the attention of those who made it their life's work to be as spiteful as it was possible to be. Later that very afternoon, she was sat in her little sitting room, to all intents and purposes engaged in trimming her old bonnet and unsuccessfully trying to take her mind off her erring husband, when her servant Bessie entered the room to say that Mrs Armstrong and Miss Fenwick had called and asked if she was at home.

"Do ask them in," Lydia replied. She did not think she could send them away; it was imperative that she should behave as if nothing unusual had happened. Besides, having their company would give her something else to think about. After all, there could be no danger of them knowing of the rift between Lydia and her husband just yet, and if there had been any hints at all, she was in a position to dispel them.

"Do come in, Mrs Armstrong, Miss Fenwick, how charming to see you," Lydia said cheerfully. She gestured towards the sofa. "Do sit down."

The ladies sat down and it was not long before they were regaling Lydia with all the gossip of the town. This is quite like old times, thought Lydia, when my old friends Charlotte and Maria Lucas used to call and have over the events of the previous night's ball.

"Have you heard the latest news, my dear?" Evelina supped her tea and raised a quizzical brow.

Lydia shook her head. She dreaded the report but reassured herself that, even if the gossip she wanted to keep quiet had reached her acquaintances' ears, they would not be so blatant as to inflict it upon her so brutally. She was quite wrong.

"We have heard this morning at the residence of Mrs Belasis, who is a very good friend of mine and a very reliable source of information, some interesting news of Miss Skinner. You know her, I am sure."

Evelina paused long enough to see the crimson blush spreading over Lydia's cheeks as she nodded in assent. "I know of her, though I am not an acquaintance."

"Miss Skinner is carrying on an illicit liaison with a gentleman," whispered Evelina, as though Miss Skinner must be standing at the door eavesdropping. Mrs Armstrong looked from side to side before delivering the worst. "She was seen cavorting in the gardens in the dark whilst we were all dancing!"

"Are you quite sure?" asked Lydia. "How is it possible she was seen in the dark? You do know how people love to gossip."

"Oh, it is quite certain," Lucy interjected, "though, by all accounts, we have little information as to his identity, or indeed, exactly what they were up to in the gloom of the gazebo."

"More's the pity," added Mrs Armstrong, "the man needs thrashing! We may not have his name yet, though there are rumours abounding that he is a married man."

"Though to be fair, Evelina," her friend remarked, "he is not the first and, I daresay, will not be the last. Miss Skinner likes to entertain all the handsome officers."

Lydia did not know where to look and picked up her teacup with shaking hands. She had an idea her visitors knew very well the identity of Miss Skinner's lover and were enjoying watching her squirm.

Evelina sat triumphant with a smug expression of assured satisfaction. "Now, to get to the point of my visit this morning, Mrs Wickham. I hope you will accept my invitation to a little soirée on Wednesday, for a light supper, some cards, and dancing, with your dear husband, of course. How is he?"

"He is quite well, thank you." Lydia put down her cup for fear of revealing the state of her nerves. Her pulse pounded in her ears, and she grew more anxious by the moment.

"He is so charming, such a one with the ladies, is he not? And he is such a good dancer. But talking of dancing, weren't you the popular one last night?" said Mrs Armstrong, fixing Lydia with a beady eye. "You must be quite worn out with so many partners!"

"Oh, I cannot recall, I am sure," Lydia answered and, attempting to change the subject, said, "I do admire your gown,

Mrs Armstrong. Is it crêpe? It is cut so beautifully; you must give me the name of your seamstress. You always look so elegant, such a picture of perfection!"

"I saw your husband dancing with the milliner," Evelina added with a smirk as she ignored Lydia's question and made a close study of her countenance.

"Yes, she is an excellent dancer, is she not?" Lydia replied and picked up her cup again in the hope that the strong tea would give her the courage she needed to withstand this conversation. "Wickham enjoys dancing so much!"

"Aye, and that's not all by some accounts!" chuckled Mrs Armstrong, smiling conspiratorially at her friend Lucy. "Well now, we cannot sit here all day; we really must consider taking our leave. You will be expecting your husband home for nuncheon, will you not?" Evelina picked up her gloves.

"Oh no, do not hurry on his account," Lydia answered politely, though she was quite desperate to be rid of them. Her mind was racing as she digested Mrs Armstrong's comments. "I never see him before five o'clock, he has so much to do with the regiment. There is always plenty to occupy a soldier."

"He had business in town early this morning," pronounced Evelina. "Indeed, I have seen him walking in Percy Street every day this last week."

"I expect he has had business in town. I really do not know all the pattern of his day," Lydia answered as brightly as she could. A nagging thread of suspicion tugged at the back of her mind, but she told herself not to be silly. She was sure her friends had only called on an errand of mischief. They were trying to unnerve her.

"Well, we really must be going," said Evelina, pulling on her gloves and standing up. "Come along, Lucy, we mustn't delay any longer."

Off they went, leaving Lydia's mind in turmoil. She watched from the window. They were hurrying down the street, their heads bowed together, and their bonnets shaking, as though laughing at some shared amusement. It was quite clear that word had got out and Wickham's dallying was known by all.

Chapter 23

LYDIA PENNED A LETTER immediately to her sister Lizzy begging that she might be invited to Pemberley House in Derbyshire, though she did not divulge her true reasons for wishing to flee from Newcastle in such haste. She wrote that she wished to include a tour of Derbyshire before her Christmas visit to Netherfield, professing that she longed to see Pemberley and could break her journey comfortably, whilst saving on her travel expenses if she combined the two visits into one. What Mr Darcy said on learning of this new scheme of his sister-in-law's can only be conjectured, but news came to Lydia from Lizzy soon after informing her that, whilst she was welcome to pay a visit, the same hospitality would not ever be extended to her husband. Lydia knew that Mr Darcy would refuse Wickham an invitation, and this suited her purposes exactly; she needed some time away from her husband and from Newcastle. So, at the beginning of November, with happy feelings of escape, Lydia journeyed south to Derbyshire. Pemberley was everything she expected, and Lydia was soon enjoying her sister's good fortune and society whilst tolerating her brother-in-law's company. After a fortnight she was feeling very happy again and more disposed to think kindly towards her husband. By the beginning of December, she had some exciting news, which she could not wait to impart. She wrote to her mother as soon as the arrangements were settled.

Pemberley House, Friday, December 3rd
Dearest Mama,

Please forgive me for not having written lately, but I have been away from home, enjoying the hospitality in Derbyshire. I am happy to report that my sister Lizzy is well and that Mr Darcy continues to improve under her influence. I am now able to spend thirty minutes in his company without the need to reach for a bottle of something fortifying!

I have some very good news that I cannot wait a minute longer to share! Mr Wickham is raised to a Captain with all thanks due to Lizzy, I am certain. She has been aware for some time of the lack of funds and dire financial straits to which Wickham and I have succumbed, through no great fault of our own. I daresay she must have told Darcy; he must help us and of course, no sooner does my sister express a wish than it is granted. I must say her husband is very attentive to all her needs—it quite puts me out of countenance! Well, I am vastly happy about it all, and I daresay George is thrilled too, though I have not had a line from him to know one way or t'other or if he is even aware of his good fortune. Husbands do not make good letter writers it seems to me, but I can hardly complain, as I have not written a word to him either. I am never certain of his exact direction; I believe he moves from place to place. In any case, he is in Bath on regimental business until the middle of December and will meet me at Netherfield, where we plan to stay for at least two months complete!

Pemberley is a great place, though rather too large in my opinion; I am sure I should not like such a cavernous dwelling to call my home. I am thankful I will not be here for Christmas—you could get lost out in the wilderness amongst the high peaks, which seem to make up the landscape round about, and if there is snow, I am certain we should have to be dug out!

The shops are far more appealing to my way of thinking, and Lizzy has taken me to Bakewell where I have made friends of the draper, the glovemaker, and the milliner if you understand my meaning! My purchases are all charged to the Captain, and Lizzy has been most generous also, insisting that she settle most of my bills. I cannot think why she is so anxious about such trifling matters; Wickham can afford a few treats for his wife now he has been promoted.

We went to Buxton yesterday, in the box barouche, which has the family crest emblazoned on the side. I could very easily get used to being treated like royalty. People fawn over my sister wherever she goes! We took the waters and walked along the crescent; it was a pleasant outing. Lizzy treated me to silk and muslin for three new gowns, which were given directly to Mrs Reynolds to supervise their making up. I shall certainly look the part of a Captain's wife!

Please send my love to papa and tell him that I would welcome a letter from him occasionally. Well, I daresay he is

too busy to spend the time writing to me, and I shall see him
soon enough at Netherfield. Send my best and most affectionate
felicitations to my sisters. I do miss them, even Mary!
    Your devoted daughter,
    Lydia Wickham

It was time to leave Pemberley for Netherfield. Lydia left with some reluctance; she was enjoying herself very much and thought more than once about extending her visit by a few more days, but Mr Darcy had kindly sorted out her travelling arrangements. The improvement in his manner to her was such that he would brook no refusal when it came to accompanying her to the inn at Lambton where she was to meet the post chaise, and he even insisted on seeing her into the carriage, instructing the postillions to drive swiftly. Lydia was most impressed!

Jane welcomed her sister with her usual grace and charm. It was not long before Lydia was recounting all her activities in Derbyshire and describing for her sister the grand way of life that was Lizzy's existence. Lydia met up with her husband at Netherfield who was greeted affably by Mr Bingley and with true affection by Jane. Relations were strained between the Wickhams, but Lydia tried to make the best of the situation, and Christmas passed as happily as it could. She managed to see her old friend Isabella, who was still keeping house for her brother Alexander, a clergyman in a village not far from Netherfield near Amwell. Isabella Fitzalan was the unmarried sister of Lydia's dearest friend Harriet Forster. She had acquainted Isabella with her misfortunes on their seeing one another again and took every opportunity to confide in this young lady, discussing her troubles when they met. Isabella was a good listener and a dear friend.

The Wickhams frequented the Assemblies in Meryton, and despite the disapproval from her papa, Lydia fancied herself as a matchmaker when it came to finding suitable beaux for Kitty, though she insisted on trying out her sister's partners on the dance floor.

"Believe me, Kitty, if a man cannot dance, he is not worth knowing, and if I can judge one thing, it is a man with a talent for prancing, even when he is standing still!"

All in all, Lydia enjoyed her visit and managed to come to an understanding with her husband. Although they were able to stay for a month and see the New Year in, Mr Bingley managed to sort out their travel arrangements back to Newcastle sooner than either of them would have liked. Visiting Netherfield and Pemberley had been a joy; Lydia loved her sisters' style of living, which was exactly suited to her taste. Therefore, as soon as Wickham announced that he had business to attend in far flung places once more, she was off on her travels again. Her solo expeditions gave her a sense of freedom, independence, and more pleasure than she would admit.

Monday, May 2nd

I am here again in Hertfordshire at Netherfield to see Jane
and Isabella. Captain Wickham is to meet up with me after
his jaunt to Bath, which is an arrangement to suit us both.
As far as anyone in Newcastle is concerned, we leave
together and come home together, which provides no fuel for
the gossips, and I do not have to answer to anyone. I
cannot say I am truly happy or unhappy about our style of
living and arrangements; my husband does not treat me
badly, and my marriage, though sinking into indifference on
both sides, gives me respectability if not much else.
Marriage to George is not as I had imagined it would be,
but I must admit that fault is entirely my own. I have made
an imprudent marriage; I understand that now, especially
when my sisters' own successful alliances are observed first-
hand and appear to be in such great contrast to my own. I
do envy my sisters their attentive husbands; even Mr Darcy
is a paragon in that respect. Bingley is an angel—I once
thought my George to be such a man, but I have lived with
him long enough to discover the truth. He does not love
me—he never did. George has never felt the same about me
as I do or did of him. I should have realised when he
admitted to me all that time ago that he was not capable of
loving anyone. But I was blind. My passion was all
consuming and overrode every other consideration. I was
incapable of seeing the truth, a young fool who is now
paying heavily for my mistaken folly. And though I am
loath to admit it, I have none to blame but myself.

There are few to whom I would admit these thoughts, and on days like this, when I am consumed with sadness for what might have been, I find it hard to be at peace. For my own sake, I keep up the pretence that I am as giddy and light-hearted as ever; I would not give the world the satisfaction of knowing anything else—in my heart, I am still the young girl who believes that perhaps my husband will realise that he has been in love with me all along and cannot do without me. But, I suspect my longings are all in vain.

Chapter 24

AT NETHERFIELD, MRS WICKHAM and the Bingleys were sitting in the pretty breakfast parlour at the table, having finished their early morning toast and chocolate. Lydia was holding court as usual, talking nineteen to the dozen, Charles Bingley was doing his best to appear attentive to his sister-in-law's every word, and Jane was trying to run through a list of tasks she had to accomplish.

"I hope you do not mind, Jane, but I wrote Isabella to say she might call today," Lydia announced. "I do not want to put you out. We could venture abroad, but then I cannot be bothered to walk as far as Meryton, and you know I am not a great walker. I cannot think why you both wish to surround yourselves in so much countryside. It is too quiet for my taste. Give me the hustle and bustle of town life any day. You would simply adore Newcastle for its lively ambience. Even when Wickham and I lived in that dreadful Eastcheap, I must say I preferred it above any existence I have ever suffered in the country."

"It is a good thing we are not all the same, Lydia," her sister professed, putting aside her notes. "For myself, I could never be happier than when I am at Netherfield, with all its associations. I would not wish to bring my children up in the town."

Lydia cast a sideways glance at her sister who was the very picture of contentment. She was expecting their first child, and though she was apt to tire easily, Lydia envied her increasing beauty and healthy bloom.

"I think I like to be in town almost as much as the country, Mrs Wickham," added Mr Bingley, smiling at Lydia, "and though Netherfield will always have a special place in my heart, we must fix on getting properly settled somewhere soon and secure a place of our own."

"I hope it will be in the country somewhere, not too far from Lizzy perhaps," said Jane.

"I always think Yorkshire a pleasant sort of county," added Bingley.

"Oh yes, my love, if we settled in Yorkshire we would be so close to our dear sister and brother. We should be able to visit frequently."

"I will mention it to Darcy when they get here. He might well know where the best houses are to be had."

The conversation was halted when Mrs Garnett, the house-keeper, popped her head around the door and addressed her mistress. "There is a Miss Fitzalan and Mr Fitzalan called to see Mrs Wickham, my lady. Shall I show them in?"

"Oh Lord," Lydia declared, "Isabella has brought that dull stick of a brother with her." She sighed. "What's his name . . . Alexander?"

"Lydia," admonished her sister, "that is unfair. Mr Fitzalan is a very pleasant young man. He is a little quiet perhaps, but there is no harm in that."

"Silent and dour, you mean," cried Lydia. "Well, I have so much to tell her, and I just won't be able to speak to Isabella properly, if you take my meaning."

"Mrs Garnett, do show in Mrs Wickham's guests. Would you like some more tea, Lydia?" Jane asked. These civilities over, she and her husband rose to leave the room.

"Thank you, Mrs Bingley, you do think of everything. Though if we could have some more delicious plum cake and bread rolls, Mrs Garnett, that would be wonderful. I am still feeling a little peckish. Lord! I have such an appetite, it must be the country air!"

Isabella was as beautiful as ever, in a pink pelisse with a straw bonnet adorned with pale blush roses and sweet ribbon to match. Her brother stood at her side. In complete contrast to the fair Isabella, he was dark like his sister Harriet; a tall, well-built, raven-haired man with the same startling forget-me-not blue eyes as his siblings. Lydia would have called him good looking but for his expression, which was always severe. She did not think she had ever seen him smile. Lydia thought him more sombre than cousin Collins and twice as dreary. She half expected him to fetch out Fordyce's sermons and sit her down to read them, there and then.

"Isabella, it is a tonic to see you," Lydia cried. "How are you? The country air is certainly suiting you."

"My sister looks well, does she not?" Mr Fitzalan added.

"Alexander, you would say that, you are always such a kind person," his sister laughed. "He never has a bad word to say about anybody, truly."

"A paragon indeed," Lydia answered, her eyes meeting his across the room. He always looked at her with distaste, as though she were something he had just scraped off his highly polished boot. "Do take a seat."

"How are you, my friend?" asked Isabella.

"I am well enough, thank you. Wickham has gone to Bath to enjoy his usual haunts and other pleasures of which, thankfully, I am unaware, though truth be told, I should like to go to Bath myself. But there it is; that is how we rub along, and I daresay it is for the best. At least it keeps his 'other interests' out of Newcastle and my hair."

Mr Fitzalan coughed with embarrassment and shifted his feet on the Turkey rug.

Lydia did not understand why Isabella had brought her brother along with her; how on earth they could conduct a conversation together with him spluttering every two seconds she could not account. There was a silence. Lydia looked across the gravel walk for inspiration whilst she tried to think of a topic more suitable for discussion with a clergyman. "Have you heard from Harriet or Pen lately? I have not heard a word from either of them, though I daresay I may have missed some letters, which have gone to Newcastle. Is either of the Miss Harringtons engaged yet?"

"Both of the Miss Harringtons have had the luck to find young men and are settled in Harrogate with a twin brother each. I believe they are both in an 'interesting' condition. I am surprised you had not heard they were now married."

"Heavens above!" Lydia cried. "Is it really that long since I heard from them?"

"Harriet and Henry are in Brighton again, enjoying the sea air and she is very well," Isabella went on. She looked sideways at her brother before making a gesture with her hands aimed at Lydia, indicating an increasing girth.

"Good Lord," said Lydia laughing, "is the whole world at it?"

"It would seem so," Isabella grinned. "I should not say it, but I daresay you will be soon swelling the ranks also."

Mr Fitzalan got up out of his seat and went to the window and seemed to be studying something of great interest down the drive. Why he had decided to invite himself, when it must have been obvious to anyone he would be in the way, Lydia could not tell.

She took his seat next to her friend. "I doubt it quite honestly; it's not for want of trying, believe me, but I would have thought something might have happened by now," she whispered. "To be truthful, it does not upset me in the least. I am not maternal, you know; I consider it a blessing. And with Jane and Lizzy both increasing daily, I shall have all the babies I want to dandle on my knee. Besides, Captain Wickham has all the endearing qualities of a demanding child, I can tell you."

"Oh, Lydia, you have not lost your sense of humour anyhow," said Isabella with concern.

"No, I am fortunate that my spirits remain high, despite much provocation. Tell me, how is your mother?"

"Her health is not good, but she is as well as can be expected. We are fortunate that Bertha, our housekeeper, is a very good sort of girl. She will always sit for a while if I wish to go out."

"Well, that is good to hear because I have some exciting news which I am sure will put you in good spirits," said Lydia. "My sister is giving a ball; she says it will be the last she will give for a while, as it will not be long before she is too fat for dancing. I am allowed to invite my friends, so you must come."

"Alexander, did you hear?" cried Isabella. "We are invited to a ball at Netherfield! How very exciting."

Lydia had not meant to include Alexander in the invitation also. She could not bear the thought of having to entertain the rector. Cousin Collins was bad enough, but at least he approved of dancing. On the last two occasions Lydia had been at a dance in Meryton and witnessed Alexander's behaviour, he had been austere; she had not seen him dance once, and when she had hinted that he might take a turn with her, he had muttered something incomprehensible and shot out of the room. Her dislike for him had increased tenfold from that moment.

Mr Fitzalan turned from the view and bowed in Lydia's direction with a little nod of his head. What was that? Lydia wondered. Is he accepting my invitation or has he a nervous twitch? For the life of her she could never understand why Isabella seemed so fond of this brother. If this was what one had to expect, she was pleased she had none. What a perfect ninny! "It is to be held on Friday and will go on all evening and into the next morning I shouldn't wonder," Lydia boasted. "My sister's hospitality knows no bounds; there will be champagne and lots of food, wonderful dancing, and Hertfordshire's finest beaux. We will have you married before the night is out!"

"I should think such a match would be most imprudent," Mr Fitzalan remarked. "Not a recipe for success I would have thought. You would not recommend such a marriage yourself, would you, Mrs Wickham?" His eyes were like ice—cold and glacial—as he returned to his seat to stare at her uncompromisingly.

Lydia wanted to shake him. She was sure he was making some veiled reference to her own nuptial arrangements. She would show him she did not care to be intimidated. "You do not believe in love at first sight, I take it?"

"I do not, Mrs Wickham," he answered, with a grim, unsmiling expression. "I think one should be very cautious of feelings which only obey the emotions of the heart. Quite frankly, I do not believe in the kind of false love which you describe. Poets and writers seem to rate it highly, but for myself, I have never experienced such a state of confusion nor do I wish to."

Lydia looked him up and down with distaste. She did not think she had ever met anyone so wholly unattractive. There was nothing about him she could like, and she found it impossible to imagine that anyone else would ever see anything of any merit in him. She was most decidedly persuaded that the single state was one he should certainly get used to; he was never going to fall in love nor inspire love in another.

"It takes time to know one's future partner," he insisted. "I must confess, I am an avid advocate for long engagements."

Lydia could quite believe it; he had made it very clear that he had no passion in his soul whatsoever. He was a cold fish. No doubt Isabella had given him a hint about her own hasty and imprudent marriage. That he did not approve of elopements, she was sure.

"Promise me you will come and visit us at the rectory," Isabella interrupted. She hated to see those she loved at odds with one another. "Please come tomorrow if you are not engaged."

"I should like that very much," Lydia answered. She bit her lip but was tempted to voice her hopes of Alexander's absence. With luck he would be out and about seeing to his parishioners.

"I am so very glad you are here, Lydia," Isabella professed on rising. "We will make the most of our time together, but I must get back for mother. Until tomorrow; then, we will have a nice long chat." She kissed her friend, Mr Fitzalan bowed but uttered not a syllable and off they went.

Despite Mr Fitzalan's unwelcome presence, Lydia felt better for seeing her friend. She missed her company and that of Harriet too. There was nothing like a true friend for sharing confidences. Being married to a man like George was hard work, and once the novelty of being called Mrs Wickham had worn off, she thought there were few delights left. Isabella would listen to her troubles with understanding; she would just have to wait till tomorrow to hear her news.

Chapter 25

MR AND MRS DARCY, accompanied by Miss Georgiana Darcy, arrived late in the afternoon, having travelled down from Derbyshire over the last couple of days. Lydia did not see them before dinner, as they went immediately to their rooms to take some rest after their arduous journey. She was thankful that when she did see him, though perfectly civil, her brother-in-law never had much to say to her, and as he was always fussing around his younger sister, she was free to converse with Lizzy as much as she liked.

"You are looking very well, Mrs Darcy, nicely fat if you take my meaning."

"I do, thank you, Lydia."

"Your muslin becomes you very well. It is a very fine one."

"Thank you, Lydia."

"I was wondering, Lizzy, last time you wrote, you promised to send me a muslin you saw in Bakewell. Well, it never arrived, and I think perhaps it might have got lost off the carrier's cart; I have been meaning to write to you of it but it slipped my mind.

What with the ball and everything, it suddenly came back to me; you see I have nothing smart enough to wear and there is so little time to get anything made up."

"I have it with me," answered Lizzy promptly. "I had it made up for you; we were always a similar size, except of course I have left the length. You always were the tallest! Mrs Reynolds made the pattern and it is to that lady you must write your thanks."

"Mrs Reynolds will have worked very hard on your gown, Mrs Wickham. She is a marvel. Mind you, do not forget to write and say thank you," added Mr Darcy, turning from Miss Darcy to address Lydia directly.

Despite his manner, Lydia thought her sister had changed him for the better. Theirs, for the most part, was an equal partnership, which Lydia observed with some envy; each gave in turn and respected the other, which she was sure was a rare quality to be found in most marriages. There was hardly ever a cross word between them, and if there was any disagreement, it was aired and discussed in the most civilised manner. And Mr Darcy was almost certain to be the one to give in first. He clearly worshipped Elizabeth.

"Are you quite well, my dear? You look a trifle pale this evening," he asked his wife as she sat picking at her food. "Perhaps an early night might suit you."

"Yes, I am a little tired, I confess; the journey has sapped me of all my energy. An early night will restore my good spirits, I am sure."

"Miss Fitzalan is delighted about the ball," said Lydia, hardly waiting for her turn to talk, "though she is insisting on being accompanied by Mr Taciturn."

"Lydia, that is unkind," Jane remarked. "He is a man of few words, but he does not know any of us very well."

"I can't think why he wants to come," Lydia insisted. "He doesn't talk except to give his opinions, which no one cares about; he doesn't dance and will look at everyone who does with an expression of abhorrence. If only Isabella were in a home of her own, I could talk to her just as I please. He is always there, hanging about in the background. You should have seen his face when we were talking about Harriet's growing stomach."

"Lydia, I should hope you know better than to go discussing such things in front of young men; it is not seemly," Lizzy scolded.

"Well, perhaps he has now learned his lesson and will stay at home in future," Lydia retorted.

"Has it occurred to you that he might enjoy the company of his sister and her friends, that he was trying to be sociable?" Jane questioned. "He does appear to be ill at ease in company, but perhaps Isabella thinks you bring him out of himself."

Lydia scoffed. "The only reason he comes with his sister is to spoil our fun, and because Isabella is so charming and thinks so well of her brother, she cannot see that he is in fact jealous of me. He cannot bear the thought of her spending two seconds together with anyone else and wants her time and attention exclusively. Between him and their mother, poor Isabella is worn to a frazzle."

Mr Darcy sighed audibly and scraped his chair back in agitation.

"It may well be that she will have a home of her own soon," said Mr Bingley, putting down his knife and fork to raise his glass and inspect its contents.

"Whatever do you mean?" asked Lydia, dashing her cutlery down impetuously and causing a great clatter.

"I do not think Charles means to talk out of turn, and I daresay Isabella will tell you herself, but it is common knowledge that a young gentleman farmer has been calling on her," added Jane. "But I have no wish to gossip; I am sure she will tell you all about it herself."

"Yes, Frederick Rowlandson, a capital fellow; he owns a pretty property at HighCross, set in many acres," expanded Mr Bingley. "I shouldn't wonder if she is not made a very happy woman—a very prudent match indeed. Your friend is a sensible girl I think."

"I wonder at her not telling me about him this afternoon," Lydia answered, ignoring Mr Bingley whom she was sure was trying his hardest to vex her, "but then we were not able to be confidential with one another. Well, I hope for his sake our dreary rector is out tomorrow when I call on Isabella. Sister, may I have a carriage?"

Lydia quite missed the exchange of raised eyebrows that passed between her sisters and brothers as she excused herself with great speed from the table, declining dessert or any more wine.

"Yes, of course, there will be a carriage at your disposal; after breakfast if you wish it."

Jane and Lizzy were both relieved to see her go. Jane always felt uncomfortable at the tensions which family life inevitably incurred and particularly those that abounded when Lydia came to stay. Lizzy was well aware that her sister's presence irritated Mr Darcy, throwing him out of all good humour, and once Lydia had removed herself, he became cheerful once more. It was pleasant for them both to have some time with Jane and Bingley, and being here would introduce Georgiana to more society. She was more than a little quiet this evening. Lydia's presence, Lizzy was sure, always brought back unpleasant memories for Miss Darcy. Not that Lydia had ever given her cause to regret the past, but an incident concerning Captain Wickham, before Mr Darcy was intimate with the Bennet family, made it very awkward to have his name mentioned within Miss Darcy's earshot. Lydia had been advised of the circumstances shortly after her marriage and been told that on no account was she to discuss her husband in front of Miss Georgiana. Lydia had, at the time of discovery, been shocked at the disclosure that her husband had forced his attentions on Miss Darcy, made her believe that he was in love with her, and suggested an elopement. Apparently, he had followed Miss Darcy to Ramsgate, but fortunately, before Captain Wickham could persuade her to run away, Mr Darcy had appeared to save the day. This episode had naturally led to the withdrawal of all connection with Wickham; Mr Darcy had never forgiven him, though he had been obliged on his wife's account to make some reparation.

Lydia retired to her room to mull over the events of the day. She reclined on a sofa at the foot of her bed and plumped a silk cushion behind her head. She was not quite ready for sleep, and her eyes sought out the view, resting on the wooded landscape in the distance, the tops of trees tinged with copper at the end of a beautiful day.

So Isabella had a young man. Strange to think she had not mentioned him in her correspondence, but then they did not write as they used to do. There was always something else to do and she just never seemed able to find the time. Besides, it was not always easy to write in the happy vein she would have desired. She was quite excited at the prospect of seeing her friend on the morrow. Lucky Isabella, thought Lydia, to have attracted a young farmer who had both property and land. To be near to her beloved mother, but quite far enough away from her brother, would be a great advantage, Lydia considered, with amusement. She could not wait to hear all of Isabella's news!

Chapter 26

AS SOON AS SHE had breakfasted, Lydia hastened away to her carriage and was soon bowling along the drive and ascending out of the park where, for an instant, she looked back at the house in all its handsome grandeur. They cantered through the wood and out into the lanes, heading for the rectory at Monks Holt just two miles away and were soon stopped before the gates of a very ancient looking house, not as modern as Lydia's preference would have had it, but large and substantial nevertheless. She walked up a path of old mellow brick with tiers and banks of flowers nodding on either side before lifting the huge iron knocker on the old oak door.

There was silence. She was sure they were expecting her; Isabella had insisted she come as early as possible. She knocked once more as loudly as she could. Again there was silence, but eventually, she heard distant footsteps, then the door opened, and there stood a short, plump girl, wheezing with all the humour of a very good housekeeper, who showed her in with a welcoming smile.

"Forgive me, Mrs Wickham. I was sitting with Mrs Fitzalan upstairs and, what with there being so many steps to come down and me not as agile as I should be . . . well, come in and I will show you to the sitting room. Miss Isabella asked me to say that she is sorry she is not here in person to greet you, but she has just stepped out in order to fetch her mother's tonic draught and won't be long. I'll tell the rector you are here."

"Oh no, do not disturb him. I am quite happy to sit and wait," Lydia replied anxiously. She wished to avoid Mr Fitzalan if she could.

They passed along a panelled hallway, dim and gloomy after the bright light outside, before Lydia was shown into the pretty sitting room. With oak beams and mullioned windows, the house was very old and of a bygone age. Bars of sunlight blazed over the furniture, large stuffed sofas covered in old, faded damask graced either side of the fireplace, carved tables were set in the alcoves, and ancient throne-like chairs with rush seats ranged along the walls. Lydia was very fond of Isabella's home, though she thought how she might improve it with some alterations to the structure and a few choice modern fittings. It was a charming family house. Lydia walked over to the casement window to look out onto the terrace and formal garden, which was still laid out in the old style in hedges of knots. White doves pecked at the intricate pathways and flew beyond the high yew hedges into a painted dovecote and a sleepy cat, sunning himself on a seat, stretched his limbs and rolled over to luxuriate in the warmth. She was admiring the view when a figure turned a corner around a hedge, appeared with a trug and a garden fork, and busied himself by the garden wall. Lydia craned her neck to see. The tall muscular gardener, clad only in a white shirt, tucked into his breeches, with the sleeves rolled up, displaying a very fine pair of legs to Lydia's way of thinking, was partly obscured by the hedge. He stood, his back towards her, tying up a straggling rose that had fallen away from the wall. She could not help thinking what a fine figure of a man he made. His dark hair was almost wild; the breeze shook his curls and billowed at his chemise, so that his strong, lean body was exposed. In the next moment, he turned and Lydia could not hide her astonishment. Her mouth fell quite open as it became clear exactly whom she had been ogling with such admiration. That he had seen her expression she was sure, for despite dipping behind the curtain as quickly as she could, their eyes had met. Alexander Fitzalan had fixed her with his piercing blue eyes and his mien was one of gravity.

She could not think how she had not recognised him; she should have known his dark head anywhere, but to see him in such a state of undress and without his clerical black, which seemed to be as much a part of him as a beetle's black armour, had taken her completely by surprise. She sat down, feeling flustered, and prayed he would not come and speak to her. After five minutes, she began to feel quite safe and was ready to breathe again without turning in alarm at every creak of the floorboards and every footstep that passed by the door. She began to loll in the chair, closing her eyes in the warmth of the sun and admonished herself for her folly. But the turning of the door handle was enough to set her upright once more, and to her dismay, her composure disintegrated as the person she least wanted to see stepped into the room.

"Mrs Wickham, I had no idea you were here," Mr Fitzalan declared. "I hope you have not been sitting long on your own."

He stood before her in his usual black garb, and Lydia could not help but wonder if she had seen an apparition out there in the garden. "My sister had an errand to attend to, but she thought she would be returned before you arrived. I cannot think what must be detaining her."

This was quite a speech, and more words than Lydia thought she had ever heard him utter, though she felt it devoid of the necessary enquiries and flatteries on her health, her beauty, and her person, which young men of her acquaintance usually emitted. He sat down opposite her and fiddled nervously with the fringing on a fat velvet cushion.

"You have a beautiful garden, Mr Fitzalan," Lydia remarked. "You must be a great gardener I think."

Alexander did not know where to look. He was clearly mortified by her comments, though she was not to know that merely the recollection of his being seen in his shirt and breeches was enough to confound him. Why did Mrs Wickham always seem to take so much pleasure in his discomposure? He could not think what to say and was immensely grateful for the fact that his sister chose that instant to burst in on the pair of them.

"Oh, Lydia, I am so sorry to have kept you waiting on my company," she cried as she came flying into the room, throwing her cloak and her bonnet onto a chair before falling into a seat. "The apothecary could not be found, then I was delayed by Miss Wynn, who always has a week's gossip to impart, and then I saw Miss Rowlandson, who begged for some advice about a new bonnet."

"You saw Miss Rowlandson? How is she? Were you helpful in your advice, Isabella?" Mr Fitzalan sat up with instant attention, prompting his sister with more animation than Lydia had ever seen in him.

"Suffice to say, she entered the shop and bought the very hat I recommended, so yes, I would say so. Do not worry, Alexander; for your sake, I would not put her off."

Lydia looked from brother to sister. Mr Fitzalan must be smitten with this Miss Rowlandson, judging by the daft expression spreading over his countenance and his sister's coy smiles. She hoped the poor woman knew of his designs; it would not bode well to have Mr Fitzalan take one by surprise with declarations of affection, but that could hardly be the case. He did not know what it was to be in love; he had professed as much.

"I must go and attend my duties, forgive me, ladies," he said as he rose, colouring instantly and bowing stiffly before leaving the room in such haste as made Lydia nearly burst out laughing.

At last they were left alone, and in the natural course of conversation, Isabella had soon taken Lydia into her confidence. "Miss Eleanor Rowlandson is a good friend of ours; indeed, I hope she may be more than just that—a sister too perhaps."

"Is your brother in love with Miss Rowlandson?" Lydia asked, trying to keep the astonishment out of her voice.

"I cannot say, though it is clear he likes her well enough. No, Eleanor has a brother, Frederick. Oh, Lydia, it is towards this excellent fellow that my desires tend and my hopes lie."

"You sly thing, not a word did you divulge to me in any of your letters. How could you keep such a secret?"

"To be truthful, Lydia, he has only just declared his intention of courting me, and I did not want to say anything until I was really sure. Lydia, I do love him, more than anyone ever."

"Is he handsome? Is he rich?" Lydia quizzed laughingly, keeping up the pretence that she knew nothing about him.

"Both! I am so lucky; I cannot believe my good fortune. However, we are not married yet, nor even engaged, but I have high hopes."

"Isabella, I am so happy for you. You deserve to be so blessed. Tell me all about him."

"I danced with him at an Assembly in Meryton, though I had already been introduced to him by his sister. They live at HighCross, which is only down the road, and she was one of the first to call when we moved here to be with Alexander. The family owns much of the farmland hereabouts; Eleanor lives with their parents close by, and Freddie has the running of Home Farm. Lydia, I know you will love them both as much as I do."

"I'm sure I shall. And do you think, when you have gone to live at Home Farm, Eleanor might be set up in the rectory?"

"I wish it more than I can say, but you know my brother, Lydia. For all my love of his endearing ways, he does not have that knack with ladies that others possess. He does not know what to say to them. He is truly awkward with strangers, and how any young lady is to come to know him on a more intimate basis I do not know. He cannot make any small talk nor get past saying 'how do you do' or have any idea of how to flatter or compliment. If only he had a teacher, a girl of his acquaintance, someone with whom he feels comfortable who could teach him the art of conversing on subjects lighter than those which only interest clergymen." Isabella looked with intent at her friend. "Yes, that is what he needs: someone to show him the way."

"Surely if Eleanor is interested, she will be the person to do that," Lydia replied, picking up the cushion Mr Fitzalan had abandoned.

"Perhaps, but I fear she may not be aware that he has even the simplest regard for her, based on his behaviour thus far. No, what he needs is someone to instruct him in the ways of love and teach him to flirt a little."

Lydia was at a loss as to know what to say as she sat smoothing out the cushion's fringe between her fingers. She thought Isabella was asking the impossible. It made her giggle to think of Alexander even attempting to flirt with any poor unsuspecting female, let alone encourage anyone to take on the task of instructing him in the art of seduction.

Isabella was staring at her with a look somewhere between recognition and amusement. "I am forming a most excellent plan as I look at you, my dear friend. You know Alexander quite well enough, and you are just the sort of person to encourage him to almost anything. You could do it."

Lydia laughed out loud. "I cannot agree with you, Isabella; what on earth gave you that absurd idea? I would think if anyone should instruct Alexander on how to behave towards young ladies, it is you. He needs to hear such advice from his sister, believe me. I am certainly ill qualified for such an exercise. Besides, Alexander does not like me. We can never have a conversation without one upsetting the other. It is quite clear how much he detests me."

"However can you say such a thing, Lydia?" Isabella looked astounded. Her fair curls shook around her neat coiffure in agitation. "Has he ever given you cause to think he dislikes you? What has he said? Has he behaved badly towards you?"

Lydia shook her head. "I wish I had not mentioned it; I am truly sorry, Isabella. No, he has never said anything amiss nor behaved in any way improper. Please forget I said anything at all."

"Dear friend, tell me what you mean," Isabella begged.

"If I am honest," Lydia said sighing, "I think he looks at me as one looks at a truly wicked woman, and I suppose, in a way, I have at one time had my share of wickedness. That is altered anyhow; I am a respectable married woman."

"Truly, Lydia, I think you are mistaken about my brother. I am sure he has mentioned his regard for you as my friend, and in any case, it would be going against the grain. He does not judge his fellow man. He is a clergyman after all."

"Precisely," Lydia answered, "I am quite used to the ways of clergymen. You forget my cousin is a man of the cloth."

Isabella looked most put out.

"I will try at least to engage him in some conversation if you like," said Lydia, "but I warn you, I do not think I am up to the job. I cannot promise to aid your brother's chances of romantic liaison with any exchange we are likely to have. I truly believe you would be much better off having this talk with Miss Rowlandson."

They were interrupted by a knock at the door and Bertha entered with a grin on her face that stretched from ear to ear. "Mr and Miss Rowlandson have called, miss, shall I show them in?"

"There, Lydia, now you shall meet them!" Isabella giggled, as she ran round the room picking up her belongings, rearranging the chairs, and inspecting her reflection in the glass. "Bertha, do hurry and show them in."

Freddie and Eleanor Rowlandson waltzed in with such an air of confidence and affable good humour that Lydia was taken by surprise. He was a very handsome man with a pleasing address and charming manner. Mr Rowlandson might be a farmer, but he was certainly something more than the country bumpkin Lydia had anticipated. His sister was something of an eye opener too; a beauty, all blonde curls and emerald eyes, and though Lydia could not tell why she took an instant dislike to the girl, one thing was certain: Miss Eleanor Rowlandson was not at all the plain young woman Lydia had expected to see. She was dressed in white muslin, with a Spanish cloak of the same swinging from her shoulders, and on her head a Persian hat with green feathers framed her pretty face, setting off her eyes, which Lydia thought were exactly the same shade as the eyes of the cat she had seen in the rector's garden.

"We have heard so much about you, Mrs Wickham," Mr Rowlandson enthused. "Miss Fitzalan was so delighted to hear you were to be in this part of the country again and so were we— thrilled at the thought of meeting with you at last. I hope you will forgive our speed at coming over to get a look at you, but we had heard such reports that we couldn't wait a minute longer, we just had to come and see for ourselves. I might add, Mrs Wickham, that I need hardly say that we are not disappointed in the least, are we, my dear? You are every bit the woman of beauty and fashion we have heard so much about!"

Miss Rowlandson smiled and nodded in the right places, though Lydia noted it was not done with the same enthusiasm. The door opened again and there was Mr Fitzalan, turned up quite like a bad penny, Lydia thought, though she imagined it would be fun to watch his attempts at courting Eleanor. She could see, to her great amusement, that Miss Rowlandson was staring at him a great deal, smiling far too much, and fluttering her eyelashes at every chance, but these antics seemed to have no effect on her intended suitor, who either was not aware of her attempts to captivate him or chose to ignore them.

"Your sister is mistress of Netherfield, is she not?" Mr Rowlandson continued. "I am slightly acquainted with her husband Mr Bingley, as fine a fellow as ever lived."

Lydia nodded and smiled; she was quite used to hearing praise of her relatives in such a manner. She surmised it might be easy to be thus distinguished by one's fellow human beings if one were as rich.

"We have heard there is to be a ball at the house," added his sister. "How I should love to be a fly on the wall at such a gathering and see all the beautiful gowns."

Isabella looked anxiously at her friend. Lydia knew what she was thinking—that she would love to have Mr Rowlandson there, to twirl away the hours. Isabella looked down at her clenched hands with resignation; she knew it would be too much to ask her friend to invite him, and in any case, it was more than likely not in Lydia's power to be able to do so.

"It would be my pleasure to invite you to the ball; it is my great privilege to invite whomever I choose," Lydia announced, pleased to see the expression on Miss Rowlandson's face who was now regarding her with a mixture of envy and admiration.

"Mrs Wickham, you cannot mean it!" Eleanor declared, jumping up from the seat, the ostrich feathers in her hat waving in her excitement. "Oh, tell me I have heard correctly; am I really to go to the ball?"

"That is very generous, Mrs Wickham," her brother cried, grinning at Isabella who beamed back with sheer joy. "We would be delighted to accept your very kind invitation."

Lydia could not have felt happier if she was mistress of Netherfield itself. It was most agreeable indeed to offer such generous hospitality at someone else's expense. She only hoped that Jane would not mind too much when she told her what she had done. Everyone continued to praise her for showing such beneficence, all except Mr Fitzalan, who had not spoken throughout but merely watched her, with that same disapproving and unforgiving countenance, with those eyes that matched the sky outside.

"Do you dance, Mr Rowlandson?" Lydia asked. "No, do not answer me; I pride myself on my ability to discern a man who dances like a dream, and I would lay a bet on my best bonnet that you are such a creature."

"High stakes indeed, Mrs Wickham," laughed Mr Rowlandson.

"Do not laugh, sir. You clearly have no comprehension of the great store I lay by my headwear. Tell him it is so, Isabella," she asked, giggling, but did not pause for breath long enough to allow her friend to speak. "I always love to dance, you know, and I hope once I have had my try out with all my favourite beaux, you shall save me a dance too. I do love to dance with a well-looking man." Lydia could not help herself; he was so very charming and was clearly enjoying her flirtatious manner, as his eyes did not leave hers once. She did not notice her friend's close observation of the pair of them, and even if she had, it would not have deterred her.

"My sister Isabella is an excellent dancer, the most accomplished in Hertfordshire I should say," Mr Fitzalan butted in, and

Lydia noted not only Mr Rowlandson heartily agreeing with him but regarded Alexander's smug air, as if he rejoiced in detracting all attention from her own good self, which appeared to have been his object.

She was quite sick of him and decided she would have a little sport with him. "Mr Fitzalan, are we at last able to coax you into your dancing slippers? You cannot come to a ball at Netherfield and stand about you know; it is simply not allowed. You must not show your disapproval. Even Mr Darcy condescends to partner all, from the highest in the land, to the most lowly farmer's daughter."

Alexander stared back at her inscrutably before her steady gaze forced his eyes to look down at the ground, yet his jaw remained set firm and his mouth unsmiling.

"But Mr Fitzalan does dance, Mrs Wickham, and with great style I might add," Eleanor interjected. "I cannot think where you got the idea from that he does not. Indeed, I have danced with him several times at the last two Assemblies."

Lydia was most vexed to find that the man who had refused to partner her had not only agreed to dance with Miss Rowlandson but had accompanied her more than once. "I am sure he does dance after a fashion; I am just a tease, you know. But I think if we press him, he will admit that he was always reluctant to exhibit and frowned at those who did. I must say I am glad to hear of this change and to be told that he has a talent for dancing is music to my ears."

"Perhaps there were reasons for my reluctance to dance on the occasions to which you refer, madam," he said brusquely, before rising from his seat. "Forgive me, I must beg to leave you all." He was gone instantly from the room, leaving the others staring at one another, stunned by his abrupt departure and the exchange between him and Mrs Wickham.

There was an awkward silence for a second or two before Lydia spoke. "Dear me, I appear to have touched a raw nerve; I was only funning you know. I do hope it won't stop him performing at the ball. Now I shall be more anxious than ever to witness this rare display." She laughed, but when the others hesitated before half-heartedly joining in, she had a notion that they were only doing so to be polite.

Miss Rowlandson was keen to restore the equilibrium. She surmised that Isabella was not happy with her friend for laughing at her brother, and despite the fact that Mrs Wickham had suggested that farming folk were lowly, she also did not want to jeopardise her invitation to the ball, where, apart from witnessing the wonderful sights and sounds, she would be sure of parading her beauty before an audience that would previously have been denied her. "Men never can suffer to be teased. They are hopeless creatures, are they not? Isabella, I think it so good for them, I really think you should adopt some of Mrs Wickham's jests with my own dear brother; he certainly would benefit from such quizzing!"

"Oh yes, Miss Fitzalan, it would be my pleasure to have you teasing me at any time." He laughed and winked at her, which produced a hint of rose upon her creamy complexion. "And if I might be so bold, may I engage you for the first two dances at the Netherfield ball?"

Isabella's spirits were entirely recovered. "It would be my great pleasure, Mr Rowlandson."

"Well now, we had best be going," he declared, rising reluctantly from his seat. "It has been a pleasure to meet you, Mrs Wickham, and thank you; we are indebted to you for your kind invitation."

"We are indeed," enthused his sister. She shook Lydia's hand warmly before turning to Isabella. "I expect we shall not see each other until the ball now. Oh, there is so much to be done before the big day and so much to accomplish, I hope I might manage. Mother will be so pleased!"

Lydia was a little concerned that her friend might scold her for her behaviour after the Rowlandsons had departed, but Isabella had already forgiven her. "That was so kind, my dear friend, to invite the man I love to the ball. You knew how much that would mean to me, and to invite Eleanor too, for dear Alexander, thank you."

"It was selfishly done, I confess, as much for my own pleasure as for yours," Lydia admitted.

"That I do believe," laughed Isabella, "and I will certainly allow you to dance with Freddie if you promise not to steal him."

"Oh now, Isabella," Lydia said, giggling. "You know my wicked reputation. I cannot promise all that!"

Friday, May 13th

The house party is not yet complete. Mama and papa, Mary, and Kitty are to arrive this afternoon and will be staying till tomorrow. Mr Bingley's sister, Caroline, who has recently become engaged, has been staying for a month at the home of her fiancé's parents and will also arrive, with her lover in tow, at a similar time. After my sister's wedding, Miss Bingley did not enjoy playing second fiddle to Mrs Bingley, who took prece-

dence over her, and so, Jane soon hinted that Charles look around for a suitable match for his sister. It was soon found in a Mr Heathcote, with whom Bingley was at school. This fellow, though not of noble birth as Miss Bingley would have preferred, has made his fortune through trade, is almost as rich as Mr Darcy, and owns property in the west country. Miss Bingley will soon be able to live in the style that she feels her inherent right, amongst neighbours she considers inferior, and at a suitable distance from her brother, his wife, and family, so that calling frequently and being on intimate terms with Jane will be made impossible. If I were Jane, I should be very happy.

I must confess that I am not very comfortable with the idea of seeing Miss Bingley again. She is the rudest woman I know and has the most unfortunate manner. Thank goodness her sister, Mrs Hurst, is indisposed with a baby at present; I could not bear the two of them looking at me with disdain. At least Wickham is not here, and I am thankful he is not due for another fortnight at least.

Chapter 27

THE ENTIRE COMPANY WAS sitting in the drawing room after breakfast when all members gathered were suddenly alerted to the sound of horses and wheels. The prospect through floor-length windows afforded an excellent view across the gravelled drive and Jane expressed her surprise at the sight of a carriage approaching.

"Who can this be?" she asked, looking across at her husband. "We do not expect anyone till this afternoon, do we, my love?"

Lydia jumped up to take a closer look, observing from behind a curtain draped back over ornate gilt finials that it was a carriage she recognised.

"It is mama and papa, Kitty, and Mary," she announced. "I daresay mama could not wait a moment longer. Yes indeed, my mother is stepping down from the carriage as I speak and scolding Kitty for sneezing."

"Goodness, what can bring them at this hour?" asked Jane. "I must find Mrs Garnett. I do not know that their rooms will be quite ready."

Lydia observed with some amusement that Mr Darcy had raised his eyes to the heavens, that his wife was doing her best to placate the onset of his imminent irritability, that Charles Bingley was out of his seat and running round after his wife, and that Jane was trying to keep everyone calm, though unsure what to do next, standing up one moment and sitting down the next.

Mrs Garnett appeared at the door. "Mr and Mrs Bennet and the Miss Bennets, ma'am."

Mrs Bennet was through the door in a flash. "Jane, we are come a little earlier than I said, but I thought you might like it, as you will be rushed off your feet, and visitors do not always make themselves as useful as they ought. I should have thought about it when I wrote to say we should come in the afternoon, and then before I knew it, I had sealed the wafer and it was gone. Never mind, we are come and are here to help you."

Lydia braced herself for her mother's ministrations and rose to greet her. She certainly seemed to be the same Mrs Bennet, but Lydia thought how her mother had aged lately; there was more grey flecked in the hair at her temples and new wrinkles about her eyes, but all in all, she was still a handsome woman, despite her agitation. Having confided in her mother about the state of her marriage after the first incident in Newcastle, Lydia had regretted doing so ever since, for Mrs Bennet had the habit of reminding Lydia about her husband's conduct whenever they met. Lydia's heart sank at the thought.

Kitty was at her sister's side in a moment. "Lydia, it is so good to see you. Isn't it all exciting? And you will meet my new beau, Mr Coates. He is a cousin of Maria Lucas and so handsome."

"Oh, Lizzy," shouted Mrs Bennet hailing her across the room, "how you are grown, my dear. I shouldn't wonder if it is not twins. Look, Mr Bennet, is she not very fat? Sit down, sit down my dear, take the weight off your feet."

"I am quite well, mother, thank you," Lizzy grimaced, suffusing pink with embarrassment at her mother's insensitivity.

Mrs Bennet turned with a smile to address Mr Darcy. "It is a big, bonny boy, I shouldn't wonder, looking at the size of her and with a virile man like you for his father. An heir for Pemberley, isn't she a clever girl?" Jane stepped forward to remove her mother from his vicinity and helped her to a chair. "And Jane, elegant as ever, even as she is increasing," gabbled Mrs Bennet, running on without a pause. "Why, you would hardly know. Are you wearing a corset? I do not recommend it, though in my day it was done. Well, we would never have laced our gowns you see. You are fortunate that high waists are fashionable. I said so to Mr Bennet, didn't I, my dear?"

Mr Bennet was talking to Lizzy. He had never recovered from the shock of her marriage and the fact that she had left Longbourn for good. Although he was pleased with her chosen partner, he had never found anything or anyone to fill the aching gap left by the absence of this favourite daughter.

Jane opened her mouth to speak, but as she did so Mrs Bennet's eye fell on her youngest daughter. She crossed the room at a pace, threw her arms around Lydia and hugged her till she thought she might have no breath left. "My poor, poor Lydia," she cried, "what has that man done to you now, my dear? Goodness, how ill you look, how you have aged!" She held Lydia's face up to the light and shook her head and clucked in dismay. "Tell me what has happened this time. Why have you left all your friends and your home? Mr Wickham did not beat you did he, dear? I have not had a letter from you these five months to know the truth of anything for certain."

"Mother!" Lydia shouted in frustration. "Keep your voice down! You might let me speak. You have not paused for breath since you walked through the door."

"Well, that is a nice way to greet your mama, I'm sure, with not a word of how do you do or please sit down. Shouting may well be considered as good manners in the North but it will not do here." Mrs Bennet sniffed loudly in contempt before seating herself opposite her daughter.

Jane fussed around the others and sent Mrs Garnett back for some tea. The gentlemen quickly excused themselves as soon as they saw an opportunity, taking Mr Bennet with them.

"I always knew he was a bad lot," Mrs Bennet continued, "first dallying with my dearest girl to get his hands on Mr Darcy's money and now getting his hands on all the drink and as many women as he can to satisfy his nasty appetites. And to think how I always preferred him to Mr Darcy, who is the kindest, most gentlemanly and courteous man that ever walked the land. Now I am not saying that Wickham isn't entirely to blame, but Lydia, have you never asked yourself why he strays? Is everything at home all it should be? A man must have his needs met. Well, I daresay it is not your fault, but I do think if you were expecting a happy event, he might be a little more settled. Still, I suppose if you are content to ignore his dallying for the sake of your marriage, what am I to do about it? And he is to come here and I suppose I must be civil, though I should like to give him a piece of my mind." She did not pause for breath for ten minutes and by the end Lydia felt she had endured enough.

An early dinner was served for the Bingleys and their guests at three o'clock, in order for everyone to have thoroughly digested its contents and make preparations for the evening's celebrations. Miss Bingley and Mr Heathcote did not arrive until four, much to Lydia's relief; she did not think she could withstand both her mother's and Miss Bingley's enquiries in the same afternoon. They took to their rooms immediately and a light meal was sent up.

Kitty came to Lydia's room, bringing her clothes for her sister to inspect.

"Tell me all about Mr Coates," Lydia demanded. "Is he rich and good looking? Is he 'the one'?"

"I think I can safely say he is the man for me. I am in love, I declare, and expect an offer any day!"

"Do not be in such a hurry to get wed, Kitty. Take time to make your choice. Being married is not the be all and end all, you know."

"You talk as if you didn't enjoy being married, Lydia."

"I like it well enough."

"But?"

"There are always vexations; it happens in the best marriages, you know. Oh, Kitty, enjoy your youth; have fun whilst you can without any cares or ties. But let us not talk of that now. Show me what you are wearing and how you are to dress your hair."

"What fun, Lydia! It will be just like the old days, do you recall?"

She did remember and with more affection than she cared to disclose.

Chapter 28

THE SUN HAD SHONE brightly from first light and continued to radiate all day so that, by the close of it, the warm temperatures remained, exuding not only heat rendering the rooms quite airless but the scent of exotic perfume, which emanated from the floral arrangements in every room, the flower-filled urns on the terraces, and the clusters of scented petals in the ladies' hair. Lydia thought it would be like dancing in the garden; French doors were opened to the outside and strings of candlelit crystal shades illuminated the water cascades as well as the ballroom. As the carriages rolled up, and the horses steamed in the heat under the torches and flares, which lit up the grand edifice, the strains of music floated high up to the woods and tree tops beyond.

Lydia could not help but feel excited; she had never witnessed such a sight, and even the last Netherfield ball she had attended had been nothing to this. She had refused to listen to her sister, who had requested her presence in the reception party, and was instead standing under the portico entrance leaning over the balustrade, eager to watch the arrivals mounting the staircases, busy making a note of all the fine fashionable clothes. It was quite a display of nobility and gentry all attired in their finest, the women like the gardenias in the grove, all white, dressed in the sheerest muslins and silks, shimmering under the glow of moonlight.

And the men! Such a display of well-dressed peacocks, they were as beautiful as the women to Lydia's mind. She shrieked with delight as she caught sight of Isabella stepping down from her brother's carriage and ran down the stairs, heedless of those who might get in her way.

"You look a picture," enthused Isabella, standing back to admire her friend.

"Do you like my turban? It is the very latest. I could not resist the pink ostrich feathers. I feel like an eastern princess."

"But thankfully, you are my own dear Mrs Wickham, and this is such a treat. I have hardly slept these last nights for imagining how it would all be."

"On such a night dreams do come true, I am sure," Lydia laughed, winking with great solemnity at her friend. "Perhaps Freddie will declare himself on bended knee. You know the dark walks around the grounds are very pleasant for a couple courting, and a girl might just persuade her lover to press his suit further if she gives him a hint of what might follow from an arousing kiss in the arbour."

"Good evening, Mrs Wickham," said Mr Fitzalan, stepping up to break them apart as Isabella hooted with laughter.

"Good evening, Mr Fitzalan." Lydia curtseyed before inspecting his feet. "I am pleased to see you have your dancing shoes on. Will you dance with me?"

At once he excused himself with a bow, saying he had spied an old friend, leaving Lydia in stitches and Isabella watching his departing figure with some concern.

"Oh Lydia, I think you frightened him. He is not used to such boldness. Please don't tease him so. I am worried that he might just go home and then poor Eleanor will not get her chance to dance with him."

Lydia did not think "poor Eleanor" would be that put out. She thought she would be very well able to hold her own with any of the young men; she would put money on it. "I did not mean anything. I do not know what comes over me when I am faced with your brother's stern regard, it makes me want to be devilish."

"For my sake, please try to be kind. I know he is not as lively as some young men, but if you knew him better, if you would give him a chance, I am sure you would like him."

"But would he ever like me? Now there is a question. Isabella, you must admit he does not approve of your friend."

Isabella said nothing. She knew it was useless to argue with Lydia, and she was determined not to have this evening spoiled for anyone. She took Lydia's arm in hers and patted her kid glove. "Shall we go in?"

They followed the crowd up the steps and Lydia joined the queue to greet her own family as she stood with her friend. Mr Fitzalan joined them just as they reached Mr Bingley and the introductions began. Jane and her husband were as gracious as ever, welcoming Isabella and her brother with great affability. Following on in the line was Miss Bingley, her fiancé at her side. Lydia would have liked to laugh; she was tickled to see that he was several inches smaller than his mate, and had a countenance which she could only describe as weasel-faced and a shock of unruly hair which fell in lank strands over his pale, pink-rimmed eyes. Lydia steeled herself, knowing it was not possible for her "sister" to make conversation without caustic remarks.

"Good evening, Mrs Wickham, are you here again? It must be but two months since I saw you last. And where has Captain Wickham business to attend to this time? Let me think, would it be Ramsgate or Brighton? I think those are his usual stamping grounds when he is intent on employment of a certain nature."

"Captain Wickham is in Bath on regimental business at present, Miss Bingley; he hopes to join me in a week or so. If it was not so important, he would have been here with me now."

"Ah yes, I had quite forgotten. We saw him, did we not, my dear?" She turned to her fiancé but made no attempt to introduce him to Lydia or her friends, who hung back, more than a little over-awed by the whole proceedings.

"You saw my husband?" Lydia asked, quite dreading her reply.

"Yes, indeed, we even spoke to him. We were in Bath this last week. We were walking up Gay Street and he bumped into us on the way down. He was so surprised to see me, and I think quite flattered that I remembered him; he blushed quite red in any case. He was with his sister, yes, I am sure that is how he described the lady. They are not at all alike are they? What with him so dark and she so fair, but it is easy to see how attached to one another they are, how close. She never left his side for a moment and hung onto him like a limpet."

Lydia was well aware that George had no sister and was quite sure that Miss Bingley knew it too. "Ah yes, dear Sophia, I hope my sister was well?" Lydia kept her nerve, determined to out-bluff this odious woman.

"I would say she was blooming. Do send on my good wishes for her future happiness."

Lydia felt the room sway, Miss Bingley's face seemed suddenly to blur, and if it had not been for Mr Fitzalan, who steadied her with a firm hand in the small of her back, she later thought she might have fallen over. Lydia uttered her excuses, they passed on, and though she did her best to ignore Miss Bingley's words, she kept hearing them run round her head.

"Lydia, you are as white as a sheet, are you quite well my dear?" Mrs Bennet asked. "Did you eat anything at dinner? It is not one of your fad diets again, steak and ale or such like, is it my dear? You must eat properly. This is what comes of living in Newcastle, so far away from your own dear mama."

"A banishment to any part of the country would be apt to pale anyone's cheeks I wouldn't wonder," added her sister Mary who always spoke as she thought. "I would have liked to say married life is treating you well, Lydia, but it is clear to see that the old adage, 'Marry in haste . . .'"

"Thank you, Mary," Lydia cut in. "I would have liked to say that time might have improved your manners, but the old adage, 'keep your breath to cool your porridge' might be worth remembering." Lydia was anxious to avoid detaining Mary or her mother any longer, and having no wish to sit with either of them, she steered her party to the ballroom.

"Are you quite recovered, Mrs Wickham?" Mr Fitzalan asked. His expression was all concern and Lydia suddenly felt quite unnerved. His looks told her that he had read the situation and that he had heard all of Miss Bingley's conversation. He knew exactly what sort of woman was accompanying her husband and that she was not his sister.

"I am well, thank you," she replied but found for once that she could not meet his eyes. She supposed that Wickham's flaunting himself around Bath with some floozy or other was bound, in the end, to have been generally discovered. But that it should have been Caroline Bingley who was made aware of the scandal was too insulting. Lydia was mortified. She would not think about the other hints she had so willingly supplied. She would not dwell on it.

"Have you seen any sign of the Rowlandsons yet?" Mr Fitzalan asked his sister.

"No, I have not," Isabella replied, her eyes darting anxiously around the room.

"I am sure I just saw Miss Eleanor," Lydia declared, scanning the room as though she expected sight of her at any moment. "She was surrounded by officers, quite engaged." This was not strictly true; though she had been in conversation with a young man, Lydia wanted to see Mr Fitzalan's discomfiture at the thought of his beloved being paid attention by other suitors. She could not think why she wished to be so spiteful, but she couldn't bear the idea that he had been kind to her out of pity. She would ensure he kept his concern to himself.

"You should have said, Lydia," Isabella responded a little impatiently. "I have been looking everywhere for my sweet friend. Alexander, see if you can find them."

The small orchestra, arranged on a platform at one end, had rested after their introductions and were tuning up their instruments once again. Isabella looked round frantically but there was no sign of the Rowlandsons. "If you don't hurry, we shall miss the first dance," Isabella urged.

"Stay here then, or I will not be able to find you." Mr Fitzalan moved off to search the room and the girls were left behind, watching the rush of people swarming through the doors whilst looking for familiar faces. Lydia had never seen so many people gathered at Netherfield. This was certainly an occasion to end all others, and the Bingleys had spared no expense.

After a minute or two, Isabella could bear it no longer. "It is no use, Alexander never can see further than the end of his nose. I will go and look for them myself. She rushed away, leaving Lydia to her own devices and her own thoughts. It was not long before old acquaintances, former beaux from the days before her marriage, had appeared at her side, begging for a dance and lifting her spirits.

"We thought it was you, Mrs Wickham," Mr Wooton declared with a bow. "How delightful! And is Mr Wickham with you?"

"No, the Captain is away at present on business, though I expect him in a day or two." She could not resist informing them of her husband's promotion. "How are you gentlemen? Am I to suppose you have not succumbed to Cupid's bow as yet? I do not see any ladies dangling from your arms."

"Alas," Mr Edwards lamented, "since you left, Mrs Wickham, we haven't had the heart to be in love, let alone go courting."

"Oh, you always had a silvered tongue, you wicked man," she laughed.

"Mrs Wickham!" A voice she recognised as belonging to Mr Rowlandson hailed her as he advanced through the French windows across the floor. "How glad I am to have found you at last. Is Miss Fitzalan with you?" He stood before her looking dismayed, and Lydia realised not for the first time that his regard for her friend was genuine.

"Well, she was here just a moment ago. Dear me, where has she gone? I cannot see her anywhere, can you? Nevermind, keep me company until she returns. I am sure she will be along in a moment. Here are some old friends of mine to amuse us. Mr Edwards and Mr Wooton are here to ask for a dance."

"Dash it all, Mrs Wickham," Mr Rowlandson cried, nodding in the gentlemen's direction, "that Miss Fitzalan should have disappeared like that. We were to have the first dance."

"I would hate for you to be upset, but rest assured, I will oblige if she doesn't return. We cannot have you miss the first dance. You must decide, Mr Rowlandson. Will you be my partner? And then," she said, looking up at Mr Edwards from under her lashes, "who will be next?"

Just as she spoke, Mr Fitzalan stepped up and stood before them all. Lydia laughed out loud; even though his expression was severe, she could not help but be amused. Although she knew quite well it had not been his purpose, it certainly looked to everyone else that he wished to partner her and she was immensely diverted by the absurdity of the situation.

"Mr Fitzalan, I did not know you were so keen to dance," she suggested with a giggle, glancing round at her audience who laughed back.

"No indeed, forgive me, Mrs Wickham. My intention was not to ask for a dance; you have more than enough interest in that pursuit which I beg you will give me leave to deny you." He turned to address Mr Rowlandson and stood with his back towards her. "I wondered if I might have a word in private?"

The opening bars of the first dance were being played. Mr Rowlandson bowed, sidestepping Mr Fitzalan, and offered his arm to Lydia. "Can it wait, dear friend? I have just promised Mrs Wickham the first dance."

Lydia was astounded by Mr Fitzalan's rudeness and the cold manner in which he had addressed her. She knew his disdainful expression had been reserved for her alone. Even Mr Rowlandson appeared to be much embarrassed. "Take no notice, Mrs Wickham," he said, taking her arm and leading her to the floor. "I do not know what has got into the fellow, though Mr Fitzalan was never much of a one for dancing."

"He clearly disapproves of such a heathen activity," Lydia cried scornfully. "Why did he come here tonight I should like to know? Clergymen should be banned from all types of amusement if you ask me. How dare he try to spoil our fun!" She was more cross than she could say, especially as she observed him—his tall figure watching her from the side of the dance floor—with such a look of distaste that she felt she should retaliate. She stared triumphantly right back at him when she was assured of his blue eyes' fullest attention and was instantly rewarded, as he was forced immediately to look away.

Freddie was the very dancer Lydia expected him to be, and she could not resist a little flirting with such a well-looking man. To tell the truth, she was more than a little jealous of her friend's good fortune in finding such a man, and though she would not steal him for long, surely a few harmless dances would not hurt. Isabella's face said it all as they came off the floor; she was so disappointed to have missed the first dance.

"Mrs Wickham is an excellent dancer, is she not?" announced Mr Rowlandson.

"She is indeed," smiled Isabella, trying her hardest to look happy. She generously thought that Lydia probably did not consciously set out to divert all young men's attentions towards herself, but Isabella wished that, for once, Lydia would leave her beau well alone.

"And now, my dear," Mr Rowlandson said, turning to Isabella, "will you do me the honour of dancing with me?"

Lydia watched as Isabella and her partner moved off, happy in one another's company. Mr Edwards was there in a second, but before he could proffer his arm, Mr Fitzalan had taken her by the hand, had dismissed any other bystander, and was marching her onto the floor. He had not spoken one word to her and one look at his countenance told Lydia that it bore all its usual hallmarks of ill humour.

"I think you are very rude, Mr Fitzalan, to butt in on another gentleman. Mr Edwards and I were about to take a turn," Lydia pronounced crossly.

Mr Fitzalan ignored her and, fixing her with an expression of cold civility, bowed in her direction. "What do you think you are doing?" he demanded as the music started and he steered her reluctantly down the set.

"I do not know what you mean, Mr Fitzalan, I am sure."

"I warn you, you do not fool me. I know everything is a game to you."

"What are you trying to say, you ridiculous man? Why do you find it necessary to spoil other people's fun all the time?"

"You are flirting outrageously with Mr Rowlandson, with no regard for Isabella. She is not only my sister but your loyal friend."

"Lord! It is just a little harmless teasing."

"But it is at my sister's expense, and I will not have her hurt for the world. Just because you feel wronged, it does not give you the right to hurt others."

"It is nothing, sir, believe me. I love Isabella as you do. Forgive me, but you presume too much."

"But I know your kind better than you think. You have no morals; you are precisely the sort of woman who is never content with her lot and is not happy unless she is pursuing some object which is not hers to own. I will not permit it, madam."

"You know nothing about me," she said, flashing her black eyes at him in anger. "How dare you presume that I should wish to see your sister suffer or imagine you know anything about me. I am perfectly content with my life, thank you very much, and I would ask you to keep your opinions of my affairs to yourself in future. Let go of me!"

Lydia wanted to walk away, run from the dance floor, but to do so would indicate quite clearly to the assembled company that something was amiss. She forced herself to stay, and when he gripped her hand, she wrenched it away as surreptitiously as she could.

As soon as the dance was over, she excused herself and slipped out into the garden. Once away from the house, she ran as though her life depended on it. She was close to tears but determined to compose herself. How dare he speak to her like that? She would show Alexander Fitzalan that he could say what he liked; she was not to be upset by him. Why did all men seem to take their pleasure from being cruel? To pronounce that she had danced with Mr Rowlandson because she felt wronged was hateful of him, and she could not get his words out of her head. For the life of her, she could not think why she was so bothered by his opinions; he was such a po-faced, mealy-mouthed, arrogant ninny, not worth her consideration. When she was halfway down the front drive she paused, knowing it would be folly to go much further. It would be hateful if she was missed and they sent out a search party for her. She started to turn back, and it was then that she thought she heard footsteps on the gravel behind her. Stopping to listen, the crunching of stones underfoot was heard again.

"Who is there?" she cried. She swung round, her fists up ready to lunge at any footpad or vagabond who might be lurking in the dark.

A lone figure, dirty and unkempt, stepped out onto the path looking for all the world like a wild gypsy, with straggly hair and several days' growth of beard.

Lydia opened her mouth to scream but the assailant was upon her in a second, his hand clamped over her mouth. "How about a kiss from a pretty lady for a poor weary man," he whispered hoarsely.

Lydia kicked and struggled but it was no use. His hands were everywhere and his mouth was on her neck.

"Come on, my lovely, you cannot say no to me," he said, releasing his hand from her mouth and clamping his lips on hers.

"Good God, Wickham!" shouted Lydia as she pulled away crossly, recognising his voice. "What on earth are you doing here?"

Chapter 29

EVEN IN THE DARK, Lydia could see Wickham's dishevelled appearance. He was grimy, unshaven, and dusty, as well as rumpled as though he had been sleeping in his clothes.

"Lord above, Wickham, what has happened to you?"

"It is a long story and one which I have no desire to bore you with, suffice to say all my money is gone, stolen from my person. I have only the clothes on my back."

"Just look at you, George. I have seen better turned out beggars."

"Thank you for your compliments, my dear. I am delighted to see you too."

"Were you gambling? Did you lose all on the cards? And why do you keep looking at me with such a guilty expression? Do we have anything in the world left?"

"Truly, my dear, I was attacked. Pounced on by a cutpurse and a damned woman to boot."

Lydia's imagination conjured up a picture of the woman described to her by Caroline Bingley and wondered if she was responsible for his misfortunes. "Well, I do not know what we are to do. Mr Darcy is here, and if he or my mother should discover that you are in the house, there will be hell to pay. Lizzy and her husband are not due to leave for a day or two yet, and my mother has let it be known that she is to give you a good thrashing."

"I have no desire to be sociable I can tell you. At this moment, all I wish for is a decent night's sleep in a soft bed. I have slept under hedgerows for the past three nights."

"You must not be seen, do you hear? You will have to slip in by way of the servants' entrance."

"Anyone would imagine that you are displeased to see me. Tell me in truth, how much have you missed me?"

"I suppose I will have to tell Jane you are here," she continued, completely ignoring his question. "She will no doubt tell Lizzy and then the whole house will be upset. Really, Wickham, this is most inconvenient. You are not due for another week, and I have not yet fulfilled all my plans. You vex me exceedingly."

"Well, that is a nice way to greet your husband, I'm sure. Where's my sweet kiss?"

"Left on the cheek of your hussy in Bath, I daresay! And that's another thing . . . whilst I couldn't care less who she is, I would prefer not to be told about her by Caroline Bingley of all people. If you wish to have these liaisons, then I desire you not to strut them about the vicinity for all to see. No one is fooled by the story that she is your sister, and I expect the tittle-tattle has circulated the entire ballroom this evening."

"Upon my word, Lydia, I am taken aback. You wound me in your misjudgement. Miss Bingley must have misheard me. The lady she saw accompanying me down Gay Street was my cousin Nancy, whom I just happened to see that very morning. We were talking over old times. Trust Miss Bingley to put about such poisonous rumours."

"Do you swear that is true?"

"On my last breath. How could you doubt me? Now, which way shall we go in?"

They had walked the length of the gravel drive towards the house and now took care to keep within the dark shadows made by the trees along the avenue. The dogs started barking as Lydia urged him to hurry.

"Have some food sent up," he said as they reached the side door. "Don't be up too late, Lydia; you know how I hate a cold bed."

She watched him steal up the back stairs before going in search of some food for him. The last thing she wanted was to find him making an appearance downstairs. She was in desperate need of some fortification. In spite of the heat, she felt cold to her bones and thought a little warm negus might do her some good. She set forth to the orangery, which was beautifully illuminated with coloured lamps, sending long shadows across hothouse palms and plants; tables were laid for supper, groaning under the weight of turkeys, hams, fricassées, and ragoûts, poached salmons, jugged steaks, pyramid creams, and syllabubs. Lydia needed some time to gather her thoughts; she could hear the strains of the orchestra and the noisy accompaniments to a country dance, but her mind was racing, all thoughts of Mr Fitzalan's scolding having been completely eradicated by the shock of seeing her husband, and she determined that, above all, tonight if she could help it, she would sleep in another bed. What a fuss there would be when

Mr Darcy discovered that Wickham was in the house. She could not think what she should do. Perhaps it would be wisest not to mention that he was in the house except perhaps to her sister Jane who would know best how to handle such a difficult situation. She helped herself to a plateful of food and a glass of wine before instructing a servant to take it up to her room for her husband, and then, deciding she had done all she need, she hurried back to the ballroom. After all, there was no reason why Wickham's appearance should spoil her fun; the evening was young and she would like another dance.

"Lord, I'm fagged," she declared, as she threw herself into the seat next to Kitty. "Are you not dancing?"

"Mr Coates has danced with me twice and has gone in search of ices," her sister answered as she observed the dancers. "Who is that dancing with Lord Howard's son? They have danced three times in a row."

Lydia surveyed the scene. She could see Jane and Charles Bingley, dancing as animatedly as possible, looking much the picture of matrimonial bliss and at great odds to the people next to them, who barely had a civil word to say to one another. Following on in the line after them were two dancers who appeared to be very smitten with one another. Never had Lydia found herself so interested in watching another couple's behaviour. She observed the way the lady looked into the eyes of her partner and how she whispered in his ear with great informality, making it clear of her wholehearted regard.

"That is Isabella's friend, Eleanor Rowlandson," Lydia answered. "Oh dear, Mr Fitzalan has missed his chance; he will never get her now."

"Look, Mr Fitzalan is watching them, pretending not to notice, and looking as if he is deep in conversation," whispered Kitty. " He does not look in the least amused."

"Oh, that is his permanent air," Lydia explained. "Have you ever seen him smile?"

"Perhaps not much, but he is very handsome and has a fine figure."

"Yes, I cannot deny him that, and in shirt and breeches he is quite a picture!"

"So you do think him attractive then?"

"Oh, do not mistake me, I think him the dullest creature," Lydia cried. "He is so correct in everything, so polite, so concerned, so dependable. If he were ever lucky enough to attract a woman, he would bore her to death within minutes of their acquaintance."

"A man with steady principles is surely preferable though," Kitty replied, looking down at her gloves to smooth out their wrinkles. "I am sure I do not wish to marry a man who cannot be reliable and trustworthy. Indeed, Lydia, I would prefer the faithfulness of a boring clergyman any day to that of an undependable redcoat, no matter how passionate and exciting. And I would rather marry Mr Collins and be the last to marry in Longbourn than suffer an expeditious marriage which ended after six months without either partner esteeming the other."

"I should be vexed with you for so blatantly giving your opinions on what can only be a judgment on my own particular arrangement," Lydia answered, "but I find it impossible. However, on two points I cannot agree. I could never love a clergyman nor marry my cousin Collins, not if he owned all the hat shops in London town!"

Kitty laughed. "To tell the truth, nor could I."

Mrs Bennet appeared. "Do let me have a share in the conversation. What is it you two are amusing yourselves with? I could hear you laughing on the other side of the house." She eased herself into the space between them and gestured to Kitty to move further along the seat. "I know, it is Miss Bingley's gown, is it not? Such a hideous shade of yellow, it quite washes out her complexion. If that is what is considered to be à la mode, I would rather be à la dowd!"

"We were talking of commonplace clergymen, mama," said Lydia who winked at her sister, knowing that her mother's wrath would be soon incurred at the thought of Mr Collins.

"There is nothing funny whatsoever on that subject, to my mind, and it is a good thing that those persons who consider themselves the rightful owners of Longbourn House have taken themselves off to Kent and are too frightened to show their faces in Hertfordshire very often. And when he does call, he only puts his head in to assure himself that I have not sold the best silver for my own profit! I have half a mind that Lady Lucas is doing the same thing when she calls, and I am sick to death of answering queries on her daughter's behalf. Don't talk to me of clergymen."

Lydia's attention was drawn to the sight of Mr Fitzalan and Miss Rowlandson, who were now dancing in the set. "Mr Fitzalan is a very good dancer, do you not think, mama?" asked Kitty. "And he is a clergyman."

"Is he indeed?" her mother exclaimed. "I am surprised, I confess. I never saw a clergyman so nimble on his feet."

The three ladies were silenced as they watched him. "And he has a pretty leg!" their mother exclaimed.

"Oh, do look what a comical pair Miss Bingley and Mr Heathcote make," Kitty giggled. "He will have his eyes poked out if he is not careful."

"Well, I do not think there is much danger of that," quipped Mrs Bennet. "I've seen more bosom on a cold-pressed turkey."

"Lizzy is dancing with a lot of vigour," Kitty commented, suppressing a laugh at her mother's forthrightness.

"She'll regret it in the morning when her ankles have blown up like pigs' bladders, all puffed and swollen, you see if I am not mistaken," nodded Mrs Bennet, the plumes on her head shaking with the agitation. "When I was having you, Lydia, you gave me no end of trouble. I blew up like a Montgolfier balloon and looked like a ship in full sail. Not that much has changed; you are still a cause of worrisome heartache for me." She paused to gaze at her daughter. "Cat got your tongue, Mrs Wickham? You are very quiet this evening. Have you nothing to say?"

The truth was that Lydia was transfixed, unable to tear her eyes away from Mr Fitzalan and his partner, despite all entreaties to do otherwise. She was surprised to see that, despite all expectations, he was a very good dancer. She could almost envy Eleanor for his manner alone, which was not at all the behaviour he had exhibited when dancing with her. She had no recollection of their dance at all, apart from how she had been scolded and the memory of his hateful words. He was now smiling at Miss Rowlandson and escorted her with such care that Lydia was made to recognise the feeling that quickened her breathing and churned her stomach as a stab of pure jealousy. She didn't think Wickham had ever looked at her with such sincerity and could not help imagining how it would be to have a partner in life whose attention was entirely her own, someone who was not just looking for the next pretty face or the next flirtation. The dance came to its conclusion, and Lydia noticed that just as he was asking to partner her again, Ralph Howard was stepping up to claim her once more. Eleanor's attentions were swiftly diverted, and Lydia observed the disappointment with which Mr Fitzalan regarded the pair of them taking to the floor.

Mr Bennet appeared before them. "Kitty, come along, you have been sat here too long in idle chatter with your sister. We will find some refreshment; a glass of punch is what I require."

Lydia knew full well that her father took every chance to separate the two sisters and that he did not relish her expeditions back into Hertfordshire, feeling that she was a bad influence on Kitty. Both girls were careful to meet in secret whenever they could, though Lydia admitted she liked to vex her papa by flouting his rule that they were not permitted to spend any time alone.

"I must go and find Jane while I think on it," Lydia said, remembering that her husband was upstairs and that her sister needed to be informed of his arrival. She took in her father's ill looks and, excusing herself, found she was crossing the floor, deliberately walking past Mr Fitzalan. She did not move that way for him to ask her to dance, she told herself, and when he ignored her, she felt more vexed than she could say. He did not acknowledge her in any way; he averted his eyes and turned to walk in the opposite direction.

She could see Jane in the distance, looking hot and bothered and rather perplexed. She did not have her usual composure, and when it became clear that she was engaged in heated conversation with a lady, Lydia's curiosity was more than a little aroused, as was a large section of the assembled company. Jane was purposefully running round after a lady who seemed to be in a state of some anguish. Indeed, Lydia thought, she was not the sort of person her sister usually consorted with; she was buxom, blowzy, bedecked, and be-ribboned in the most outlandish dress. Her face, which was painted with smudges of rouge, peered out from under a large puce bonnet over which waved a dozen ostrich feathers of the most garish colours Lydia had ever seen.

"Where is he? I know he's here. Mrs Bingley, you had best let me see him!"

Jane, who was doing her utmost to talk calmly to the woman, was now joined by her husband, who became almost agitated in his efforts to calm her. The woman shrugged off his arm as he tried to steer her out of the ballroom, and she began running round the room, her large bosom wobbling with the exertion as she waddled about shouting her head off. "Wickham, Wickham! Where are you? I know you are here! George Wickham! Come out where I can see you!"

Lydia was rooted to the spot with horror. She could see Lizzy now, heading off the woman before she ran another circuit, letting her know that she would be listened to if she calmed down. It was suggested they go to the library where they could talk properly.

"Come out, George," the woman shouted, "I know you're hiding. You didn't expect to see me did you? Wickham, where are you? Wickham!"

Jane and Lizzy carried the woman off, an arm each, as she shouted continuously and dragged her heels, despite Mr

Bingley's gentle requests for quiet as he brought up the rear. Lydia had a horrible feeling that she knew exactly who she was, but she could not bear to think of it.

"Ah," said Miss Bingley in Lydia's ear, "I can always recognise a woman of gentility at fifty paces. It is Wickham's sister, I believe, and looking as elegant as when I saw her in Gay Street. You must introduce me some time."

Lydia spun round, aware that the whole room had stopped to see the fracas. Everyone, it seemed, was engaged in observing her countenance. Miss Bingley made a hasty retreat as she caught sight of Mrs Wickham's expression. Mrs Bennet started to cross the room with speed and Lydia turned on her heel in response, anxious to make her escape and determined to follow the others to the library. Mr Darcy took charge in the ballroom, instructing the orchestra to resume playing, and a lively country jig soon had everyone marching to the dance floor, there to have over what had gone on a moment before.

Lydia stood at the library door in fear and trepidation, debating whether she had the nerve to go in as Mr Darcy swept past her into the room and stood before the woman who had collapsed, looking worn to a frazzle and as crimson as the port in the punch bowl, with her hat sliding off the top of her head. Jane administered smelling salts.

"For all our sakes, madam," Darcy boomed, "I would ask you to calm down and state your business. How may we help you?"

"I'm here to see Captain Wickham, sir, George Wickham. I know he's here, so don't tell me nothing different." She took a large slug of wine from the glass Mr Bingley proffered.

"And who are you, madam? Whom do I address?" Mr Darcy continued as he stared at her in contempt. She drained the glass, bit into the apple puff Jane had presented on her other side, and pronounced her identity between gobbled mouthfuls, as she spat crumbs down her dress, "Mrs Wickham, sir. My name is Mrs Molly Wickham!

Chapter 30

IF ANY STRANGER HAD walked in at that exact moment, it is likely he would have thought himself arrived at Bedlam. There was an uproar. Lydia screamed and flew across the room in seconds and had to be restrained by Mr and Mrs Darcy from attacking the bovine creature who was now sprawled across a chaise longue, looking considerably worse for wear from having guzzled too much wine. Mrs Bennet was experiencing palpitations, threatening to faint, but as vocal as ever. Jane was endeavouring to keep calm whilst her husband rushed about, determined to be useful but quite unable to be effective.

"I am Mrs Wickham!" Lydia cried, shrugging off restraining hands and thrusting her countenance into the woman's face. "Who are you? That you are come to make mischief is plain for all to see. Explain yourself. Exactly what do you want with my husband?"

"Your husband? I don't know nothing about your husband," the woman replied, getting rather red and agitated in the face. "I only know about my own, useless lump that he is. I know he is here, but he don't know I am. No, he did not think I had the wherewithal to find him, nor the money!" She produced a leather pouch, which she waved under Lydia's nose.

Lydia gasped. "That belongs to my husband. How did you get your dirty hands on it, you thieving strumpet?"

"Lydia, please, you are not helping matters," Lizzy said leading her sister away. "Let us try and resolve this in a more civilised manner."

"It's my money, what I'm owed," protested the woman. "He's never paid me a penny since he married me, and I'm entitled to what's due to me!"

"Did you take Captain Wickham's money?" asked Mr Darcy.

"I did and I'd do it again; he's never paid a penny for his board, all the years I've known him. It's mine, I earned it!"

Mrs Bennet moaned loudly. "My poor, poor Lydia. To what depths of shame must she be plunged?"

"Captain Wickham is in Bath, madam. Is that how you came to be in possession of his purse?" Mr Darcy added.

"He is not in Bath!" cried Lydia. "He is here." She swallowed hard as she took in his expression.

"What do you mean, he is here?" Mr Darcy's face looked thunderous.

"He is upstairs sleeping."

"Good God! Well, let's have him fetched."

"I'll go," shouted Bingley, springing to attention.

"Wait for me," said Darcy in a measured tone. "It may well take two of us to bring him to order."

With the gentlemen gone, the ladies were rather at a loss to know what to do and say next, though they were all relieved to see that the woman calling herself Molly Wickham was quiet at last, content to sup on yet another glass of wine as she regarded her fellow females with suspicion.

Lydia spoke up first. "You say you are married to my husband, is that right?"

"I am married to George Wickham, as God is my witness, madam. Married at Walcot Church in Bath."

"You have the certificate to prove it?"

"I don't have no piece of paper, but I swear it's true, on my life. He was keen on it too; keen enough to get his hands on me and my money at the time. He was in a bit of a bother, debts to pay and such. I was working in the Saracen's Head Tavern, and he was one of my regulars—as regular as George Wickham can be—and then he comes to me one night, declares his love for me, and begs me to marry him."

"When was this?"

"Two years ago next month, though to tell the truth I haven't seen much of him since. No, he upped and left as soon as he could. But he visits every now and again, eases his way back into my bed and my affections. Well I can't say no to him, no woman can I'm sure, and he has had plenty."

"Stop," cried Mrs Darcy, who had heard quite enough. "We do not need to know any particulars, apart from the details of your marriage."

"My husband told me he'd been set upon by a cutpurse, and he will verify your story as lies," cried Lydia. "He is being fetched now. Tell me you are lying, and I will see you are in no more trouble than necessary."

"I ain't no cutpurse, ma'am, though my husband has nearly driven me to it. I swear I am married to George Wickham. You can ask Tobias Hughes and his missus. He's my landlord, and they witnessed our marriage, no word of a lie. Now he's what I call an honourable gentleman. If not for him, I wouldn't be here now."

"Well, it would be easy enough to discover a gentleman's movements if you were intent on pursuing him," said Lydia crossly.

"Not Wickham, he's as slippery as an eel and never in the same place twice!"

As I know to my cost, thought Lydia. "How did you track him down?"

"Well, he begged Tobias for money for the stage, as he was out of pocket, being as his money had gone. Wickham gave him some twaddle about having to leave to see a dying relative in Hertfordshire but was no more specific than that. Mr Hughes obliged him with a little, but knowing what a tricky customer he can be, told him to forget about paying him back and asked if he could send any more on to him. He said yes, of course, gave his address as Netherfield Park, which Tobias, bless him, passed on to me as soon as he could."

Lydia was feeling far from well again and was just beginning to take it all in. She opened her mouth to speak and managed to whisper, "If this is true then I cannot be married."

Mrs Bennet writhed in her seat, threw back her head, and groaned, emitting huge sighing lamentations and crying out in hysterics before Lizzy could reach her side to calm and reason with her. "Not married!" Mrs Bennet cried. "Not married!"

"I am not married," muttered Lydia again.

Darcy and Bingley appeared at the door. "He is gone!" Bingley shouted. "I have instructed the grounds to be searched, but his bed is untouched."

"If he was here," declared Mr Darcy, "I think we may surmise his reasons for not stopping."

"He was here," cried Lydia, "I saw him, spoke to him. But he has no money, nothing, not a penny."

"Well, it is certain that he has now," Bingley continued. "He has had a change of my clothes and replenished his funds."

"She is not married!" shouted Mrs Bennet, pointing at her daughter and stabbing the air with a finger. "He has sullied my dearest girl and left her without a thread of decency or respectability. I rue the day you set eyes on him, Miss Lizzy!"

"Mother, please! You will make yourself ill," cried Lizzy, fetching out Mrs Bennet's salts to waft under her nose.

A servant appeared at the door. "Mr Bingley, sir, one of the horses is missing from the stables, but we cannot see anyone about the immediate area."

"Upon my word, Lydia," wailed Mrs Bennet, "can it get any worse? Oh, I feel faint, my heart, such a pain. I think it's stopped, quick, help me!"

"Thank you, Thomson. Tell the men to keep looking," Bingley said, with one eye on his mother-in-law who was now writhing in her chair.

"I doubt very much if we shall see anything of Captain Wickham this evening," said Mr Darcy.

"No, I think it quite clear he has absconded. However, I feel I have neglected my guests for too long," said Bingley. "Will you hold the fort here, Darcy? I will return, though heaven knows how this can be hushed up."

"I am sure you can think of something, my love," Jane soothed. "I will stay here for the present and see to mama."

Darcy interrogated the woman once more, with the benefit of Mrs Bennet's advice ringing in his ears. Molly Wickham was looking more terrified than ever and extremely cross to find out that her husband had disappeared.

"Take pity on a girl, sir," she appealed to Mr Darcy. Until that moment he had not considered what was to be done with the woman. "These pennies are all I have in the world!"

"We cannot very well send her on her way at this time of night," whispered Mrs Darcy, "and for all we know she may be telling the truth."

"Of that I have no doubt. Even if the only fact is that Wickham has had some dealings with her, we are obliged, I think, to ensure her safety and well-being," answered her husband.

"She will have to stay here," said Jane.

"No," argued Darcy, "that is not to be borne. She will have the house stripped in hours; who's to say she hasn't a dozen accomplices waiting without, and whilst Wickham is not here to deny or confirm her story, I would prefer to be cautious of her claims. Perhaps I can get her set up at the inn at Meryton. In the morning I will put her on the first stage to London."

"We'll all be murdered in our beds," wailed Mrs Bennet. Jane left Lizzy in charge and went in search of a sedative. Mrs Garnett had some laudanum, and she was sure a few drops in a cup of tea would do the trick!

Mr Bennet appeared at the library door at that very moment with a look of astonishment on his face and a glass of wine in his hand. He had come to escape the dreary company by whiling away a few hours with a fine drink and a good book. "What on earth are you all doing in here?" he asked. He had never seen so many members of his family intent on being in a library.

"We have been tricked, Mr Bennet," cried his wife. "Come, sit here and be some comfort to me whilst I tell you of our misfortunes, which are more vexatious than you can imagine!"

Jane returned with the draught for her mother and Isabella for her sister. Though anxious not to be in the way, she was most concerned for her friend. Lydia gave her the worst of the details and could not help giving herself up to tears.

"I will return in just a little while," Isabella said gently, offering her handkerchief as Lydia sobbed once more. She left, returning two minutes later with her brother. Lydia was horrified. What on earth was Isabella doing? She could not bear to look at him. What must Alexander think of her now? Was it any wonder that he did not address her in any way or attempt to talk to her? He just went straight to Mr Darcy and spent the next ten minutes in conversation with him. No doubt they were both declaring that nothing less than this outcome would ever have surprised the pair of them.

Isabella returned to her friend's side. "We have arranged it all, Lydia," she declared. "I hope it is to your satisfaction for it is our dearest wish to help you. You are to come back to the rectory now and stay with us for a while until it is all sorted out. Alexander has spoken to Mr Darcy and will speak to your father. Everyone is agreed it will be for the best. That is, if you wish it, my dear."

"But Alexander will not wish to become embroiled in my scandal, surely?" Lydia asked, looking up at her friend.

"It was his suggestion. He is as anxious as I to help you. Believe me, Lydia; he would do anything for a friend of mine and especially for you. Now do not worry; all your bags are being taken care of and put into the carriage waiting at the door as I speak. Mrs Bingley seems to think you would prefer to leave by a side door; I am sure she is right."

Lydia hesitated. She did not know if she felt strong enough to face Alexander and his penetrating eyes. Surely they would reveal all he really thought on the matter. But she knew she could not refuse. "Thank you, Isabella. I do not deserve such a friend, truly."

Lydia thought she was fortunate indeed to have such friends, and though she found it difficult to believe that her removal to the rectory had been at the suggestion of Mr Fitzalan, she was grateful to be leaving Netherfield and the tittle-tattle behind her. She had been assured by Jane that, although speculation was rife, no one was any the wiser and not only had Mr Bingley been able to convince people that the woman was some poor family retainer who had run mad, but he had announced supper in the orangery with immediate effect. In their haste to fill their stomachs and their glasses and make the most of Mr Bingley's generous hospitality, the company was occupied only for a few moments more with the odd woman who was clearly deranged. Soon after, she was quite forgotten as the heady consumption of copious amounts of food and the contents of the wine cellar rendered the majority insensible.

Lydia was surprised at her family's kindness on parting. Everyone had good wishes for her and even Mr Darcy bade her a cordial goodnight; no doubt, she thought, because if indeed it turned out she was not married to Captain Wickham after all, the connection with his family would be finally severed forever.

Lydia was thankful that her mama had retired to her bed as soon as she could. She did not think she could have kept her composure. Her papa had the same weary expression on his face that he always reserved for her alone and could only say, "Never mind, Lydia, he duped us all."

Outside, Isabella was waiting in the carriage, and it only remained for Mr Fitzalan to hand Lydia in. He was very gentlemanly, and she knew he had behaved with consideration. She was unsure whether the extra gentle pressure of his hand was her imagination, but she was certain that the moonlight did not play a trick as he smiled reassuringly before she stepped up to take her seat. No doubt Isabella had told him to be kind.

Saturday, May 14th

I am relieved to have left Netherfield. Not only have I escaped the gossip and prying eyes but also I am pleased to have said goodbye to my family, who I consider most trying at the best of times. I swear if my papa were to find me dying of a putrid infection he would only say, "nevermind."

However, despite the comfort of my room here in the rectory and the hospitality of my friends, I know I have to find some way to get out of the mess I find myself in and discover once and for all the true nature of the situation. My initial reaction was tears and mortification, though I am proud to say that I suffered such distress for no more than five minutes. To discover Wickham is possibly already married is a great shock and to be at the centre of yet more scandal knocks my pride, but after recovering from these first sensations, and before I lay down my head this night, I will acknowledge my true feelings.

I am not ashamed to say I feel immense relief. I ceased to love George Wickham some time ago, and the thought of release from my marriage is to imagine I have wings and can fly away, free, despite the scandal that will inevitably ensue. I was certainly head over heels in love with him in the beginning, but there have been so many unpleasant discoveries and hints at infidelities that I am numbed by it all. Never was anyone so happy to learn of her unhappy predicament! My greatest fear is that Wickham might be found to be my husband after all; therein lies the key to my problems. It must be settled. I must find out the truth of the matter!

Chapter 31

ON ENTERING THE BREAKFAST parlour the following morning, Lydia sat down to stare at her empty plate and watch her tea go cold. "I must go to Bath, Isabella," she said, looking at her friend's countenance to judge her reaction. "I cannot rest until I know the truth of the affair."

"But is that wise?" her friend answered, brushing toast crumbs from her lap. "Surely someone could go in your place? I should think Mr Darcy is already making plans on your behalf."

"No, Isabella, I will not be easy until I have seen the marriage register for myself. Besides, I cannot just sit here and do nothing, I will go mad. Mr Darcy may go running after Wickham if he chooses, but I am only interested in the legalities."

"Are you really so disinterested in your husband?"

"I would not care if I were never to see him again."

"And if he is innocent?"

"If he is innocent, then I am a wealthy countess."

Isabella hooted with laughter. "I am sure I would not be so sanguine."

"You forget, Isabella, I have lived with his guilt for months now."

Alexander chose that moment to join them, helping himself to a dish of chocolate and fresh bread rolls.

"Lydia means to go to Bath," Isabella announced.

Lydia searched his face, expecting the usual critical response and could not help staring when he answered most unexpectedly.

"Yes, it is imperative; someone needs to go to Bath, and I understand you may wish to go yourself," he said. He broke a piece of bread, and liberally buttering the generous portion, he went on gravely, "But you cannot go alone."

"I must go," she said firmly, waiting for him to talk her out of her scheme.

His cerulean eyes met hers across the table. "Then we will all go to Bath."

"All of us?" asked Isabella.

"I had suggested that I make the journey to Mr Darcy," Alexander continued. "He was willing to accompany me, but I assured him it was not necessary. Forgive me, but I had presumed to go myself. I will make any enquiries you wish on your behalf if you would like that, Mrs Wickham. It may be easier for me to obtain the necessary documentation we require. It will all be discreetly done, I assure you."

"Please call me, Lydia, Mr Fitzalan. I cannot bear to hear his name spoken. I hope you understand."

"If that is what you wish, Miss Lydia, and you must call me by my given name also. It is only fitting. You and Isabella have been as sisters for many years. I hope I may act for you as a brother might."

Lydia could not believe his kindness. That he understood the mention of her married name to be an anathema to her touched her beyond words, and that he had instigated help for her was a pleasant surprise. "I cannot thank you enough, Alexander," she said, returning the compliment, and was rewarded with a smile.

"I had best sort out the arrangements for mother with Bertha and think about packing," Isabella said, rising from her seat. "Alexander, I think you need to have a few details from Lydia, do you not? I will leave you to it." She left the room and there was an awkward silence.

"I am so sorry to put you to so much trouble," Lydia said at last.

"You have no need to apologise. It is not your fault. Let me take some information about Captain Wickham and make sure I have everything I need, his full name, etcetera."

Mr Fitzalan took charge and, once started on the business in hand, achieved all with efficiency and thoughtful attention. He seemed more at ease now he had a job to do, as if he could finally talk without reserve, and Lydia was impressed with the confident way in which he proceeded. His manner was most congenial, his voice quiet, and his words carefully chosen.

"I cannot thank you enough for all your help on my behalf," Lydia responded. "I must be taking you away from your duties and from Miss Rowlandson."

"I have nothing much to do at present that will not keep for a day or two," he answered. "And as for Miss Rowlandson, I am sure she will not be impatient for my return. I do not think she will want for company." He busied himself by sprinkling sand on the paper in front of him. Picking up his pen, he wrote at a furious speed on a fresh piece.

Lydia wished she had not mentioned Miss Rowlandson; he clearly thought that Eleanor had turned her attention elsewhere.

She did wish she could help him, however. He was being so very kind and she wanted to show her appreciation.

"Alexander, forgive me for being so blunt; I speak only as someone who wishes to help you. Love is not always a matter of chance you know. It requires a little nurturing to fan the flames along, which might otherwise die if left or neglected."

"I do not play games, Lydia."

"But are you content to let another steal the girl you admire? Will you not fight for her? Surely if you do not act now and claim her there is a danger that someone else may step in."

He looked up and gave a rare smile that reached his eyes. "I thank you for your concern, Lydia, but as you know, I do not rate the state of love highly. Miss Rowlandson will be better off with Ralph Howard, believe me."

She could not help but feel compassion for him. "Then indeed, I am truly sorry for you. Even in my reckless alliance, I believed I was in love and yes, a state of confusion it might be, but I submitted to it and felt my regard most wholeheartedly. And though I now believe my love was not truly returned, that I was misled, I still believe in the power of true love. To adore another person heart, body, and soul is a predicament worth enduring at least once in a lifetime. Believe me, I would suffer its pangs again for the happiness I felt, however fleetingly."

Alexander shuffled his papers together and coughed as if to cover embarrassment. He opened his mouth to speak and then closed it again. As his face reddened, his looks told her that he was immensely displeased. Lydia could see how uncomfortable he felt and wished she had not said anything. She knew she had probably said too much. He ran his fingers through his dark mane before standing abruptly. He bowed and, without uttering another word, left the room.

Lydia retired to her room to gather her thoughts and her belongings, wishing she could make the journey to Bath on her own, though she knew that would be impossible. She would never be allowed to travel such a distance by herself. Oh, to have to sit opposite Alexander Fitzalan and have him looking at her with such disapproval all the way; the thought was unbearable. She laid the last few things in her trunk, ready for their departure in the morning. She had always wished to go to Bath, but she could not imagine any circumstance more dreadful than the one she now faced and decided Bath would never live up to any expectations she once had. It would be forever spoiled and she could not help but think of George Wickham with abhorrence.

Their journey went off well with no delays. The roads were good despite the misery of rain and, thankfully, as far as Lydia was concerned, no one seemed eager for too much conversation. She tried not to dwell too much on the past as she stared out at the drizzle, but she could not help thinking back to a time just a short while ago when she had been the happiest girl alive, in love with the man she adored above any other.

The horses were fast, and they reached Devizes with ease by four o'clock. Isabella and Lydia were to share a room at the Swan Inn and found themselves very pleased and comfortable in their room, which was quite large, with two beds and a view onto the street. Lydia changed her gown for a fresh, sprigged muslin and rearranged her hair with a white silk ribbon. Isabella was not ready to go downstairs for dinner, so Lydia thought she might have a wander round and get her bearings. Downstairs, there was the usual bustle to be found in such a place: strangers arriving or departing, servants hoisting baggage on their shoulders and admitting guests to their rooms or seeing them off into chaises.

Lydia discovered a snug parlour off to one side with cosy chairs and sofas, a fireplace with a fire just lit against the cool, damp evening, jugs full of country flowers, and a table groaning with an assortment of newspapers and books. Best of all, there was no one sitting there, and she wondered if she was at liberty to go in. After some hesitation, deliberation, and then encouragement from a passing maidservant, she took herself in and sat down in a chair by the fire. She could see the rain was still teeming down outside and wondered whether she would have felt quite so miserable if the sun had been shining.

She fetched out a book from the shelf in the alcove at her side, and finding it had plenty of pictures to amuse her and not too many words, she settled down to idly turn the pages. Most who observed her as they passed by the door would have believed her to be entirely engrossed. Of course, she hardly attended to the pictures, and she bit her lip more than once to stop herself from crying. Her sadness had turned once more to anger and she wished she could see George if only to give him a piece of her mind. She did wonder where he had gone and guessed that he would more than likely be making his way to London with all haste. Good luck to him, she thought bitterly. I would not have him back if he begged me. I will never be fooled by such a man again nor give my heart away so readily. She did not think she would ever be so silly as to fall in love again.

Perhaps Alexander Fitzalan was right after all. She would be more careful in future to keep her feelings in check.

A voice at the door broke her reverie. "May I join you?"

She looked up to see Alexander regarding her from the door and she started a little. He was dressed like a country gentleman in breeches and a blue coat, which made his eyes appear as blue as the cornflowers in the jug by the window. He looked younger than usual, she thought, and decided he must leave off his black clothes more often, especially if he was ever to capture Miss Rowlandson's heart, though she quickly realised she must avoid that subject again if she were to make her peace with him.

"Of course, do come in. I was waiting for Isabella and I thought this looked just the place," she answered.

He walked in, took a newspaper from the table, and sat in the chair opposite. He spent some considerable time arranging himself and the paper to his satisfaction, and all the time Lydia observed him surreptitiously. She was pleased he did not seem to be in the mood for conversation, and she wished Isabella would hurry up before the silence prompted him to speak. She went back to her pictures and didn't look up even when it became clear that his eyes were upon her. Why did he stare at her in such a fashion? She could not think what she had done now to upset him, and though she could feel his gaze still upon her, she continued to look at her book with an air of study such had never before been seen.

"I owe you an apology, Lydia," he stammered, his words tumbling out almost incomprehensibly.

"I beg your pardon," Lydia answered, quite sure that she must have misunderstood him.

"I wish to tell you something, and I must apologise to you."

Lydia looked at him and waited. She could not quite believe her ears.

Alexander got up to look out of the window, and she wondered if he had changed his mind about talking when he did not speak again for some time. Finally he turned to face her, and she could not help noticing that his blue eyes were clouded, as if in sympathy with the greyness of the day. There was an air of great sadness about him and she smiled at him in reassurance.

"Forgive me, I have not told you the truth." He took a deep breath before beginning again. "Would it surprise you if I admitted that I too have loved as you have yourself?" he asked.

Lydia was astonished, and she feared her expression would give her away.

He hung his head. "I lied to you about my past . . . and when you were doing your best to advise me, to be kind to me, I chose to avoid the truth."

"Oh no, please. I do not want to hear anything you do not wish to tell me. I did not mean to force a confidence," she entreated.

"I will tell you the truth. I did love a girl once," he continued, as he looked out of the window once more and stared at the coaches rumbling past. "I would have gone to the ends of the earth, yes, even died, for her. But it was not to be. She did not love me as I thought and . . . well, there were other complications."

"You too have suffered," Lydia whispered in response.

"I fought for her and lost. I am not so unfeeling as you suppose, and I am well acquainted with loving where hope of being loved in return is gone. I have felt such sorrow as made me want to deny the existence of such an emotion. I have lied to myself, Lydia, and buried those feelings which consumed me."

"I am astonished," Lydia answered, "though it is easier now to understand your behaviour towards Miss Rowlandson. Does Isabella know what happened?"

"She knows all about it, the whole sorry tale. I could not bear to have Miss Hunter talked about after everything that passed, and I made Isabella swear to deny her existence. She was not able to discuss the affair with anyone, I made sure of that, not even with her closest friends. Indeed, I have not talked of Susan or even spoken her name these two years—not until today in fact."

"But you need not have said anything at all. I am sorry to have made you confess, to bring back a past which must be so unpleasant for you."

"No, I am glad you made me talk of it, made me think of her again. I admit, I am now a cautious man and I would have to be convinced by a very constant heart before I gave myself up to such folly again, but I can think of Miss Hunter without too much sorrow now."

"Then perhaps you will allow yourself to fall in love again."

"Oh no, Lydia, I do not believe I am ready for such a step. Love is too fickle for my constitution, I confess."

"But believe me, constancy of affection does exist," Lydia insisted. "We have both been unlucky, I am sure. I believe there must be someone for everybody. You may yet find happiness with Eleanor. Perhaps she is unsure of your regard for her. If another is making his feelings more certain and paying her more attention, she is likely to think he is the right one to make a claim and she will turn to him."

"Ralph Howard has more to offer; she will be the lady of the manor, she will have everything she desires and far more than if she opts for a mere clergyman."

"But you would be offering so much more, do you not see? I never thought I should say so, but truly, gowns, jewels, and riches are one thing, love, constancy, and fidelity are quite another. The true prize, I should say. To be loved without condition and give the same in return must be quite wonderful. You must give yourself another chance."

Alexander looked at her for a moment, a frown on his countenance and all Lydia could think was that he must be wondering what on earth she could know about any of it to be giving him such advice.

The door opened and Isabella marched into the room. "What are you two about? I am starving, and if we do not hurry, they shall feed our lobster and asparagus to the horses!"

Lydia did not get another chance to speak to Alexander that evening and they were soon off on the last leg of the journey to Bath early next morning. Isabella prattled on about the wonderful dinner and the cheesecakes they had finished for dessert, but Lydia noted that Alexander was as thoughtful as ever. No doubt two young ladies, namely Miss Hunter and Miss Rowlandson, consumed his thoughts, but she was pleased to see that he appeared on the whole to be more cheerful.

The weather had improved, and her first view of Bath lived up to all her expectations. The view from the top of Kingsdown could not have looked more romantic to her ideas; all was vapour and mist, and the buildings, as fine as palaces, glittered white in the sunshine. At last they entered Bath at one o'clock and were settled in lodgings in Quiet Street, which suited the girls perfectly for its proximity to the shops in Milsom Street and the Pump Rooms, which were just a little further down into the town.

Tuesday, May 17th

Though we are not come to be merry, Isabella wants to show me all the delights of Bath and from what I have observed so far, I am as thrilled with it all as if I were a young girl in my first season. I am very pleased with my little bedroom on the first floor, which is neatly fitted up with a bed, a cupboard, and the sweetest dressing table, all draped in muslin and ribbon. We have a view giving a glimpse of Queen Square—not the most fashionable district, but splendid nevertheless. I have been standing at the window to witness the afternoon sun shining on the passersby, conveyed on foot or by carriage, phaeton, or gig. Two ladies in gauze cloaks caught my eye, the fringe on their parasols swinging in rhythm, their white muslin dresses fluttering back outlining their pretty figures. A gentleman in a green coat swaggered along on the opposite path and hailed them with a wave of his hat and a bow. The constant clattering of the horses' hooves, the rumble of coaches, and the cries of tradespeople can be heard all around, and I cannot help but be fascinated by all I see. If only circumstances were different, I might enjoy myself in Bath immensely.

I am very nervous about what the next few days will bring, and I feel a dreadful sense of obligation to my dear friend, Isabella. Alexander is being so kind, and I find my opinion of him changing. To discover that he has been crossed in love, as I have myself, and to hear him confess that he wished to enlighten me of his past has made me realise why he always seems so gloomy and irritable. However, I could never be like that myself; misery is not a state I enjoy. Perhaps we will be able to cheer him up a little whilst we are here, though working on my behalf and having to deal with the legacy of my past folly is hardly to be described as an amusing occupation! I cannot believe how different Alexander appears when he is not dressed as a clergy-man. He looks so much softer and very vulnerable somehow—it makes me feel almost protective towards him. I think I am beginning to understand what it must be like to have a brother for a sibling and almost envy Isabella and Harriet!

Chapter 32

THE VERY NEXT MORNING a visit to the Pump Rooms was resolved upon. Lydia was feeling more than a little anxious when Alexander announced that he was to go to Walcot Church to make his enquiries, and so it was at Isabella's suggestion that they should go out.

"The waters will help calm your nerves," she said, "and besides all that, seeing all the fine company will give you something else to think about."

"You do wish me to act for you, Lydia?" begged Alexander. "You are quite sure that you desire me to go to the church?"

"Yes, of course. I thank you, but I admit I am concerned at what the outcome may be. I could hardly sleep for thinking last night. In my heart, I must admit that I shall be far from upset if I am to discover that Wickham is already married. I must confess that I long to be free. Is that very wicked?"

"No one could blame you for feeling that way, Lydia," Isabella declared, taking her friend's hand in a gesture of comfort. "You are not to think you should answer for your husband's activities."

Lydia looked across at Alexander who said nothing. It was clear his opinion of her had not changed. "At the same time, if indeed it is found he is already married, my worries are for my future. What will become of me? I dare not think on it. And worse still, my greatest fear is that Mrs Molly Wickham is no such creature and that I will be bound to George Wickham for eternity. To have to return to Newcastle with him is a fate I cannot endure."

"I must go," Alexander announced, picking up his hat and an umbrella, for the sky beyond the window displayed grey clouds that threatened more rain. "If I were you, I should go out now Isabella, before it pours and the streets become too dirty. Here, you take this," he said proffering his umbrella, "you will have more need of it than I. Now, do you have enough money for everything you need? I know you young ladies will not be able to resist the shops. Isabella, take what you need, do not argue. Let us meet here again in two hours." He paused to pull on his hat and turned to address Lydia. "I hope I will have some news for you, some news you would like to hear."

Lydia thought him generous in his remarks. He had that grave expression again, but at least he was being compassionate. She thought his attentions towards his sister very thoughtful and envied Isabella for having someone to think about those things for her; indeed, she thought how she too would have liked such a sibling. Four sisters were all very well, but to be looked after and cared for by a sympathetic brother, who saw to all the small necessities, would have been something else entirely.

They set off for the Pump Rooms but made slow progress for the shops were there to tempt and tantalise, and though Lydia protested several times about being far too upset to shop, she found after little more than a yard and a half, she could hardly pass one without stopping to look in a window or encourage her friend through its doors.

"Didn't I tell you we would see some frights?" declared Isabella laughing after leaving one of the milliner's shops.

"Quite so," agreed Lydia, giggling as well. "I thought I'd come across a rare hybrid tree till the young lady who bore half a hundredweight of apples and cherries on her head moved to step on my toe."

"And I am not at all sure about Parisian bonnets, are you? I would not like to be seen with such a helmet on my head." Isabella chuckled at the thought.

"Still," said Lydia sighing, "I am vastly happy with my sprig of orange blossoms which will become my bonnet very well. You were right, Isabella; a little shopping has certainly improved my constitution!"

They carried on down the town and had soon joined the crowds, entering the doors of the Pump Rooms, which were very full. Ladies and gentlemen glided about the floor as though in some intricate dance, meeting and parting, greeting friends and old acquaintances amidst a cacophony of chattering sounds. The girls did not know a soul, and after walking up and down a while, as Lydia attempted to give the impression that this was not her first time in Bath, they decided it was time to try the waters.

"Follow me," urged Isabella, grabbing Lydia by the hand so as not to lose her, "I think this is a queue of sorts. They weaved their way through the crowds, which eventually jostled and pushed them to the front of the pumper's counter, and were handed cups of water which they dutifully drank.

"Good Lord!" gasped Lydia, pushing out her tongue in a most unladylike manner. "I would have not ventured on such folly had I known how disgusting it would be. Does anyone actually drink this foul tasting stuff for pleasure?"

"You will see how good it is for you in time," insisted Isabella, draining her cup to Lydia's astonishment, "though we should need to be here for several weeks to enjoy its true benefits."

They sat on a bench under the Tompian clock and watched the fashionable set, the ladies like butterflies alighting on lavender scented beaux, flouncing and flirting, flourishing and flitting from one group to another.

"I hope you do not think it unkind of me, but I have written to Harriet to tell her what has happened," admitted Isabella.

"No, of course not, and I am sure she will not be very surprised to hear of it, having acquainted her in my letters with many hints and instances as to the state of my marriage."

"She will be most concerned, I know."

"Well, enough of my circumstances! We haven't had a chance to be on our own, and I haven't had a moment to ask you about your beau. Did Mr Rowlandson get his chance to propose at Netherfield?"

"He did not. I think he was more than a little embarrassed by his sister's behaviour. I am sure you must have seen her throwing herself at Ralph Howard. You know Freddie and I had hoped there was an attraction between Eleanor and Alexander, that something may happen between them. But now I am not sure if he ever liked her that much."

"I believe I have been mistaken in some ways about your brother," Lydia ventured.

"Whatever do you mean?"

"His manner, his reserve, his disdain for love, for dancing and flirting, his dislike of all the pleasurable pursuits, I did not immediately understand him. I had not realised he had been wounded by a former love."

"Did he tell you about Miss Hunter?"

"Not in any great depth, but I now understand his caution."

"I admit, Lydia, I am surprised he confided in you. I am sure he has never told another soul."

"I forced his confidence," Lydia confessed. "I did not mean to, but there it is. I hope he will forgive me."

"I am sure he has already, indeed. Alexander does not disclose any information he does not care to impart. And perhaps I should not be so surprised. If anyone could make him talk, I am sure it would be you."

"We are easier in one another's company now, I think."

"Good, I am glad to hear it."

Lydia frowned. "Alexander seems to think Ralph Howard has more to offer Eleanor; he is backing off without a fight."

"My poor brother does not think very highly of himself and, for all his lamentations on being a mere clergyman, does not give himself credit. He may not have Ralph Howard's manor house, but he is to inherit in his own right one day, you know."

"Is he really?" asked Lydia, quite intrigued.

"Why yes. Our uncle has a sizeable estate near Amwell and Alexander is his heir. It is true he cannot compete with Ralph

Howard at present and our uncle is only fifty, but one day Alexander will be quite a wealthy man and a match well worth consideration."

"I suppose Eleanor must be ignorant of this information or she might be more attentive to your brother."

Isabella laughed. "That is quite true, Lydia. I am sure it has never cropped up in conversation, and I think I am not inclined to supply her with such intelligence either. I hate to say it, but my opinion of that young lady is quite changed."

"But you have not answered my question," begged Lydia, changing the subject. "Freddie must have left you with some feeling of his regard for you."

"There was a note left at the rectory before we came away, I confess. I did not tell you because you had other things on your mind."

"Did he tell you how much he loved you?"

"Not in so many words, but he did say he was looking forward to seeing me soon and that he would miss me much more than he could express on paper."

"It's high time I attended another wedding and one which promises much happiness!" cried Lydia, hugging Isabella, her eyes shining with delight.

"To marry Freddie would be my dream, I confess, but I do not really know of the strength of his feeling, Lydia. In any case," Isabella replied, standing up to take in the position of the hands on the clock, "it is time to go and meet Alexander. Come, let us hope he has some news."

Half a minute had them through the Pump yard to the archway opposite Union Passage, but as usual, they were detained at Cheap Street by the constant rumbling of carriages and carts and prevented from crossing by the approach of a gig, driven along at speed, so that the girls felt in danger of their lives. The smartly dressed coachman who galloped past without a care for anyone who might be at the side of the road looked back at them as he raced by, and although Lydia had not been especially observant of the driver so in fear was she of her life as she jumped back out of the way, she could not help feeling completely overwhelmed as she recognised his face.

"Wickham!" she cried. "What on earth is he doing here?"

They watched the departing gig disappear in a spray of muddy water, but there was nothing they could do apart from speculate on his reasons for being there, which were most perplexing. Ever since his abrupt departure from Netherfield, Lydia had wondered whether he had known of Molly Wickham's pursuit of him. Perhaps he had been alerted by the sound of her voice or a vision of her ambling up the drive as he chanced to look out of the window. Perhaps it had never been his intention to stay at Netherfield and that clean clothes, money, and a horse were his only purpose for turning up at all. Lydia might never know, but one thing was clear: George Wickham was not in Bath by accident; he was there for a reason and the thought filled her with foreboding.

Chapter 33

ANOTHER FIVE MINUTES FOUND them in Quiet Street again. There was no immediate sign of Alexander, and Isabella laid a table in preparation for his return with some of their morning's purchases, bread rolls, cheese, and a plate of ham, whilst Lydia made herself useful by dressing a salad and cucumber.

"What on earth can Wickham want in Bath? You would have thought with all that has passed it would be the last place he would appear," she said to her friend. Any nervousness she might have felt about the outcome of her married state had intensified with that gentleman's appearance. "What can he be doing here?"

Before Isabella could give her answer, they heard the knock on the front door announcing Alexander's return from Walcot and waited nervously as his footfall on the stairs grew louder. One look at his face was enough to stop the exchange of conversation between the girls. Isabella took his coat before he sat down at the table. He looked directly at Lydia with the same grave expression that had become very familiar to her over the past few days. "It is not good news, I am afraid."

For a moment, she thought she might faint and steeled herself to hear the words that she was still a married woman, that her name would be Lydia Wickham forevermore. She was not feeling well; her heart was beating too fast, as though it might burst. Perhaps if she sat down for a moment to calm her nerves, she would recover. Her ears started buzzing, and as a wave of nausea overcame her, the world became as black as a night sky and quite as star filled. She heard her name being called, but she could not see. Lydia called out in blind panic before she slumped, only to be saved by Mr Fitzalan, who jumped out of his seat and caught her in his arms.

Alexander Fitzalan did not know what to do; he had not expected this. She lay in his arms; that she had fainted he was sure. He searched her face for any sign of life—she was at least still breathing. Her lips, which had taunted him so many times, pink as rosebuds, were pale and parted, her breath coming in short darts. It is a pretty face, he thought. How vulnerable she looked. He became more concerned when she did not immediately come round. "Lydia, are you quite well? Please open your eyes and tell me you are not ill."

Lydia's lashes fluttered open; her black eyes were startled and round. She was astonished to see him, and as she recollected the circumstances, she struggled to stand. Alexander aided her with strong arms until she was upright, keeping his hand at her elbow lest she should relapse.

"Please do not upset yourself," he begged. "Come, sit down. I must tell you all my news. Forgive me, I did not mean to distress you so; I had not finished telling you everything. There was a robbery at the church early this morning and several important documents, including books of registers, banns, and so forth were stolen, though the poor rector cannot think why such items would be taken or how they could be of any importance to a thief."

"So that is why he is here and dashing about so urgently upon his gig!" Lydia managed to say as she recovered her breath, still gasping for air.

"Who is here?" Alexander asked looking puzzled.

"We were almost run over by Captain Wickham in Cheap Street," declared Isabella. "He is here in Bath!"

"Good heavens, I must alert Mr Darcy at once," cried Alexander. "He will wish to know of it, I am sure. I will send a letter by express. I need paper and ink."

"I did not bring any with me," sighed Isabella waving her salts under Lydia's nose. "I am sorry. We were in such a hurry, and I did not give my writing box a minute's thought."

"Do not worry, I will go out and get some. I will return in just a moment! Look after her, Isabella." He flew from the room immediately, not stopping for bread and cheese, and the ladies were left looking at one another.

Lydia could not eat a morsel. Though she was feeling much better, her mind was running on other matters. "Wickham must be married to that woman," she said, speaking her thoughts out loud. "Why else would he go to the trouble of stealing church records?"

"That may be the case, Lydia, but I hate to raise your hopes. We do not know that he has stolen them, though it certainly seems likely."

A loud report on the front door downstairs had the ladies leaping to the window.

"I do not think it can be Alexander returned so quickly," said Isabella. She peered out but was not able to see the visitor hidden by the canopy below. "I will go and see."

Lydia heard Isabella's light footstep on the stairs, then Mrs Bromley the housekeeper in conversation with a man judging from the low register of the voice. Isabella was there again instantly. "It is Captain Wickham. He told Mrs Bromley he desires to speak with you. Shall I send him away?"

"No," said Lydia firmly, her eyes alert. "Send him up. I want to hear exactly what he has to say for himself."

"But will you be safe?"

"Isabella, George Wickham is many things, but he is not a murderer. Besides, it will be amusing for me. Quite how he plans to talk himself out of this pickle I cannot imagine."

Isabella showed him into the sitting room and left them alone, retiring to her room, but with the door left slightly ajar in case she was needed. Lydia had more trust in that wastrel than she possessed, that was for sure!

Lydia had already decided that she would find the whole episode far more diverting if she were to keep her counsel and let him run on in his own particular way. She offered him a seat and waited.

"Listen, my love," he started, "I know how it must all appear, but believe me when I say that my feelings towards your very excellent person are never varying; you are the love of my life and ever will be. When I quitted Netherfield, I had very good reasons for leaving when I did and I think if you allow me to explain, we can resolve it all."

Lydia sat in silence and waited for him to continue.

"Of one thing in this life we can be sure: that it is a trial and that few manage to travel seamlessly through its passage is undeniable. I admit I have committed a few errors along the way."

"Get to the point, George!"

"Yes, of course, dear. I must ask you to think back. You recall, my dear, that period of my life when Mr Darcy refused to give me the living he owed me."

"Yes," Lydia answered. "I recall that particular tale distinctly."

"Indeed, you know I was at a low ebb. I had been dropped and snubbed by a man who was as good as my brother, and I knew not which way to turn. I made a mistake; I see that now. You can imagine how it all was: a lady seduces a young fellow, hard on his luck, into thinking she has a high regard for him, plying him with drink and the promise of fortune. Next, before he knows what is happening, she has marched him up the aisle and then abandons him as quickly as she debauches him."

"To what do you refer, sir?"

"You do not know?"

"I do, but I wish you to tell me."

"Why I was married, my dear, but let me assure you, it was a marriage of convenience, it meant nothing; it's not worth the paper that declares its truth."

"Tell me," asked Lydia, "was that before or after you tried to seduce Miss Darcy?"

Wickham was discomfited by her remark, but as a gambling man knows when his luck has run out but persists in one last go, so did Captain Wickham entreat his former lady with one last attempt to bring her round. "My love, no one need ever know anything about my previous alliance, which is a marriage on paper alone. I swear on my life that I have never lived with her nor ever seen her again."

"I see," said Lydia, "so we will just continue living the lie that has become as natural as breathing: that we are happily married, that I turn a blind eye to your amorous encounters and imagine that they do not mean anything. We will continue to pretend that, since the day we met, you have not lied, cheated, or mistreated me in any way."

"I have the book, the record of this most unfortunate ceremony in my possession. No one shall be any the wiser. Listen to me; you and I will start afresh. I promise from this day forward to be the most faithful husband a girl ever wished, the most ardent lover. And look how well I am doing. With our dear brother Darcy's help, I will rise again in my profession, I know it. We will have a grand house, Lydia, as many servants as you wish, carriages, clothes, even a little pug if you desire it!"

"Captain Wickham, please stop this instant."

"As many bonnets as can fill up a smart barouche, as many . . ."

You are wasting your time and your breath. I will not listen, George."

" . . . diamonds, cameos—you know how you adore jewellery. I will cover you in precious gems!"

"Are you not attending or are you simply stupid? I am not interested."

"But you should be, damn you, Lydia. If I don't have you, whom do you think will? A girl willing to run away and live with a chap in sin, a girl past her bloom, a girl sullied as a streetwalker will find no suitors willing to call. You'll have no chance of marrying again, mark my words."

"No chance of marrying again, whatever do you mean? As well you know, I have never been married! I should like to say I am sorry to disappoint you, but frankly, I am not. You have no claim on me, which I celebrate more than you can imagine. I would not live with you again, even if you could rustle up Pemberley itself nor if I were to discover that you had married me honestly. And despite the scandal that will inevitably result, I am delighted with the outcome of this highly fortunate discovery. If I possessed the funds, I would reward Mrs Molly Wickham with an annuity for her generous and timely intelligence!"

Lydia hesitated. She could hear voices outside the door. Alexander burst through, demanding to know if she was quite well. She could have hugged him, for the expression on Wickham's face was a picture.

"Lydia, I am sorry I was away so long. I should never have left you."

"And who are you, sir?" Wickham demanded, as Alexander moved swiftly to Lydia's side. "Who are you to address my wife with such familiarity."

"My name is Alexander Fitzalan. I must presume you are George Wickham. And this lady, sir, is most emphatically not your wife."

"He has the books that were reported as stolen, Alexander," Lydia cried, fearful that Wickham, whose countenance looked thunderous, might step up and challenge Mr Fitzalan to a duel, or hit him at the very least. "I have told him that I am not to return with him. I know I am not his wife nor do I wish to be."

Alexander suddenly took charge, gently ushering Lydia out of the room and telling her he would have a private audience with Captain Wickham. He told her that she was not to worry about the books or anything else; he was there to help sort her problems out.

Once out in the corridor, she felt duty bound to warn him. "But Alexander, do not believe a word he says and please be careful." She touched his arm, and he smiled reassuringly, patting her hand as he spoke.

"Leave it with me, Lydia. I know what kind of man he is, believe me. I am now fully acquainted with his crimes against you. I will be careful. Sit with Isabella. Five minutes and it will be done, I promise."

Lydia joined Isabella in her room. They sat quietly, listening to the exchange of words, Wickham's angry voice, and Mr Fitzalan's calm, deep tones. They heard a door slam, a heavy tread on the stairs, and the front door bang shut.

It was all Lydia could do to stop herself from running up and throwing her arms around Alexander, but she knew she could not. He would hate such a display of emotion, and she felt they were getting on so well now that she didn't want to spoil their newfound amity.

"He has one hour to return the books to me and leave Bath, though I did inform him that Mr Darcy is on his tail," pronounced Alexander. "I suspect the books may be returned sooner."

"I know him," cried Lydia, "that will not be enough to deter him. There is sure to be another scheme."

"Let us wait and see. I am certain he will honour his promise; he has no choice."

Within the half hour, there came a loud knock on the door. Alexander anticipated Mrs Bromley before she managed to descend the stairs, and he returned in a moment bearing the promised books.

"I did not hear Wickham," Lydia cried. "Has he been and gone already?"

"Oh no; he is far too shame-faced to show himself here again, and if I am not mistaken, I guess he has left Bath already, taking the London Road where he imagines he will be able to lose himself easily. I should not boast of it as a man of the cloth, but I think Mr Wickham was more than a little afraid to see me again and sent a body in his place!"

"Mr Fitzalan!" exclaimed Lydia. "Did you threaten Captain Wickham with violence?"

"Not in so many words," he laughed.

The tension was broken for a moment as they all burst out laughing before Lydia plucked up the courage to see the entry that officially recognised her own marriage as null and void. It proclaimed for all the world to see that George Wickham of Walcot Street, Bath, and Pemberley House, Derbyshire, together with Molly Spratt of Walcot Street, Bath, were married in Walcot Church by license on 10 June, in the year One Thousand, Eight Hundred and One. Their signatures were there, George's unmistakable scrawl looking very much as it had done on their marriage certificate. So it was official: her husband was a bigamist; she was unmarried, now unmarriageable, a single woman with no fortune and with no prospects of acquiring any.

All of a sudden her problems weighed heavily on her shoulders; her thoughts and the small room crowded in on her, and she knew she had to get out. The day looked to be as miserable as she felt—huge dark clouds were rolling slowly over the grey skies—but though the prospect of getting wet was not a happy one, she knew she had to breathe fresh air. Lydia excused herself, saying she was to go for a walk, quickly donning her cloak and bonnet, and setting forth before she could be talked out of it. Without knowing where she was going, she just knew that she had to go and be alone with her thoughts. Heading firstly for Gay Street, she then turned off, finding her way to the Gravel Walk, and as she started to stride along the path, climbing higher past the backs of houses whose windows seemed to watch her every step, she felt the first speck of rain. Looking up, Lydia felt furious that she had not brought an umbrella for it was clear she was going to be completely soaked. Far from being a sharp shower, the clouds were as gloomy as one ever saw them in Bath, and before long, the heavens opened and there was a deluge. She ran under the cover of the trees, which only afforded partial shelter. Lydia was starting to feel extremely cross with herself and wondered what could have possessed her to have such a silly notion. This was not her favourite pastime. A walk in the sunshine was one thing, but standing in the rain with wet feet and water trickling down inside one's bonnet was not the sublime experience she craved. Searching the skies for a break in the clouds, she was just contemplating running to the next set of trees when she saw the figure of a gentleman she recognised running towards her, umbrella in hand, with an air of great urgency.

Chapter 34

IT WAS ALEXANDER. "LYDIA, you are soaked through; please allow me to present my umbrella. I never go out without one in Bath."

"No, you are very wise, Mr Fitzalan, but you see before you the eternal optimist who believes that, because she does not wish it to rain, it will not happen."

He laughed and insisted she take it before pulling up his collar against the large droplets that found their way through the canopy of leaves, spattering on his hat and down into his coat.

"Mr Fitzalan, you cannot stand so in the rain, I will not allow it. Please shelter with me under the umbrella, sir, I beg you."

"Please do not be concerned. A little rain never hurt anyone," he said, drawing his coat around him.

"I insist or else I shall leave this place instantly, leaving you here on your own with this instrument!" She proffered the handle towards him and it was with some reluctance that he took it. "See, there is room for two," she said, as she stood next to him under the shelter of the brown cloth. They stood side by side, as they looked out at the scene in silence. Lydia felt Mr Fitzalan's shoulder brush against her own; she was very aware of the intimacy but found that she had no inclination to move away. She spoke at last. "It is very beautiful, is it not? Even in the rain."

"It is, indeed, quite delightful," he said and turned to look into her eyes.

They were so close she could feel his breath on her cheek.

"Mr Fitzalan, I want to thank you for everything you have done. I know we haven't always seen eye to eye . . ." She did not know how to continue, and when she saw his expression, she noticed that all the good humour had gone out of his face.

"There is no need to thank me, Lydia. I only hope that you feel I did the right thing—that you have no regrets. I would not want you to think that I interfered or acted in any way that you did not wish."

"But of course not, you have acted exactly as I wished. I desired it, believe me. He is nothing to me; he has no claim on me. I have known his true character for many months, and I own ours has been a miserable existence. But I have no one but myself to blame. I was so taken with the idea of being in love and of getting married that I didn't stop for two seconds to consider whether I was doing the right thing. But when I first fell in love with him, truly I had no idea. I really fell head over heels in love, you see. I worshipped the ground he walked upon and was swept away by my feelings. I was very naive and easily persuaded; I know that now. My father always said I was one of the silliest girls in England. However, I would wish you to know that, despite my propensity for folly and frivolity, I am not wholly without principles. Indeed, I am constant and truehearted, at least I could be or would be . . . if I had ever been truly loved. You do believe me, don't you?" She was not sure why she wanted Alexander to see her as a character she hardly recognised herself, but she could not bear the thought that he would only ever think of her as a wicked creature. It suddenly seemed important to her that she should change his mind and that he should see her in a different light.

"Yes, I do," he said softly and turned to face her, his blue eyes crinkling as he smiled. "I do not doubt you have a true heart, and I am sure, if you were ever given the chance to be loved in return, you would discover all that you hoped love would be. You might even surprise yourself."

"You are too generous; it is clear you do not know me very well."

"Perhaps you do not know yourself as well as you think. Shall we walk?"

He offered his arm, Lydia took it and had to admit, if only to herself, that the sensation of walking with Alexander in such a way was not unpleasant in the least; he was quite like the elder brother she had never had. Perhaps they might be friends after all. She was certainly beginning to understand how Isabella came to rely on him so much. He was so very different from any other man she had ever known; he was a man of his word and a man of action. He was also a very good listener, and she had to admit, she could not help liking someone who let her run on as she wished. If he would only enjoy a better humour, he might be quite attractive. They walked along in companionable silence until they came out onto the Royal Crescent.

"I have been meaning to speak to you, Lydia, to apologise for my behaviour on the evening of the Netherfield ball."

Lydia remembered that evening with a sentiment closely resembling shame and now recognised that she had behaved badly. "You have nothing to apologise for, believe me. If anyone should be asking for forgiveness, it is I. The truth is, I am a dreadful flirt; you were quite right. I couldn't bear to see Isabella so happy whilst I felt so miserable."

"But had I known, if Isabella had informed me sooner of the cruelty you have suffered, I would have behaved with more understanding, and I own I scolded you, not so much because I felt justified in my actions, but because you reminded me of someone else."

"Are you talking of Miss Hunter, the girl you loved?"

"I confess, I am. But I have given you quite the wrong idea. The fault lay with me. I lost her through my own folly, my own jealous nature."

"But Mr Fitzalan, we are all inclined to such jealousies, especially in the case of love. It is human nature, and we all have our failings."

"Well, I now know what my nature can be and I am not proud to admit my weakness. I drove her away because I could not bear another man to talk, dance, or even look her way. She was a great favourite with many young men. Like yourself, she was a girl full of life and spirit, and I wanted to tame her, change her into a person she could not be. I drove her into another's arms by my own stupidity. You know I am not an easy man in company, and I thought at every moment she might leave me. I thought if I did not cage her she would go and I would never find another. Indeed, I wonder if I ever truly loved her. If I had, surely I could not have behaved so badly. There now, can you see why it is impossible for me to risk any such involvement ever again?"

"But you might find true happiness with Miss Rowlandson. You will learn to curb those feelings, I am sure. If you recognise your mistakes, that is a certain step towards happiness. I too have learned the hard way and with far more misdemeanours than you have ever been guilty of I daresay."

"You are too generous, Lydia, but you do not know of my mistakes, my thoughtless actions, my folly."

It is indeed fortunate that you know so little of mine, thought Lydia.

They had walked down Marlborough Buildings and were cutting across the fields. The rain stopped, and with it all confidences seemed to cease. Mr Fitzalan's expression became as closed as the brown umbrella, which he snapped firmly shut before hooking it over his arm, and all too soon, it seemed to Lydia, they were back in Queen Square and around the corner from their own front door.

On their return, they found Isabella in a state of some excitement. They had received callers whilst they had been gone. "You will never guess who has come to Bath for a visit," she cried as she grasped Lydia's hands. "Mr Rowlandson has been here with his mother and Eleanor. He has followed me to Bath! Of course, I am sure he would not have done any such thing had he known of our true circumstances for being here, but to know that he could not stay at home whilst I was here means so much."

"Isabella, I am happy for you, but I do not know why you are so surprised. I should think he would follow you to the ends of the earth! And Miss Rowlandson is here too? I wonder why she wanted to come?" Lydia asked mischievously, looking up at Alexander. "Perhaps she too is here to set her cap at someone we know."

Alexander blushed and looked quite out of humour. All his appearance of good nature disappeared with a scowl, and he excused himself, saying he had more letters to write.

"Oh dear," Lydia sighed, "and we were getting on so well."

"It is not you, Lydia; sometimes there is no accounting for his black moods," Isabella whispered. "Why, when I suggested we should now head back for Hertfordshire, he stomped about for five minutes before he declared that he had no intention of removing from Bath. Mind you, it seemed that he said so out of some consideration for you."

"Why, what did he say?" Lydia asked, intrigued to know what Isabella meant.

"Alexander thinks we should stay a little longer to give you a holiday, and let Mr Darcy decide what is to be done with Wickham and tie up all the loose ends. That way, when you go back to Netherfield, everything will be sorted out and you will have less to worry about."

"Did Alexander really say all that?"

"Yes, did he not tell you? I imagined that was why he went running out looking for you."

"No, indeed, he said very little."

"But we shall go home tomorrow if you wish it. You must be exhausted. It is very selfish of me to expect you to stay here, especially with all the associations Bath will have forevermore."

"But I am not in a hurry to go home, I assure you, Isabella. All that waits for me in Newcastle is grief and vexation. I would prefer to stay here for a little holiday, truly. I never have been able to make a visit before, and I wish to see everything!"

"Then it is settled. Thank you, dear friend. I know you do this for me; you are too good."

"No, you should know me better than that." Lydia laughed. "I intend to make the most of it!"

Wednesday, May 18th

Isabella is surprised that I have not collapsed as a result of the many trials that I have endured this day, but I find that I feel quite restored. My spirits are not low, and I feel a new energy, an excitement for which I cannot account. The relief I feel to have finally seen the proof of Wickham's infamous marriage on paper is indescribable, though I know that there will be new anxieties to face which I am loath to confront.

But I am not the only person with problems. Poor Alexander—I fear he will never recover from his disappointment, and now I know a little more of the circumstances, it is clear he is a troubled man. Though we are quite different characters, I have discovered he has quite as many flaws as I. And he a clergyman! Well, I take great comfort from the fact that he is not the faultless man I had presumed, and though his errors may not be as great as mine, he is certainly made more human by having some. Alexander's motives were as heartfelt as mine I am sure. He believed if he did not keep a check on Miss Hunter that she would leave him. His greatest folly was a desire to take too much control, to restrain and restrict the behaviour of the one he loved in an attempt to keep her. And if only I had shown some control over my actions and curbed my obsession with George, perhaps my own great folly could have been avoided. Well, we have both come to a better understanding of life as a result, and though first attachments, it would seem, are not always the best, I hope Alexander will find his heart's desire one day.

I am glad we are to stay longer in Bath. Isabella will be able to see Freddie, and I will not mind spending a little more time with her brother. I would like to know him better and help him if I may.

Chapter 35

THE FOLLOWING MORNING BROUGHT the expected missive from Mr Darcy. He had made good progress, was on Wickham's trail, and had intelligence of him being seen in the Boar's Head Tavern in London where he had been in company with friends.

"I daresay that will be Mr Draper and crew—gentlemen of the navy whom I met in a former life," said Lydia sighing. "I expect he has thrown himself on their mercy, though I should expect they will soon tire of his friendship when they realise he hasn't a penny to his name."

"I expect Mr Darcy will soon find him," said Mr Fitzalan, folding the letter, "though exactly what he means to do with him I cannot guess."

"I have no doubt he will find him," Lydia commented.

"He has done it before, and I am sure will manage again. Wickham had best beware; I do not think Darcy will be letting him off lightly on this occasion."

They planned to start the day with a trip to the Pump Rooms, but Isabella was clearly more excited than she had been previously at the thought of meeting Mr Rowlandson. They hastened down to the town, with Alexander in tow urging them both to slow down, and were instantly gratified to see their friends already there and waiting for them under the clock. The usual felicitations preceded a request from Miss Rowlandson to take a turn about the room. She latched onto Isabella and pulled Lydia over to her other side. "We must walk together so we will cause a little stir, will we not? See how the gentlemen cannot help but be drawn in our direction?"

Lydia glanced behind her to see Alexander and Freddie deep in companionable chatter and could have laughed out loud. It was clear they were not impressed by the ladies' efforts to attract the notice of young men and were completely oblivious to their charms.

"We are planning to go to the Upper Rooms tomorrow evening," said Eleanor. "I confess I am excited at the prospect. Will you be going too?"

"I am not sure if we will be able. Mrs Wickham is here for her health and has been quite unwell. I do not think she will be up to dancing," answered Isabella, conscious that Lydia, for all her brave words, might prefer to remain at home.

"Nonsense," Lydia cried. "I insist that you go, Isabella, and besides, I am sure I shall enjoy some dancing. It will be good for my spirits. I am determined to enjoy my holiday and am feeling much better, I assure you."

"Can you guess who else is in town?" Eleanor said, but did not wait for an answer. "Ralph Howard, that lovely man who danced with me at Netherfield, is here and not far in Laura

Place, which is as elegant as it is exclusive. He has called a few times at HighCross recently and mentioned he was coming here for a couple of weeks, but I daresay we will not see him."

"I am sure you will," responded Lydia as she and Isabella exchanged glances. Her mention of Ralph Howard calling at HighCross had not been missed by either of them. "Bath is a big town, but it seems everyone follows the same pursuits, just like they do in Brighton."

"Oh, I should like to go to Brighton," Eleanor declared, "but there is never enough money for too many expeditions."

"What are you talking of, my dear?" asked her brother Freddie.

"I was just saying I should like to go to Brighton, but visits are so expensive, it is impossible to go everywhere one should like."

"Aye," said Freddie, "but you were as keen to come to Bath as I, were you not, Eleanor?"

She blushed at his words and quickly turned the conversation to join Lydia and Isabella, who were discussing the morning gowns of the fashionables.

"We are going for a walk this afternoon," Isabella commented. "Nowhere too far away, just around and about. Would you like to join us?"

"I would love to, but unfortunately I am engaged. I have an appointment with a mantua maker. She is just going over an old gown, but I would like to look my best. I will take mother; she is very good at making decisions about clothes. The journey was so fatiguing that she is resting this morning, but she has assured me she will be well enough for a little trip out later."

"And now, Miss Isabella," prompted Freddie, "you promised me you would assist me in procuring a glass of this superior water

I have heard so much about. Tell me, am I supposed to drink it all in one go?"

The rest of the morning passed as well as expected, and Lydia was glad to see her friend thoroughly enjoying the company of her handsome beau who was as attentive as ever. However, she was not impressed at all by Mr Fitzalan's efforts with Miss Rowlandson. He clearly needed more than a hint if his romance was to progress any further or if he was to divert Miss Rowlandson's attentions from a certain quarter. Lydia decided she must try again to give him a little advice on the best ways to capture a young lady's affections.

In the afternoon, Isabella and Lydia set out for their walk to promenade on the Crescent Fields, which lay in front of the elegant sweep of the Royal Crescent. This was a popular place for a stroll, and there were large numbers of people taking in the air, their fellow creatures, and any new scandal to be had. Isabella was just asking Lydia what she thought Mr Darcy would do once he got his hands on Captain Wickham when the former stopped abruptly and froze, rooted to the spot. Lydia soon followed Isabella's astonished regard as she contemplated the spectacle before her.

Walking towards them, arm in arm, were Miss Rowlandson and Ralph Howard with Eleanor's mother trailing just a little behind them. Miss Rowlandson leaned on Mr Howard's arm, at once expressing her intimacy and familiarity, whilst he held her parasol, taking care to shade her skin from the glare of the afternoon sun. Eleanor greeted Isabella with open arms, declaring what an honour it was to meet again and swiftly presented her companion.

"Ralph Howard at your service, ladies," he said bowing deeply. "I am delighted to meet you. Any friends of Miss Rowlandson are always a joy to meet with. I trust this will be an occurrence to be oft repeated."

"I misunderstood," said Isabella, who was shocked to see the obvious understanding between her friend and Mr Howard, "I thought you were engaged with your mantua maker this afternoon."

"Yes, but the sunshine and Mr Howard called us out. Indeed, we could not stay inside on such a day," enthused Miss Rowlandson, "and a walk is always such a felicitous occupation for diverting conversation, is it not?"

Mrs Rowlandson looked keen to be gone and excused them all as soon as she could. "There may just be time to catch your appointment, Eleanor, if we hurry. Mr Howard is so kind to accompany us. Forgive me, Miss Fitzalan, but we must take our leave. Shall we see you tomorrow at the Rooms? I do hope so. Mr Howard will be attending; he has promised to be of our party. We shall see you there, no doubt."

Isabella watched them walk away and shook her head. "I have never seen anything so brazen in my life."

"Do you think she has set her cap at Mr Howard?" Lydia asked. "Poor Alexander, he will have his heart broken again."

"Perhaps, though I am not so certain that he admires her as much as you imagine." Isabella shook her head and her fair curls stirred in the summer breeze. "I do not think his heart will be broken. However, I do know he needs someone to love him, a girl with a true affectionate heart."

"Well, I am not convinced that Eleanor Rowlandson is the lady to fit that description," Lydia remarked.

"That is true. She has wasted no time in making her object plain."

"Wherever will you find a girl for him, Isabella? For it is certain, he will never find her on his own!"

"I cannot think," came her answer. "Indeed, it is a puzzle to bemuse us all."

Thursday, May 19th

I must admit that I feel sorry for Alexander. Miss Rowlandson appears to have her eye on riches and has thrown herself at a certain gentleman with greater claims to fortune than Isabella's poor brother. I do not think I have the heart or desire to encourage him to pursue that minx, but I do wish to advise him if I can. He has been so generous with his time in helping me, and I grow fond of him. I would not like to see his heart broken, especially by a young woman of little worth! I don't doubt she considers herself the very epitome of fashion and fair looks, with her fine silks and jade eyes, but I intend to watch that madam closely.

Isabella grows more in love with Mr Rowlandson. He is a most charming fellow, and they make the most delightful couple. I do hope he does not keep her waiting much longer. If he should ask for her hand, she would be the happiest girl alive, and if he does not act soon, I think I shall take him in hand and drop a few hints! I am certain that will not be necessary and that love will declare itself before much longer.

As for myself, although it is hard to be a witness to such happy courting, I could not be more pleased for them both, even if watching them stirs the memories I thought were forever buried in my heart. It would be a wondrous thing to be in love and feel it returned to the same degree, yet I do not consider it likely to ever happen to me. Perhaps I am not deserving of such a fate—I am not good or virtuous like Isabella or my sisters Jane and Lizzy, who certainly have earned their right to happiness. Well, at least I do not have to spend the rest of my days with George Wickham, which in its way is my prize and comfort!

Chapter 36

THEY ENTERED THE ROOMS on the following evening an elegant trio; Alexander graced on either side by such elegance as had the whole room craning their necks to follow them about the place. As soon as they could, the girls made their way into the ballroom whilst Alexander went in search of their friends on Isabella's instructions. There were so many people that there was hardly a seat or bench left in the room. Spotting a gap on the second tier, just fit to accommodate two girls, they made their way along, apologising for stepping on toes or making those not slim enough to flatten themselves against the bench stand up. Finally, they were seated between a dowager on one side and an old tough on the other and could see all before them; the fine, the lovely, the plain, the ugly, wives and husbands, mistresses and adulterers, friends and lovers, all parading and performing before them, as though on a vast stage.

Lydia scanned the room and distinguished sight of Mr Fitzalan, whom she could see conversing with the

Rowlandsons. He could not fail to arrest her attention, especially as he looked so unlike the clergyman from Hertfordshire that she recognised. She had to admit that he was more handsome than he had ever been before in her eyes; the cut of his coat was as superior as any in the room, his black hair curling into his collar, and his eyes casting as many sparkles as the chandeliers glittering above her head. Quite how long she must have been staring in his direction she had not realised until Isabella laughingly commented that she had not comprehended how much Lydia appreciated a chimneypiece. She blushed, admitting the truth of Isabella's words to herself, thinking that there was plenty to admire when Alexander Fitzalan was placed before one, even if all his attention was directed at Eleanor Rowlandson who clearly engaged him. In the next second, it was almost as if he felt the intensity of her regard, for he looked up as if he perceived her contemplation of him. The room seemed to dim. All Lydia could see was the sapphire blue of his eyes, lustrous lights as bright as any flame, glimmering on an invisible beam which flared between them. She turned away for to look another moment would have betrayed her feelings, emotions she did not dare to recognise.

"Look, Lydia, there is Alexander, he has found them. I wonder that you did not see him yourself, you were so engaged with the view in that direction," Isabella declared.

"Lord, it's hot in here. I must get some air," Lydia announced and stood up.

"I will come with you," Isabella kindly offered, and so they both struggled the way they had come, until they were in sight of the doors at last.

Out in the corridor, the heat was not so oppressive and Lydia could breathe at last, although she was pallid and her heart hammered.

"Are you quite well? Oh, I knew we should not have come." Isabella took her friend's hand. "Stay here, I will fetch you a drink; you do look most ill."

Lydia slumped against the wall. What on earth was she thinking? Why did the sight of Alexander talking with Miss Rowlandson unsettle her so? She turned to put her head against the cool surface but a hand on her shoulder made her turn. She was very surprised to see Mr Fitzalan standing there, but was so very glad to see him that she could hardly speak at all.

"Lydia, forgive me, but you appear to be rather pale. Isabella tells me you are unwell. I think perhaps it was a mistake to have brought you here. We should never have come out this evening. I will take you home."

Lydia nodded and smiled. "I am quite well, Mr Fitzalan. I was just a little overcome."

He offered her one of the glasses of wine he was carrying, his fingers brushing hers with the lightest touch as she took it, and Lydia was confounded by her reaction. As if she juggled molten glass, she instantly dropped the vessel, which broke into a thousand tiny pieces. She leapt out of the way, avoiding the worst of the spills, which fortunately missed her gown but spread quickly across the floor and formed a large pool.

"Forgive me, Mr Fitzalan. How foolish of me," she cried, discarding her gloves and kneeling to attend to the mess on the floor.

"Do be careful, Lydia, there is broken glass; allow me or you will cut your hand."

He knelt at her side, but it was too late; a small dagger-like shard had pierced her skin and blood was pouring from her finger. He helped her to stand and demanded that she should allow him to inspect the damage. He gently wiped the wound, mopping away the blood with a handkerchief he produced from his pocket.

"Keep your hand very still," he said as he gripped her fingers firmly. "I am going to attempt to remove the glass. I will try my best not to hurt you."

Lydia watched his face and felt moved by its tender expression. His very closeness made her feel uneasy, and she did not wish to think why. She would not admit that she found the curve of his arrogant mouth attractive in any way as he bit his lip in concentration before extracting the glass with consummate ease, nor would she acknowledge that his firm grasp and the merest stroke of his fingers was unsettling in the least. She was staring at him so intently that he looked back at her for a moment. It was over in a second, their conversation resuming forthwith, with all attendant anxiety.

"There, I've got it. I think all will be well now. The bleeding will stop in a moment," said Mr Fitzalan, folding the linen and binding her finger.

"Thank you for your kindness, your consideration. Indeed, I am indebted to you. But let me not detain you from your dancing. Miss Rowlandson will be waiting for you," she said. "She will not say no if you ask her to dance," she added, "and if I were you, I would not leave it too long."

"You still believe Miss Rowlandson admires me?"

"You must not give up so easily. I would say a little encouragement, a few compliments, some harmless flirtation, and the deed will be done. She will be in love with you."

His face instantly reflected that same reserve and indignant disdain as preserved as ever she had seen them. "Indeed, I am against such nonsense. Forgive me, but I must take my leave. I trust you are recovered enough."

"Quite well enough, Mr Fitzalan, do not concern yourself." She watched him walk away, wondering how she could have felt any sense of sympathy for him, and hoped Miss Rowlandson would be dancing with Ralph Howard. She would not waste her time or breath again. It made her quite cross to think how she had put herself out. She tore off the dressing on her finger and threw the handkerchief down on the floor. The bleeding had stopped; she had no use for it now. She stared at the crumpled cloth stained with her blood. It was lace-edged with his initials, A. F., embroidered in one corner in blue silk. More vexed than ever, she knew she could not leave it and snatched it up, stuffing it in her reticule. The old familiar feelings of despondency and wretchedness threatened to overcome her. Why did she bother trying to be civil to Mr Fitzalan? He was not worth the trouble, and why she allowed herself to be upset by him she could not say. But she must overcome her feelings. She must be calm if only for Isabella's sake. As soon as she had recovered her temper enough, she went in search of her friend. She quickly saw Isabella on the arm of Mr Rowlandson, who had taken her off to the dance floor, and was instead faced with the sight of Mr Fitzalan in conversation with Miss Rowlandson and Mr Howard, who beck-oned to her just as she was pretending that she hadn't seen them.

Lydia approached, said good evening, and curtseyed, trying her best to look as though she was not disturbed by the sight of Mr Fitzalan, who stared at her with what she imagined must be utter contempt. Mr Howard was fortunately in a very talkative mood, at least for five minutes, before he undertook to accompany Miss Rowlandson to the floor, leaving Lydia and Mr Fitzalan to watch them dance.

There was an uncomfortable silence. Lydia was at a loss as to know what to say. She could only observe the animated way in which Mr Howard and his partner were enjoying the dance, how their bodies moved with the other, how they only had eyes and words for each other.

"Miss Rowlandson and Mr Howard make a pretty exhibition," Mr Fitzalan commented. "They are well matched and keen to partner the other. I find I am quite happy to observe their growing affiliation; each seems to complement the other to perfection."

Lydia could not think how to reply. She could hardly agree with him.

"How is your finger, Lydia? Are you feeling better now?" he asked tenderly.

"It is much better, thank you."

"Yet you are very quiet. Forgive me. I know I am at fault once more. I apologise. I spoke harshly back there in the corridor; I am sorry."

Lydia relented. She knew she had no reason to be so cross with him. "No, I am sorry. I do not think. I just open my mouth and all the wrong words come out."

Alexander laughed. "We are both very sorry, are we not? Let us stop saying sorry and do something else instead." He hesitated. "Would you do me the honour, Lydia, of taking my arm and dancing with me?"

"I would like that very much," she answered, "if you are sure you wouldn't rather wait for the beauty with the emerald eyes."

"Emeralds are all very well in their way," he replied returning her familiar stare which immediately took her off her guard, "but I prefer the coal black of polished jet, which is far more unsettling to my mind and more beautiful than any sparkling gem."

She was completely taken aback. That he had made a reference to her own dark eyes she had no doubt, and now she struggled to recall exactly what he had said as he took her by the hand and led her onto the dance floor. To dance with Alexander was a joy mixed with so many different emotions that Lydia found it hard to concentrate on her steps. Neither spoke a word for the first few minutes, so conscious were they of impressing one another. Lydia was determined to show him that he did not miss out for not dancing with Miss Rowlandson, and he was anxious to prove not only that he could dance but also that he could do so very well.

"Well, Miss Lydia, I hope I have surpassed all your expectations," Mr Fitzalan begged. "I think you must now own that I can at least dance after a fashion."

"You are proficient, certainly," she smiled, "but it is clear you are looking for a compliment and that only makes me feel like abusing you for your arrogance. However, I will say yes, without doubt, you are . . . quite good."

He laughed. "You are too generous with your compliments, but I also know you better than you think. I am aware that you like nothing better than to tease me."

"Tease you? Mr Fitzalan, what can you be thinking? I would not dare!"

"As for myself, I suppose I must admit you are the superior in regard to dancing, but I cannot decide which of your particular talents have supremacy over all: your dancing ability or your penchant for talking non-stop, especially with a view to wounding me." He looked at her gravely for an instant before he burst out laughing at her worried expression. "You have met your match, Miss Lydia, what do you say to that?"

"Let the fun begin!" she cried. "But I warn you, it will be impossible to get the better of me!"

Friday, May 20th

I have woken from a fitful sleep and am tormented by my dreams. My friends are very good and doing their best to cheer me. Alexander was especially thoughtful last night. He even flirted with me a little, which I am sure he did to prove to me that he is capable of charming a woman. He held me so very gently in the dance, and I have to admit he is an excellent dancer. But whilst it is amusing to be in Bath, and I can pretend that I haven't a care in the world, I know that I am going to have to face certain truths. I will not be returning to my home in Newcastle ever again, and the likelihood is that I will have nowhere else to go but return to my childhood home Longbourn. I am certain that however generous Lizzy or Jane will be with money, they will neither of them offer me a perma-nent home, especially as they are intent on filling their houses with umpteen numbers of children. The thought of having to return to my parents and to have all the neighbours look at me with pity, to end my days as an old maid, is more than I can bear. I have no independence, and there is nothing I can do to gain it. To be beholden to my father and then to have to throw myself on the mercy of the Collinses are circumstances I shall not even contemplate.

Alexander's handkerchief smells of lavender and its owner; comforting smells that have a curious effect as I inhale its sweetness. If I fold it carefully and place it on my pillow next to my nose, perhaps then I may fall fast asleep.

I will ask Alexander's advice on the morrow. He is so thoughtful and sensible, and I feel I can rely on him. I am certain he will listen to my anxieties, and though he may not have a solution to my problems, I know I shall feel better for having shared them with him. I am so happy to know Alexander and so glad to find he is everything his sisters have always described. But I am sure when we return to Hertfordshire he will have little time for me. I cannot blame him. Who would wish to know me if they knew my story?

Chapter 37

LYDIA AWOKE STILL FEELING as miserable as ever, and to make matters worse, Isabella was beside herself with happiness. Listening to her friend's ecstatic effusions on the ball Lydia heard how Mr Rowlandson had danced almost every dance with her and that, at the close of the evening, he had asked if he could call early next morning.

Alexander arrived back from an outing to collect the post and interrupted his sister's animated discourse with a final letter from Mr Darcy, outlining Wickham's whereabouts. Mr Darcy had apparently made contact with Captain Edward Draper, who had been persuaded to help Wickham gain a position on his newly commissioned frigate. They were sailing for the West Indies and Mr Darcy was quite convinced that he was gone for good, saying that Wickham would not be returning to England and that he would not be surprised if they didn't see him reported in a newspaper yet, hanged for a pirate on foreign soil. As far as he was concerned, he knew Wickham would not risk a return to face the master of Pemberley House. The matter was closed. Good riddance to a bad lot had been Mr Darcy's last word on the matter, alongside a gentle-manly reference to his sister Lydia whom he hoped was bearing up, saying she was welcome to visit her sister Lizzy when she felt well enough, though in the interests of keeping any scandal at bay, it might be prudent to continue using her married name for the present. After a suitable time, he assured her, he would let it be known that George Wickham had gone to sea and met his death by drowning in a shipwreck. That way, he considered, might be the only way Lydia could be sure of finding herself a husband, and he did not see why she should not make a respectable match in time. Lydia would have preferred something a little more dramatic and fancied telling everyone he had been eaten by a great shark for his untimely demise; however, the fact that she was getting rid of him once and for all was extremely diverting. Relief washed over her. She could not say she wished George any real harm, and to know that he was gone and would not be back to taunt her was welcome news indeed. She must start to put that part of her life behind her and make a new start, and though the prospect of doing that was quite terrifying, she knew she would be capable of meeting the chal-lenge. She was mildly amused by Mr Darcy's plan for her continued respectability, but decided she would be prepared to go along with it for a quiet life. She was quite beyond trying to vex her illustrious brother-in-law further. She knew he must have had to lay out a size-able sum to get rid of her husband, and she was very grateful. Perhaps she might even be able to make an extended visit to Pemberley if she played her hand correctly.

Mr Rowlandson was as good as his word, and Lydia was sure she knew exactly what would follow after his arrival. She was proved right. As soon as he stepped through the door Freddie requested a private interview with Alexander, and having gained the necessary consent, he went in search of his beloved. Lydia and Alexander withdrew from the sitting room as soon as they could, repairing to their own rooms to leave the lovers in peace, both anticipating what was about to happen. Just a quarter of an hour had settled it all, and Freddie and Isabella were urging them to hear their tidings.

"Alexander, Lydia, come and listen to our news. Freddie has asked me to marry him; we are engaged!" came Isabella's triumphant cry.

"I could not be happier for you both," shouted Lydia, dancing her round the little sitting room, knocking into all the furniture. "Never were two people more suited. I wish you joy!"

Everyone expressed their congratulations, there were hugs all round, and in the great excitement that ensued, Freddie declared he had another announcement. "I have forgotten to tell you in my urgency to deal with the matter in hand," he admitted, "but I also have some other news to impart. My sister has received an offer of marriage from Mr Howard. I do not think it was wholly unexpected." He glanced at Alexander whose reaction was everything it should be. "She has accepted him."

"And I am sure we are all delighted for Miss Rowlandson," declared Alexander. "Do send her my congratulations."

"And mine too," added Lydia, who thought Mr Fitzalan did not look quite as composed as his countenance suggested. His cheeks were quite pink, especially when he caught her eye. Indeed, the blush deepened, and she saw him pick up a book from the table and study its leather covering intently.

At once, Isabella and Freddie suggested a walk out to Sydney Gardens to get some air. Lydia felt she could hardly refuse, everyone had been so good to her, and besides, she would like to see the celebrated gardens and get lost in a maze.

The girls hastened to get ready, Isabella calling Lydia to her room to help her choose a suitable bonnet for such an auspicious occasion.

"Oh, Lydia, I cannot believe it! I am so lucky. I am beside myself with happiness. Whatever have I done to deserve such a wonderful man? I am sure I do not know."

"It is not luck, you goose; no one could resist falling in love with you," Lydia answered. "You are not only too beautiful to resist, but you are the kindest creature in the whole world. I wish I had always been the friend you have been to me."

"But you have been the loveliest friend; you are very dear to me."

"And I am sure I do not know what I have done to deserve your friendship, Isabella."

"But what do you think of Eleanor and Ralph Howard becoming engaged?"

"I am not surprised," Lydia confessed. "She is clearly a fast madam, as my mother would say. Only I feel so for Alexander. He does not deserve to be so hurt. Did you not see his face?"

"Yes, I did notice his regard. Indeed, I have been watching him very closely of late, but I do not think he is in the least bit upset about Eleanor. In any case, he never looked at her the way he looks at someone else."

"Whatever do you mean?" Lydia demanded. "Is Alexander in love with someone else?"

"I think he is, Lydia, though I am not sure if he knows it himself yet, or if he does, he is unsure what to do next."

Lydia could not think why the notion made her feel suddenly ill at ease. She had certainly never seen him looking at another woman apart from Eleanor with anything more than disregard.

"Do you not know of whom I am talking?" Isabella asked with a wry smile.

"I confess I do not," Lydia replied as she took in her friend's expression.

Isabella laughed. "Why, it is you he admires."

"Oh no, Isabella, you are quite wrong," she insisted, regarding her friend's face closely. Isabella pinned another rose onto her hat and laughed. Lydia glanced at her own reflection in the glass and considered that despite everything she had been through, she still possessed a certain bloom. Bath air was suiting her; perhaps all that rain was good for her complexion after all. "Do you really think he admires me?" She looked sideways at her friend, hardly daring to meet the amusement in her eyes.

"I absolutely refuse to comment on any observations I may have made unless you can tell me that you might find it in yourself to love my brother."

"Isabella, I do not know. I doubt I shall ever fall in love again. I admit I find Alexander a very attractive man, and he has been very kind to me."

"And he has excellent prospects, you know."

Lydia laughed. "Be that as it may, I think you are quite mistaken in his regard for me."

"Lydia Wickham, or should I say, Lydia Bennet is exactly the sort of girl he admires most, whatever appearances might suggest. You are a vibrant personality, a girl who loves life and does not take it too seriously. You do not allow mere trivialities to upset you; you live passionately and carelessly. Though Alexander could never be like that himself and professes to dislike such qualities, he is drawn to such zeal, zest for life, and disregard for convention."

"Yes, a penchant for folly and frivolity: qualities to attract and ensnare the most sensible of men!"

"Lydia, we are none of us perfect. We all have lessons to learn in life."

"I have certainly chosen to learn mine the hard way."

"Come, let us go. The gentlemen await our company."

They set off, marching down to town, all four in step with the girls leading the way, striding out with a purpose as they chattered about wedding clothes and wedding rings. It was only when they were halfway down Pulteney Street that Lydia found herself at Alexander's side, Isabella having latched on to her fiancé to walk in raptures with him and to discuss their new situation. Mr Fitzalan offered his arm. Lydia took it without hesitation and wondered again at the ease with which they fell into a comfortable step. Once more, she thought how much she enjoyed walking with him in that way.

"Will Wickham be happy in his new profession, do you think?" Alexander asked after a moment or two.

"I hope so for his sake," Lydia answered. "I for one am relieved to think I shall not have to see or meet with him again."

"And now you must start a new life."

"Yes, I must. I admit I am a little anxious, but I will rise to the challenge. I must. I will go home to Longbourn and make the best of it. I shall be a sweet old maid and look after all my nieces and nephews as a good aunt should."

Alexander became quiet and Lydia sensed he was holding back. That he wished to say something else on the matter she was sure. He turned his head and Lydia noticed how his dark curls brushed against his brow, wild tendrils which escaped from under his hat. She would like to reach out and touch one.

"I would like to be of some assistance to you, Lydia. I may presume too much, but Isabella and I are very happy for you to continue living with us at the rectory if you wish." He looked away across the road before finding the courage to speak again. "But of course, you may have other plans and when Isabella marries, you may want to . . . well, I just wanted you to know you have a choice."

"You are so very kind, Alexander," Lydia cried, scarcely able to believe her good fortune and wishing she could throw her arms about him. "I cannot think of anywhere I would rather live and with such dear friends, even if one of them can only dance in a mediocre fashion." She smiled up at him and witnessed the laughter in his eyes. "No; jesting apart, forgive me for saying so, but I think Miss Rowlandson has made a great error. She will regret you in time. You have a true and noble heart."

"Aye, a true heart which has been forced into an uneasy acquaintance with disappointment in love."

"Forgive me, you are talking of the girl you loved and lost. I have spoken out of turn yet again."

"No, it is not Miss Hunter to whom I refer."

"Then it must be Miss Rowlandson of whom you speak. Please forgive me, Alexander. It is not my wish to upset you with reminders of all your past hopes."

Alexander laughed. "I do not think you understand, Lydia. I wish her happy with Ralph Howard. No, my heart is not broken by Miss Rowlandson." He hesitated for a moment, searching the skies as if looking for his next words. "How can it be when this heart is in love with another?"

Lydia looked up at him and did not know what to say. All she knew was that she did not want to hear that he was in love with someone else. She bit her lip and looked down the length of the road to glimpse the gardens coming into view. All at once, the heavens opened, Alexander reached for his umbrella, and the raindrops fell, spattering with a loud retort on the cloth over their heads, contrasting greatly with the uneasy silence which existed between them until he spoke again.

"Yes, I am in love with another," he said as he looked at his companion intently, "but although I am falling very much in love with her, there is nothing to be done. She does not return my affection."

Lydia's heart hammered as she returned his gaze, which seemed to melt into her very soul.

"I have battled with my feelings but I am worn down, and I cannot keep my counsel any longer, though in my heart I know I should," he murmured. "What should I do, Lydia? Should I tell her how I feel?"

"Do I know of this lady?" asked Lydia both dreading and demanding to know his answer.

He nodded, screwing up his eyes as though intent on something or someone yonder and appeared to have changed his mind about revealing her name. Lydia could only hear their feet tapping along together on the pavement, each footfall ringing in her ears, and the rain, still dripping incessantly.

She stopped him and pulled on his arm. "Who are you in love with, Mr Fitzalan?"

"Do you truly not recognise the one I love?" He stopped and taking her hand raised it to his lips. "Dear Lydia, please say it is not so. Please tell me that you know my heart beats for you, always for you, that given time you might even be able to return my affection, perhaps even consent to marry me."

Until that moment, Lydia could honestly say that she was unaware that Alexander was in love with her, but she thought she recognised the strength of his feeling now. And whilst she put her mind to it, she knew, at last, that she was not only capable of acknowledging and returning his affection but that she was a long way to already being in love with him too. Who was to say that a second attachment might not be preferable to a first and that one conducted with less haste might be infinitely more successful? Alexander, she was sure, was capable of making her a very happy woman. She would never have believed that she would consider being married to a clergyman, but perhaps the idea of being a rector's wife was not so unpalatable after all. Everybody would be delighted, though she was certain that her own family would be very shocked and surprised. When next she wrote to Kitty, she must remember to recommend clergymen for making suitable husbands. Most wonderful of all, she would have two delightful sisters in Isabella and Harriet and a home to call her own, though truth to tell, the rectory would need more than a few alterations in her opinion. In any case, when she and Alexander were married, they might take possession of the larger manor house sooner than they knew. Of one thing she was certain: He was without doubt one of the most handsome men she had ever set eyes on, and if she could just see him in his garden, in shirt and breeches once more, she had no doubt of what might follow in the summer house.

"I do know, Alexander, it is too true," Lydia cried in earnest with that thought in view, "as my heart beats for you. Always for you!"

FINIS

About the Author

Jane Odiwe is an artist and author. She is an avid fan of all things Austen and is the author and illustrator of *Effusions of Fancy*, consisting of annotated sketches from the life of Jane Austen. She lives with her husband and three children in North London.